Cradle
of
Conflict

Wings Press, Inc.

Cradle of Conflict

John was jarred from his idleness by banging on the front door, triggering Whiskers to bark while dashing to the living room. John glanced through the peep hole and quickly opened the door. He heard Geraldine's cane striking in the background. Moments later, Sally stood next to her, craning her neck, clutching a robe against her chest.

His son Brody stepped inside the house wearing a blue University of Kentucky sweatshirt and gray sweatpants, holding the hand of his very pregnant girlfriend, Ashley. She stood there in slip-on athletic shoes, her belly protruding in a long pink gown and heavy bathrobe.

"She's having labor pains," Brody said, worry etched on his fatigued face. "We're not sure what to do."

Sally hurried to Ashley, taking her hand and leading her to the couch. "How far apart are the contractions?" Sally asked as they sat next to each other.

"About every ten minutes or so," Ashley said with a pained expression.

"How long has it been going on?'

"Maybe a couple hours."

"Have you called your doctor?"

"Dr. Palmer said to wait until they're five minutes apart." Ashley wiped away tears. "But I hurt. Something doesn't seem right."

Cradle of Conflict

Michael Embry

A Wings ePress, Inc.

Boomer Lit Novel

Wings ePress, Inc.

Edited by: Jeanne Smith
Copy Edited by: Bev Haynes
Executive Editor: Jeanne Smith
Cover Artist: Trisha FitzGerald-Jung

All rights reserved

Wings ePress Books
www.wingsepress.com

Copyright © 2023 by: Michael Embry
ISBN 978-1-59088-585-7

Published In the United States Of America

Wings ePress, Inc.
3000 N. Rock Road
Newton, KS 67114

Dedication

For Bailey (2012-2022)

He brightened the lives of my wife and me with his gentle disposition and unconditional love.

"Dogs' lives are too short. Their only fault, really."
—Agnes Turnbull (1888-1982), American writer

In Memoriam

Frederick Meade "Rick" Bailey (1945-2021)
Lexington, KY

James Duane Bolin (1955-2022)
Murray, KY

June E. Bradshaw (1930-2022)
Leitchfield, KY

Sheila M. Carwile (1956-2022)
English, IN

Richard A. Embry (1949-2022)
Wallingford, PA

Bobby Flynn (1927-2022)
Lexington, KY

Delma Francis (1954-2022)
New Hope, MN

Jack Funk (1948-2022)
Bardstown, KY

Eric F. James (1943-2023)
Danville, KY

Timothy M. Kelly (1947-2021)
Lexington, KY

Joan K. Klein (1940-2023)
Richmond, KY

Steven D. Lutz (1966-2023)
Henderson, KY

William F."Billy" Reed (1943-2022)
Louisville, KY

Mary A. Troedel (1933-2022)
Frankfort, KY

Christine Wilcher Wilbert (1947-2022)
Bloomington, IN

Richard G. Wilson (1937-2023)
Frankfort, KY

One

John rolled over in bed and put his arm around Sally's waist. She moaned softly and eased closer to him. They lay silently in the darkness for several minutes. John softly kissed her slender neck and backed away, planting his feet quietly on the floor as he sat on the edge of the bed. He glanced at the illuminated digital clock on the nightstand that glowed four-thirty-two in thin red numbers.

John found the pants he had tossed on the dresser before going to bed, pulled out a T-shirt from the drawer, and slipped on house shoes next to the bed. He stood outside the bedroom to put on the clothes, not wanting to disturb Sally.

Whiskers, his forever friend, must have heard his movements as he was waiting at the bottom of the stairs, tail wagging. John bent and gently ruffled the doggie's furry mane for a few seconds.

"Ready to go potty?" he asked Whiskers, opening the front door. The dog darted to the side of the house and disappeared as if he couldn't hold it any longer. And probably couldn't.

John stood on the porch, feeling a slight shiver in the crisp March air as he waited for Whiskers to return. It was too early for the newspaper to arrive, something that seemed to get later each month as the paper grew thinner. It had been more than two years since he'd retired as sports editor.

He remembered arriving at the newspaper in the early hours to prepare for another edition, and staying until the final product rolled off the presses before calling it a day and heading home, only to go through the same routine the next day and every day after that in what seemed like an endless loop. He smiled to himself, thinking that was something he no longer missed, even though he was still an early riser. The mornings belonged to him, something he savored and treasured. No more deadlines. No more meetings. No more office politics. Simply "me" time.

The street was relatively quiet. A few porch lights were on at the darkened homes. A car moved slowly down the street, perhaps someone heading to an early work shift. Or maybe someone canvassing the street to steal items left in front yards. Even the neighborhood wasn't what it used to be. It was thought to be a good place to live and raise a family when he and Sally bought their modest tri-level many years ago.

John snapped out of his break down memory lane and clapped his hands lightly several times. Whiskers bounded from the corner of the house and ran up to him. John patted the top of the pooch's shaggy head and opened the door. Whiskers licked his hand several times before they entered the house.

"Let's get something to eat, little buddy," John said as he followed the hungry pet to the kitchen. He filled the bowls with kibble and water, then went to the counter and poured himself a cup of coffee. Whiskers wasted little time munching down his food and taking a few laps of water, then disappearing to his pad in the downstairs den, leaving John alone at the bar.

Unsure when the paper would arrive, John thought about going back to the bedroom and getting his smartphone to see the newspaper's website. He decided not to disturb Sally from her slumber. He could go to the den and turn on the television but that might wake up Geraldine, his mother-in-law, who was a light sleeper. He wasn't ready for that. She'd probably be up soon enough, her cane tapping on the floor heralding her presence. He preferred quiet and solitude for as long as possible, clutching his warm cup and taking a sip of coffee in the somber silence.

John was jarred from his idleness by banging on the front door, triggering Whiskers to bark while dashing to the living room. John glanced through the peep hole and quickly opened the door. He heard Geraldine's cane striking in the background. Moments later, Sally stood next to her, craning her neck, clutching a robe against her chest.

His son Brody stepped inside the house wearing a blue University of Kentucky sweatshirt and gray sweatpants, holding the hand of his very pregnant girlfriend, Ashley. She stood there in slip-on athletic shoes, her belly protruding in a long pink gown and heavy bathrobe.

"She's having labor pains," Brody said, worry etched on his fatigued face. "We're not sure what to do."

Sally hurried to Ashley, taking her hand and leading her to the couch. "How far apart are the contractions?" Sally asked as they sat next to each other.

"About every ten minutes or so," Ashley said with a pained expression.

"How long has it been going on?'

"Maybe a couple hours."

"Have you called your doctor?"

"Dr. Palmer said to wait until they're five minutes apart." Ashley wiped away tears. "But I hurt. Something doesn't seem right."

"Nothing feels right about having a baby," Geraldine chimed in as she sat on the easy chair across from the couch. "You ain't seen nothing yet, girl. Pretty soon it'll feel like you're passing a watermelon."

"Mother, please," Sally said, her brows furrowed.

"Well, it's the truth."

Sally turned toward Ashley. "Anything else?"

"I had some blood."

"What?"

"I saw it after I talked to the doctor."

"We're taking you to the hospital now," Sally said in a controlled voice. She looked at Brody. "Call the doctor and let her know you're on the way."

Brody pulled his cell phone from his back pocket and dialed the number. He informed the doctor's answering service of Ashley's condition.

"Let me get dressed," Sally said, rising from the couch. "It won't take a minute."

Brody sat next to Ashley, placing a hand on her lower back, rubbing gently.

"That blood doesn't sound good," Geraldine said, breaking the momentary silence in the room. "Thank god that never happened to me."

John closed his eyes and shook his head. "Everything's going to be fine," he said softly to Brody and Ashley.

Sally returned, wearing gray jogging pants, a lavender sweatshirt and pink running shoes she had worn the previous day when she and John had walked to Shipley Park, a popular neighborhood destination. She grabbed a light windbreaker from the closet next to the front door. "Let's go," she said without looking at anyone.

Brody stood and helped Ashley up from the couch and they followed Sally out the front door.

"I'll be here with your grandmother," John said to his son, holding open the storm door. "I'll be over at the hospital as soon as I can. Keep me posted."

Brody nodded with an unsettled look, his mouth closed tightly. He held Ashley's hand as they walked slowly to his car and opened the passenger door for her while Sally went to the back seat. Brody glanced back at John, got into the vehicle, and drove down the shadowy street.

John went to the kitchen where Geraldine was already seated at the bar. He poured her a cup of coffee and sat across from her.

"Do we have any pastries" she asked.

"Huh? What?" John said with a baffled look.

"It is time for breakfast."

"No, we don't have any pastries, Geraldine."

"Can you go get some?"

"Can you wait a bit? I don't want to leave the house until I hear back from Sally or Brody."

"That could take several hours."

"I don't care," he said with a measure of irritation. "Be patient. Eat some toast."

"Well, just be that way," Geraldine said, scrunching her nose. "She's not the first person to have a baby."

"I don't see your point." John walked over and poured another cup of coffee.

"Men just don't understand."

"If this happened to Sally, would you be saying the same thing?

Geraldine face reddened. "No," she said meekly. "But she's my daughter."

"And Ashley is about to give you a great-grandchild."

"I know."

"Doesn't that mean anything to you?"

"I guess it does, since you put it that way. I almost forgot that."

"Then let's wait until we hear back from them. Okay?'

"Okay."

"Thank you."

"Uh, will you go get some pastries then?"

John held his breath for several seconds and let it out slowly. "Of course, Geraldine."

"Thank you, John."

Two

Thirty minutes later, John convinced Geraldine it would be wise to go ahead and eat breakfast. She was unhappy with the advice, but after a few minutes, relented and allowed John to make her toast and jelly. However, he promised to pick up some pastries when he was out for the next morning. That brought a tiny smile to her fussy face.

His phone rang as he was about to butter her toast. He handed the plate to her and answered the call. It was from Sally. Geraldine gave him a hard stare.

"What?" he mouthed silently to her.

"Jelly," she said slowly.

John sighed, got the jelly from the refrigerator and handed it to her. For a moment, he wasn't sure if she wanted him to spread it on the toast. He turned his back to her to let her know the queen had to do it this time.

"Are you still here?" Sally asked.

"Sorry," he said. "I got distracted by your mother for a moment. So, how's Ashley?"

"She's doing better," Sally said. "Her doctor says it was false labor."

"Really? Even the blood?"

"She's going to keep her in the hospital for observation, but said it wasn't that uncommon on a first pregnancy. Besides, her contractions have stopped."

"How about Brody? How is he handling it all?"

"He's been at her side the entire time," Sally said. "It's so sweet. I know they're both worn out, but they seem less stressed after talking to the doctor. They both need some rest."

"Has anyone notified her parents?"

"Brody talked to them briefly after the doctor left. I believe her mother may be driving in from Louisville to be with her."

"Are you coming home soon?

"I'm going to stay here for a while," she said. "I may go down to the cafeteria and get a coffee and pastry."

"Don't mention that word around here when you get back."

"Coffee?"

"No, the other word."

"Oh." Sally laughed. "Mother does love her pastries."

John glanced at Geraldine with a forced smile. She was wiping crumbs off her chenille robe. "Keep me posted if anything else happens. And let me know if I need to pick you up."

"I will, honey."

After ending the call, John gave Geraldine an update on Ashley's condition. Then she asked for another two slices of toast. "You must be hungry," he said.

John put in two slices of bread in the toaster, lightly drumming his fingers on the counter while waiting for the toast to pop up.

"A person could starve around here," Geraldine said.

"Let's not get carried away," he said, grinning, as he placed the toast on the plate in front of her. "I don't think you've ever gone hungry living here."

"Maybe not, but it gets a little boring." She began buttering her toast while John warmed his coffee.

"The food selection?" he asked.

"Everything."

John sat across from her at the counter. "What's the matter, Geraldine? Is something on your mind?"

She took a small bite from her toast and chewed it slowly. "I'm just getting tired of sitting around the house all the time."

"You're getting restless?"

"You could say that," she said. "Maybe I should move back to Arizona. At least there were activities I could do to keep me busy."

"I could take you to the senior citizens' center," John said. "That wouldn't be a problem."

"That's too much trouble," she said. "Besides, I'm not sure I want to be around all those old people."

John crinkled his brows. "Oh."

"Plus, I don't know any of them."

"You would after a while. It takes time."

"I don't have that much time."

"Maybe move to a similar retirement village here in Lexington?"

"I never thought about that." A smile brightened her lined face.

"Should we look into it?"

"Let me think about it," she said. "Maybe we can discuss it with Sally and see what she thinks."

"You know they're expensive."

"Are you worried about me spending the inheritance?"

"You know better than that," John said. "It's your money to do as you wish."

"Thank you for your consent, John."

"There you go again." John shook his head. "You know I don't mean it that way. Sally and I will support whatever you choose to do. And you know you're welcome to stay here for as long as you wish. There are no time limits. We're family."

Geraldine pushed her plate with one piece of toast and the other half eaten aside. "I think I'm full." Conversation over. She grabbed her cane and headed toward the den. Less than a minute later, the recliner squeaked and the TV came to life as she got settled in, likely until lunch time.

John cleaned the counter and went to the front door to check for the newspaper. He noticed it at the end of the driveway, almost under the rear of his car. When he cracked open the door, Whiskers was there and made a beeline to the side of the house. John knew he'd be going there soon with a pooper-scooper.

After picking up the newspaper, John waited on the porch for Whiskers to finish his business. He opened the paper but didn't see any headlines shouting for his attention. Whiskers took his time coming back, sniffing and leaving his mark on several bushes along the way.

Whiskers went to his water bowl, took several sips, then returned to his pad in the den, despite the noisy chatter from the TV. John topped off his cup of coffee, sat at the counter, and glanced at the newspaper. As usual, his second stop after the front page, was the obituary section. He scanned the page and felt a small sense of relief that he didn't recognize any of the names. That was becoming his idea of good news.

John noticed it was going on ten o'clock. He felt restrained by how much time had passed since Sally had left with Brody and Ashley. He thought about taking Whiskers for a short walk, and maybe even going to the grocery store to pick up a few items, especially pastries for Geraldine. But he sensed that something might happen at the hospital, which would necessitate him going there at a moment's notice.

Instead, he put his half-empty coffee cup in the sink and went to the living room, where he kicked off his house shoes and lay on the couch, intending to rest his eyes for a few minutes.

Three

John was jolted from his nap when Sally opened the front door. Whiskers barked but quietened after seeing it was Sally. An uneven smile creased her tired face. John blinked several times, rubbed his eyes, rose from the couch and followed her to the kitchen.

"How's Ashley?" he asked as he sat at the counter across from her.

"No change. She was sound asleep when I left. Both she and Brody are beat. Poor kids. It made me remember how it was for us when Chloe was born."

"They'll get through it, just like we did."

"Of course. At least I hope so."

"How are you? You must be frazzled as well."

"I'm okay. A little tired, but that's it. Were you sleeping?"

"Resting my eyes," he said.

"Sure." She grinned. "Then why didn't you answer when I called?"

"You called?"

"Right before I called Uber."

"I left my phone on the counter," he said, pointing to it.

"I was only calling to let you know I was leaving the hospital," she said. "Anyway, I'm starving. All I've had is a cup of coffee. Do we have any pastries?"

"Are you serious?" John asked, raising a brow.

"What do you mean?"

"Never mind. I'll be running to the grocery store soon to pick up a few things."

"Where's Mother?"

"The usual spot."

Sally glanced toward the den. "Okay. I should have known."

"What are your plans today?"

"I'll go back to the hospital later in the afternoon. Maybe take a nap before then. That's about it." She covered her mouth, trying to stifle a yawn.

The clock on the wall read 11:22. They heard the recliner squeak, signaling that Geraldine was pulling it up to an upright position. She would be making her presence known soon, so they sat looking at each other without saying a word. John had thought about oiling the springs on the chair but decided it was a good warning device to alert them when Geraldine was on the move. Surprisingly, Geraldine hadn't complained about it like she did about most everything she used around the house.

As Geraldine approached the bar, John stood and moved a stool out for her to sit.

"Can I get you some more coffee?" John asked her.

"No, but you can get me something to eat. That toast didn't stick to my stomach long."

"I'll be going to the store in a few minutes. I'll get some pastries."

"It's a little late for pastries. How about a pizza?"

"Sally wanted pastries," John said.

"Well, can't you buy both?"

"I suppose I can."

"Hello, Mother," Sally said with a pressed smile.

"How are the soon-to-be parents?" Geraldine asked, resting her bony elbows on the bar.

"Ashley appears to be doing okay," Sally said. "The doctor says it was false labor, but that she could go into regular labor later today or tomorrow."

"I remember when I had you and Wendell. There wasn't anything false about it. I spread my legs in the stirrups and you babies seemed to plop out."

"That was a long time ago," Sally said.

"And I remember like it was yesterday. You never forget having babies."

"I'm sure," John said.

"How would you know?" Geraldine turned toward him with squinted eyes.

"I read about it," John said with a light laugh. "I even saw a film on childbirth."

"Well, it ain't funny."

"But isn't the outcome worth the pain?"

Geraldine frowned at him without saying a word.

John stifled a chuckle. "Oh well, I think I'd better be going. Anything else you want from the store?"

"Whatever you see," Sally said. "I'm going to take a shower and then lie down for a bit while you're gone."

"How about you, Geraldine?" John asked with a smile.

"Just hurry. A person could starve around here."

Four

Brody was slumped on the living room couch when John returned from the grocery store. His legs were sprawled on the floor and his head was arched against the back cushion.

"I didn't expect to see you here," John said, holding two plastic bags of groceries in one hand.

Brody rose, stretched his arms, and let out a light yawn. "Ashley's mom finally showed up, so I took a break. I'm exhausted."

"I bet. Are you hungry?"

"Yes and no. Don't know what I feel like eating. Any pastries around here?"

John raised one of the bags. "Right here."

Brody trailed John into the kitchen, sitting at the counter while John removed items from the bags and put them away. He handed the box of pastries to Brody, who immediately took one out and began munching.

"Uh, save some for your mom and grandmother," John said. "Have you seen your mom?"

"Nah. I only got here about fifteen minutes before you."

The TV was on in the den. John walked to the steps and saw Geraldine in the recliner, apparently watching a game shown, unless she was asleep or in a catatonic state. He went on to the bedroom, where Sally was curled under a white sherpa blanket, snoring lightly. He closed the door quietly and returned to the kitchen, where Brody was finishing a long john.

"Mom's asleep," John said. "I think your grandmother is as well. Why don't you go to the den and get some rest on the sofa?"

"With the TV blaring?"

"Or go to the living room."

Brody took another pastry from the box and took a bite. John quietly picked up the container and placed it on the kitchen counter out of his son's reach. Brody didn't object or didn't notice.

"Want some coffee?

"I probably should be going back to the hospital. I wanted to give Ashley some time with her mom."

"You just got here. Go lie down and get some rest. I'll wake you in an hour or so."

Brody scooted off the stool. "Yeah, you're right." He stretched out his arms again. "This could turn into a long day."

"Let's hope not."

"I know Ashley wants to get it over with."

"How far along is she?"

"It seems like forever, but I think eight months. Could be a little longer. But who's counting now?"

"It's about over then."

"I sure hope so. It gets to be a drag after a while."

"Has it affected her studies?"

"A little. She's got a few more things to do with her dissertation. It's strange, but she was working on it when she started having the contractions."

"Maybe there's a connection."

"What do you mean?"

"Maybe being tense about completing her dissertation could affect her body."

"Never thought about that, but she has been putting in some long hours the past few weeks trying to wrap things up."

"Just forget anything I've said," John said.

"Why do you say that?"

"We're just a couple of guys who've never experienced pregnancy and childbirth," John said. "Talk to your mother or the doctor."

"I think you're right, Dad."

"But let me know if we can do anything to help."

"With her dissertation?"

John chuckled. "You are exhausted. I mean, with anything else."

"Uh, since you brought it up, we are running a little low on funds right now. We've had some unexpected expenses in the past few weeks. And this hospital visit is not going to help matters."

"How much?"

"Dunno." Brody shrugged. "Whatever you can spare."

"Now, Brody, you need to be more specific."

"Maybe a thousand dollars."

"I'll write you a check before you leave."

"Thanks, Dad. I don't know what I'd do without you and Mom."

"That's what parents are for. You'll learn that in the coming years. Once a parent, always a parent."

"That kinda sucks."

John slightly shook his head. "Sucks?"

"I don't mean it that way." Brody flashed an awkward grin.

"What do you mean, then?"

"It's just that you'd think the children would someday stand on their own two feet instead of getting handouts. You know what I mean?"

John pressed his tongue against his teeth and turned his head away from his son. He thought it was odd to be having this conversation with his thirty-nine-year-old son who had just asked him for a thousand dollars. Was Brody totally oblivious to his own situation? Or thought it didn't apply to him?

"It's being a family. Maybe someday you can return the favor. As they say, 'pay it forward.'"

"Mind if I have another long john?" Brody asked, glancing at the box on the counter. "For some reason, I'm still famished."

John shrugged. "Go ahead, but only one. We don't want to upset your grandmother. You know how much she loves them."

"Sure thing," Brody took a few quick steps to the counter, and snatched a pastry as if John would change his mind. He appeared surprised when John took one as well.

"When did you get here?"

John and Brody turned their heads in unison as Geraldine made her way toward them and eased up on the stool at the end of the bar.

"Hi, Grandma," Brody said, holding the half-eaten long john in one hand and placing his other arm around her shoulders. He kissed her lightly on the temple.

"Did you save any for me?" she asked, glancing around the kitchen with wide eyes.

"What's that?" John asked.

"You know what I'm talking about, John. Don't play games with me."

"You'll have to ask Brody. I told him to save you one."

"There'd better be more than one," she said, lightly tapping Brody on the hand.

"I saved you two," Brody said with an elfish grin. He stepped over to the counter, picked up the box and opened it as if to prove to her there were two of the custard-filled pastries.

"I can't eat them from here," she said, holding out a hand.

Brody set the container in front of her.

"Care for coffee?" John asked.

"That would be nice," she said, taking a nibble of a long john.

As John prepared a cup for her, Sally came down the steps from the bedroom, a sleepy smile and disheveled hair.

"Coffee for you, hon?" John asked, lifting a cup.

"Please," she murmured, as she sat patted Brody on the back and sat next to him. "Any change with Ashley?"

"She's much better," Brody said, stuffing the rest of his pastry in his mouth, leaving fragments of filling on the corner of his mouth that quickly disappeared with a swipe of his tongue, like a lizard.

John placed the cups of coffee in front of Sally and Geraldine, then sat down. Geraldine finished off her long john and grabbed the last one from the container before anyone could claim it, a sly move that didn't go unnoticed.

"Any of those left?" Sally asked, gazing at her mother.

"Oh, I thought you already had some," Geraldine said, taking a small bite to stake her claim to the last one.

"That's all right," Sally said. "I'm not that hungry."

"I can go out and get some more," John said. "It won't be a problem."

"Why don't you do that?" Geraldine said, lifting her brows. "Maybe get a dozen this time. I can't believe you only bought a half dozen. You should know better."

"I can't argue with that," John said. "Especially when it comes to you and long johns."

"Oh, don't bother on account of me," Sally said, about to take a sip from her cup. "It's a little late in the day for breakfast."

"I need to return to the hospital soon," Brody said. "Ashley and her mother are probably wondering what happened to me."

"I thought you were going to lie down for a bit," John said.

"I'll get some shut-eye at the hospital. The chair reclines."

"Do you want me to go back with you?" Sally asked.

"I'll be okay. I'll call you if anything comes up."

Whiskers bopped into the kitchen and stood next to John, staring at him with his big dark eyes and tapping his shoe to say he needed to go outside and relieve himself.

John sidled off the stool and followed Whiskers to the front door, almost as if he were following the pooch's command, and in a sense he was. "I'll be back in a few minutes."

"Uh, Dad," Brody said. "Don't forget what we discussed earlier."

"What was that?" Geraldine asked. "Trying to keep secrets from me?"

"No," Brody said, with a grimace.

"Then what is it?" she insisted.

"You don't have to know everything." Brody stood and turned toward Sally. "I'll call you, Mom, and let you know how Ashley's doing." He kissed her cheek and headed toward the upstairs bathroom.

"Why is that boy so rude?" Geraldine asked, twisting her head with a scowl. "I don't know where he got that from."

"He's worn-out from being up all night with Ashley," Sally said. "He'll be okay after he gets some rest."

"You're always defending him."

"Probably so," Sally said with a faint smile. "He's my son."

"And he's my grandson."

"Then you should understand."

"Now you're being rude to me."

"You know better than that." Sally reached over and placed her hand on her mother's forearm, but she moved it over to her side.

John returned to the kitchen and poured water into Whiskers' bowl. "Is everything all right?" he asked, sensing tension in the air.

"We were just discussing Brody," Sally said.

"So, what's your little secret?" Geraldine asked John with a stern look.

"There's no secret," John said as he eased back on a stool. "I'll tell you later, after he leaves."

"It has to be money then," Geraldine said with a smug expression. "That boy always wants money."

Brody returned to the kitchen, his long hair neatly brushed back and looking a bit refreshened. "Did I hear my name?"

"We were talking about Ashley," Sally said.

"Okay." Brody glanced around the counter with a skeptical look. John picked up on it and headed to the bedroom.

"Do you need anything?" Geraldine asked Brody with a syrupy grin. "I'll be glad to help. You know you can always count on your grandmother."

"I'm good." Brody kissed her cheek.

"I just want to make sure."

John returned holding a folded check and handed it to Brody, who flashed a quick smile and turned to leave. John followed him to the front door while Sally and Geraldine remained at the bar.

"Thanks for everything, Dad," Brody said. "I'll talk to you later." Brody surprised him with a quick hug.

When John came back to the kitchen, Sally was standing next to the toaster and an opened box of cherry Pop-Tarts.

"Are you sure you don't want me to go to the grocery store?" he asked.

"Maybe later."

"So, what's the secret?" Geraldine asked.

"You're sure persistent," John said with a light chuckle.

"Was it money?"

"Yes, it was Geraldine. They've had some unexpected expenses the past few weeks, so I loaned him some to tide them over until things are better."

"Loaned?"

"Yes, Geraldine."

"When has Brody ever repaid a loan? He's never paid me back for anything."

"How much does he owe you?"

"I'm not sure."

"Let me know and I'll reimburse you."

"Now *you're* being rude to me." Geraldine, tight-lipped, grabbed her cane and got off the stool. John wondered if she was fighting back tears.

"I'm just offering to help you."

Geraldine glared at him and took a few steps, then stopped for a moment near the stairs leading to her bedroom.

"You have some long john left on your plate," John said.

"Sally can have it." Geraldine said faintly. Seconds later, her bedroom door closed. Then the lock clicked.

"It looks like you're in the doghouse now," Sally said as she returned to the bar with her breakfast on a paper plate.

"I'll apologize later," he said with a shrug. "Maybe if I run back out and buy some more long johns as a peace offering?"

"It probably wouldn't hurt."

"I'll be back in about twenty minutes." John picked up his car keys and headed to the front door.

"Oh, John—" When he didn't reply, she whispered, "I was only kidding."

Five

After breakfast, Sally took a quick shower and got dressed to go to the hospital. John returned with the groceries, picked up the newspaper on the counter and went to the den, where he was ignored by Geraldine. She was in the recliner and immersed in *Days of Our Lives*. The volume was turned up to preclude any conversation.

"Do you want to go with me?" Sally asked as she stood at the top of the steps.

"Huh?" John said, putting a hand to his ear. "Hold on a second."

He walked up the steps to Sally. "Sorry, I couldn't hear you." He looked back at Geraldine, shaking his head in amusement. "I could say she's giving me the silent treatment in reverse."

Sally chuckled. "She'll get over it."

"She always does. Now, what did you want?"

"I was wondering if you wanted to go with me to the hospital?"

"I think I'll pass. I need to take Whiskers for a walk and do a few other things around here."

Sally gave him a sharp stare with furrowed brows. "I really think you should go with me."

"What?" John was puzzled.

"She *is* Brody's fiancée, and they need *our* support."

John folded the newspaper and placed it on the counter. "If you say so. Give me a couple of minutes to get ready. You can break the news to Geraldine." He shook his head as went to the bedroom.

~ * ~

While John was out of the room, Sally picked up the newspaper and went to the den. Geraldine glanced at her for a moment and turned her attention back to the soap opera.

"Is everything okay, Mother?" Sally asked, raising her voice to break Geraldine's imposed noise barrier in the room.

Geraldine didn't respond for several seconds as if she hadn't heard her, and perhaps she hadn't by her demeanor as her eyes were fixed on the flat TV screen. Then, she held the remote, lowered the volume a few decibels and cleared her throat. A commercial break.

"I just wish you and John would show me some respect," she said, her eyes watering as she turned toward Sally. "You still treat me like a guest, and I've lived here for more than a year. I am your mother, you know. I'd like to be treated like family instead of some old relic taking up space."

"Oh, Mother," Sally said, her voice breaking. "You are family. We just don't want to burden you with Brody's problems or anything else."

"Maybe they're not problems for me, but it's just what goes on in families. Believe it or not, I've lived through quite a few so-called problems in my ninety years."

"I know you have, Mother," Sally said with a tender smile. "We both have."

John stood at the top of the steps. "Ready, hon?"

"In a minute." Sally looked intently at Geraldine. "John, why don't you go on out to the car? Or, if you like, take Whiskers for a short walk."

"I thought you were in a hurry to leave."

"John, please." Sally turned and gave him an uneasy glance that communicated she was busy with her mother and to give her some time to finish.

"Sure. Come on, Whiskers, let's go outside." Whiskers sprang from his pad and dashed to the front door.

Sally was waiting for him in the living room when he returned ten minutes later. "I'm ready," she said with a glum face.

"Let me give Whiskers some fresh water and a treat, and I'll be with you." Whiskers led the way to the kitchen.

A few minutes later, they were in Sally's SUV and on their way to the hospital. John was about to turn on the radio but thought better of it and put his hand back on the steering wheel.

"Mother is upset," Sally said. "She says we don't show her enough respect and she doesn't believe we treat her as a member of the family."

"We've already heard that from her," John said with a glance at Sally. "She'll change her tune again. She always does. Honestly, I think we've fully integrated her into the family. I don't know what else she wants."

"You're probably right. She's most likely in one of her moods."

"You know, sometimes we have to treat her as a child."

"You don't think she picks up on that?" Sally said. "I know I would if people acted that way around me."

"Well, she pouts and can be self-centered like a child."

"I know adults who are that way."

"I don't want this to sound mean, but it's really not any of her business what goes on between us and Brody," John said as he pulled the SUV onto Harrodsburg Road. "As for what happened at the house, I didn't want to make Brody feel uncomfortable. I know he was embarrassed about asking us for money. If he wanted to ask his grandmother for money, he could have done that. It wouldn't be the first time."

"You've made your point."

"Anything else?"

"She is my mother," Sally said. "I just don't want her mistreated or disrespected."

"When have I ever done that?" John asked, tilting his head toward her.

"I'm sorry. I'm just upset right now with everything going on. You've always treated her with respect."

"And love," John added. "She can get under my skin at times, but I still love her all the same. She's quite the character, but I love her for it."

"I know you do, John. I appreciate that. I'm sorry if I insinuated you felt differently."

"And, by the way, she raised a lovely daughter."

"I love you," Sally said, dabbing at a tear on her cheek with a tissue.

"I love you, too. Is there anything else on your mind we need to discuss?"

"Why didn't you want to go to the hospital to see Ashley? She is Brody's fiancée and she's carrying our next grandchild."

"I just felt there's too much going on and she didn't need to have a room full of people. That can be stressful. I thought she needed to rest. That was my reasoning."

"She needs to know you are thinking about her. This is a difficult time for Ashley. Having this problem so late in her pregnancy is stressful. She needs all the support she can get."

"You're right, Sally."

"And Brody needs to know that as well."

"I agree."

"We won't stay long unless we need to. Her mother may want a short break, although I doubt she'll want to leave Ashley's side."

John tilted his head. "Just as we are with Chloe."

"Shoot! I forgot to call her and let her know what's going on," Sally said. "I'm a mess."

"Why don't you do that now?" John said as he pulled into the hospital parking lot. "We've got time."

Sally took her cell phone from her purse and hit the speed dial for Chloe. She got her voice mail and left her a brief message about Ashley's condition.

"She's probably got something going on with Whitney at school," Sally said, putting the phone back in her purse. "That's about the only time she never answers her phone."

"She'll call back," John said as he turned off the ignition.

"I'm sure of that."

Ashley was asleep when they got to her room. Brody was watching a basketball game on the television. Ashley's mother wasn't there.

"How's she doing?" Sally whispered as she stood next to Ashley.

Brody lowered the TV sound. "She's been sleeping most of the afternoon. The doctor came by an hour or so ago and said things looked better. She said false labor can last for a few weeks. We should be able to go back to the apartment in the morning."

"That's good news," John said, standing at the foot of the bed. "Where's Ashley's mother? Taking a break?"

"She went back to Louisville," Brody said. "Probably left about thirty minutes ago. She said she'd check back with us after she got home."

"Really?" Sally said, brows knitted. "I can't believe she'd leave with Ashley still here." She took a deep breath and sighed.

Brody simply shrugged. "After the doctor said things were better, Donna thought there wasn't any reason for her to hang around any longer. She said she'll come back if anything changes. I told her I'd keep her updated."

Ashley's eyes flickered as she awakened from her nap. A drowsy smile crossed her face as she looked at Sally.

"Feeling better?" Sally asked, reaching down and clutching her hand.

"I think so," Ashley mumbled. "Where's Mom?"

Brody stepped to the side of the bed. "She went back to Louisville."

Ashley raised her head slightly from the pillow. "What?"

"Don't worry, she said she'll come back if anything happens."

"I can't believe she left." Ashley shook her head in disbelief.

"I told her it was all right," Brody said with a bright grin. "I didn't want her driving back in the dark."

"She could have stayed here tonight." Ashley's eyes began to tear.

Sally glanced at John but said nothing.

"She said you were in good hands," Brody said. "I'll take care of you."

"How about if I stay here tonight?" Sally said as she took a tissue from the dispenser and handed it to Ashley.

"I don't want to put you to that trouble," Ashley said, wiping her eyes.

"It's not any trouble." Sally squeezed her hand and smiled.

Ashley's eyes welled again.

John moved next to the bed and patted Ashley's slender shoulder. "Everything's going to be all right. You just let us know if there's anything you need."

"Thank you, Mr. Ross."

"It's John," he said with a warm smile.

"John, why don't you go and do your errands?" Sally said. "Maybe you can bring back something for us to eat. If Ashley is like me, anything beats hospital food."

"Don't forget about me," Brody said.

"Text me in an hour or so and let me know what you'd like to eat," John said.

~ * ~

After John left, Sally pulled over a chair and sat next to Ashley. Brody turned his attention to a basketball game. Sally had to ask him to lower the volume.

After several seconds, Ashley turned toward Sally, her mouth tight and cheeks puffed slightly.

"Is there something the matter?" Sally asked.

Ashley let out a breath of air. "I can't believe my mom. Would you ever do that to Brody or your daughter if they were in the hospital? I know you wouldn't because you stayed with your daughter in New York when she was getting treatments for cancer. I'm sorry, but her name escapes me right now."

"It's Chloe," Sally said. "And I probably would be at their side if they were hospitalized or in some other condition. But perhaps your mother had a reason to leave. I wouldn't be too hard on her. I'm sure she felt you were in good hands. And she's not that far away."

"That's beside the point, Mrs. Ross. You know that."

"Call me Sally. And I'm not going to judge your mother. We all have our reasons for doing things. I'm sure she'll be with you if things change."

"You don't know my mother."

Sally didn't respond, and simply smiled and patted Ashley's arm.

Six

Later in the afternoon, after picking up groceries and twelve of the usual pastry, and getting a carryout from a sandwich shop for Sally, Brody, and Ashley, John was back at home with Geraldine and Whiskers. He made the mistake of telling her about the sandwiches and chips.

"Didn't you think I might be getting hungry, too?" Geraldine asked as they sat in the den, where she apparently had been all afternoon watching TV.

"I figured we could grab a bite to eat here," he said, raising his brows with a weak smile. "I can whip up something from the refrigerator. What would you like?"

"What do we have?"

"I'll have to check."

"Why don't you do that and let me know if it's something delicious I'd like."

"Don't you trust me to come up with something to eat?"

"I might not be in the mood for it."

"Oh."

"Ever since you mentioned the sandwiches, I've had my mind on something like that."

"I suppose I could go back out and buy you one."

"That would be too much trouble for you," she said.

"Not really," he said.

"I wonder if they deliver?"

"I never thought about that, but I bet they do. There are several delivery services that restaurants use."

"It would sure save you the trouble of going back out."

"So, what would you like for me to order?"

"What did Sally have?"

"A vegetarian sub."

"Ugh," she said, scrunching her face. "I don't know where you and Sally got off on that vegetarian thing. It's not healthy."

"I beg your pardon?" John's head arched back. "It's very healthy."

"Well, I'm ninety and have lived on meat and other things you consider unhealthy."

"I never said they were unhealthy. I've always said people should eat those things in moderation. And keep off processed meats and other foods."

"Well, then, order me a turkey sub with bacon. And a big bag of potato chips."

"That doesn't sound too—

"Now be quiet," she said, lifting a hand. "You asked me what I wanted. I didn't ask for a mini-lecture on the side."

John rose from the couch, smiling. "Touché!"

"I wonder if the restaurant has cookies or brownies?"

"I can ask. Which would you prefer?"

"Surprise me."

"Are you sure?"

"Of course, John. But just don't make it oatmeal raisin."

"I'm glad you told me that."

"Anything else?"

"I guess I wouldn't mind a soft drink."

"Diet soda?"

"Now you're teasing me," she said. "I'm not Libby."

"Just checking. I'll make it a regular Coke or Pepsi."

As John headed toward the kitchen to get his cellphone, Sally returned from the hospital, holding a bag as she walked to the kitchen.

"I didn't expect to see you so soon," John said. "Is everything okay at the hospital?"

"She's asleep," Sally said, sitting at the counter. "I decided it was a good time to leave."

"What's in the bag?"

"Half a sandwich and chips. I couldn't eat it all and thought Mother would want it."

"Uh, I don't think so. She's not into healthy food."

"What do you mean?"

"We'll discuss it later."

Geraldine got up from the recliner and joined them in the kitchen.

"Have you placed my order?" she asked John.

"I was just getting ready to."

"I have half a sandwich and a bag of chips," Sally said, pointing at the bag on the counter."

"She doesn't want it," John blurted.

"How do you know what I want?" Geraldine asked with squinted eyes. "I think I can make up my mind on what I want and don't want. What kind of sandwich is it?"

"Vegetarian."

Geraldine grimaced and glanced at John. "Oh, I forgot. Go ahead and place my order."

John turned toward Sally and shrugged. "I told you so."

Sally crunched her brows. "Whatever."

"Put it in the fridge and I'll eat it later," John said, adding, "I like eating healthy."

"Quit being a smart aleck, John." Geraldine said. "Just hurry up and order. A person could starve around here."

"I'll save the chips for you."

"What's going on here?" Sally asked.

"We had a discussion about eating healthy," John said.

"I told him I know what's healthy for me," Geraldine said smugly. "I haven't been around for ninety years for nothing."

"You made your point, Geraldine," John said.

"And I haven't had heart issues like someone I know," Geraldine said looking at John. She turned her head toward Sally. "Or with my boobies."

"I don't have breast problems," Sally said defensively.

"I recall you having to go to the doctor a couple years ago about it."

"I forgot about that."

"I didn't," Geraldine said, raising her chin. "And how about Chloe?"

"I'm not sure if her ovarian cancer has anything to do with diet," Sally said.

Geraldine tilted her head. "You never know."

"Can we change the subject?" John asked. "I'd like to place this order."

"Getting under your skin?" Geraldine asked, raising her brows.

"You know, I think I'm going to drive over to the shop. It's not that far away. It'd be quicker than phoning in a delivery order."

"I just wish you'd make up your mind. A person could starve around here."

"There's a sandwich in here if you're concerned about starving," John said, lifting the bag.

"There you go again," Geraldine said.

"I'm outta here," John said. "I should be back in twenty minutes or so. I hope you don't starve in the meantime."

Sally laughed, prompting a hard stare from Geraldine.

"Anything else while I'm out?" John asked as he turned to leave.

"Just go," Geraldine said.

Whiskers followed John to the front door, apparently hoping they'd be going for a walk or that he'd be able to do his doggy thing.

"Sorry, little buddy," John said. "I'll be right back to let you out."

"I'll take care of Whiskers," Sally said. "You go on. We don't want Mother to starve."

"I heard that!" Geraldine said.

"I'm kidding, Mother."

Sally stepped out of the house with John while Whiskers dashed to the side of the house.

"I need to get away from Mother, too," Sally said. "She's still in one of her moods."

"It's probably my fault for talking about healthy foods," John said.

Suddenly, there was a rap on the storm door. They turned around and faced a tight-lipped Geraldine.

"Okay, okay, I'm going," John said, raising his arms as he stepped off the porch and marched toward the car.

Seven

John was standing in line as Geraldine's sandwich was being made at the Subway when his cellphone vibrated.

"John, come back home," Sally said in an anxious voice. "Ashley's gone back in labor and she's having problems. She's hemorrhaging."

John looked at the employee, reached in his pocket and pulled out a five-dollar bill, and slapped it on the counter. "Sorry, I need to go. Emergency." The employee gave him a puzzled look and said, "Okay. dude."

Sally was standing in the living room when John returned ten minutes later. "I'm ready to go."

Geraldine ambled in and stopped, slightly leaning on her cane. "Where's my sandwich?"

"I'll pick up one later," John said as he stood at the door.

"Well, that sure takes the cake."

"Mother, you know why," Sally said, grabbing her purse on the easy chair.

"It wouldn't have been that much trouble."

"Bye, Mother. I'll let you know how Ashley is doing." Sally and John left before Geraldine could utter another word.

Brody was in the hallway outside Ashley's room, leaning against the wall, head slumped. He looked up when he heard Sally call his name.

"She's in the delivery room," Brody said, teary-eyed. "She just started bleeding like crazy."

Sally hugged him as John placed a hand on his shoulder. "Let's go inside the room and wait for her," Sally said.

Brody opened the door, and they followed him inside. Brody stood by the large window, staring out into the empty courtyard, while John and Sally sat on the chairs. The TV was on, but the sound muted.

"We were just watching a ball game when she suddenly started screaming," Brody said, his back to them. "Then there was blood all over the place. I didn't know what to do. I ran out and called for the nurses, and then they wheeled her bed out of the room. She looked so scared when she looked at me." He began sobbing.

John walked over and placed an arm around Brody's shoulder. Brody, slightly shaking, turned and buried his head in John's shoulder. Sally pursed her lips as tears trickled down her cheeks.

A nurse entered the room, standing where the bed had been. "We've got her stabilized right now, but she has lost a lot of blood."

"And the baby?" Sally asked.

"The baby has a strong heartbeat, so everything is fine right now. The doctor will do a C-section after she determines Ashley is strong enough to endure it. She signed the consent form a few minutes ago. Right now, she is being given blood."

The nurse managed a weak smile. "I'll keep you posted on everything. It shouldn't be much longer." She left the room.

"That's encouraging," John said as he led Brody to the chair he vacated. "They've got her stabilized. Right, Sally?"

Sally wiped the tears off her face with a tissue. "I believe so. It sounds like they've got everything under control. We just have to wait."

Brody was tight-lipped, his eyes watery.

"Have you called Ashley's parents?" Sally asked.

"Oh, shit." Brody let out a long sigh. "Everything happened so fast I forgot." He took out his cellphone and punched in their number. "Damn! Voicemail."

Sally held out her hand for the phone. "Let me have it." After the greeting ended, she told Ashley's parents about their daughter's condition and urged them to get to the hospital as soon as they could.

"Thanks, Mom," Brody said when she handed the phone back to him. "I can't even think straight anymore."

Seconds later, his phone rang. He answered. "Are you serious?" he yelled and ended the call.

"What is it, son?" John asked.

Brody shook his head in disbelief. "Someone wanting to sell me an extended car warranty. Unreal!"

"I get them all the time."

"I do, too, but didn't expect one at this moment. This is totally absurd."

"I agree. Just settle down."

Sally's cellphone ringtone began playing *Beethoven's Fifth Symphony*.

"She's in the delivery room, Mother," Sally said after a pause. "We're waiting to hear from the nursing staff and doctor. Right now, she's stabilized, and the baby is okay."

After another pause, she said, "I'll let Brody know you're thinking of him. And I'll tell John as well." She ended the call and looked at Brody. "Grandmother says she'll pray for you and Ashley."

Brody smiled. "That's nice."

"She was thinking of me?" John asked, arching his neck.

"There was something else."

"What was that?"

"She wanted to make sure you didn't forget about her sandwich," Sally said, unable to suppress a grin.

"That mother of yours," John said, glancing at the ceiling. "I should have known."

Brody looked at the TV and saw an NCAA basketball game was playing. He unmuted the sound.

"Can I get something at the vending machine for anyone?" John asked.

"I wouldn't mind coffee," Sally said.

"How about you, Brody?" John asked.

Brody, his eyes still fixed on the game, said, "Coke."

John went to the vending area and got their drinks. As he was returning, he saw a nurse enter the room. He picked up his step to hear what she had to say.

"Everything's going smoothly," she said. "The doctor doesn't foresee any problems with the C-section. I hope to be back soon with some good news for everyone."

"Can I see her?" Brody asked with pleading eyes. "Only for a few minutes?"

"That shouldn't be a problem, but let's hurry. Come with me."

"I need to tell her I love her."

As Brody followed the nurse to the delivery room, Sally had a fixed smile, as if in deep thought.

"What are you thinking about, hon?" John asked quietly, standing next to her.

"We can discuss it later. Now is not a good time."

Eight

An hour passed and they hadn't received an update about Ashley's condition. Even Brody paced back and forth, muting the TV but occasionally glancing at the screen.

"What's taking so long?" he said, waving his arms in frustration. "I wish somebody would tell us something. This is ridiculous."

"I'm sure they're making certain everything is going as smoothly and safely as possible," Sally said. "Ashley had serious complications with the bleeding. It's going to take time."

"I wanted to stay with her, but a nurse told me it's against hospital policy since it's an emergency delivery. There were people all over the delivery room doing stuff. I guess I would have been in the way."

"Ashley knows you were there for her and that's what matters right now," Sally said.

"And I got to kiss her and tell her how much I love her," Brody said, teary-eyed.

"Everything's going to be fine," John said, putting an arm around his son's shoulders. "Having a baby is nerve-wracking for everyone—mom, dad, and grandparents. I remember when—"

At that moment, there was a soft knock on the door and Ashley's parents entered the room. Her father was tall and slender with a thin moustache, thick salt-and-pepper hair, and wearing khaki pants and a blue blazer over a white shirt. The mother was medium height, in a black dress that revealed some cleavage and a string of pearls around her plump neck. They didn't appear to have been waiting at home for a call about their daughter.

"Have you heard anything?" Ashley's mother asked no one as she placed her oversized purse on the floor. "We got here as soon as we could."

"We were across the river in Indiana when we received your message," her father said. "And then we hit some heavy traffic on the bridge back to Kentucky."

John motioned with his hand for Brody to stand, giving up his chair for Ashley's mother.

"The nurse was here about a while ago and told us everything was going smoothly," Sally said. "They're doing a C-section. We hope to hear something soon."

"A C-section?" Donna exclaimed. "Why didn't you tell us sooner?"

"We were only told about an hour ago," John said.

"But you could have texted or called us." Donna scowled. "She's our daughter."

"Honey, please calm down," the man said, tapping her shoulder. "It wouldn't have done any good. We were on the road."

"But we wouldn't have been blindsided like we are now," Donna said.

"I apologize," Sally said. "It's been rather hectic around here the past few hours. And like I said, we were only informed about an hour before you got here."

"Oh, well," Donna said. "I shouldn't be surprised."

"What's that supposed to mean?" John said.

"Never mind."

The man looked somberly at his wife, placing a forefinger over his mouth for her to be quiet.

"This has been nerve wracking," Brody said. "I never want to go through this again."

"And my daughter as well," Ashley's father said.

"That's what I mean," Brody said weakly. "It's been difficult. For both of us. Er, I mean for all of us."

"Can I get either of you something to drink?" John asked Ashley's parents. "There's a vending room down the hall."

"No, we're good," Ashley's father said.

"By the way, I'm John and this is my wife, Sally," John said. "I apologize for not introducing ourselves earlier."

"I'm George Garcia. And you know Donna," he said, nodding toward his wife, sitting stiffly and looking down at her clasped hands as if in prayer.

Sally rose from her chair. "I'm going to step out in the hallway for a few minutes. I need some fresh air."

"I'll join you," John said as he followed her toward the door.

Brody made a move to follow them, but John said, "Why don't you stay here in case the nurse returns?"

"I guess so," Brody said. "Can you get me another Coke?"

"Sure. We'll be back in a few minutes.

John and Sally ambled toward the vending area halfway down the hall, neither saying a word until they reached the soda machine.

"I'm really concerned," Sally said while John inserted coins into the machine. "We should have heard something by now. I could understand if she was in labor, but since she's having a C-section, it shouldn't take that long. I pray there haven't been any complications. I didn't want to say anything around Brody or her parents."

"I'm sure her parents understand," John said. "You know they've experienced this. And isn't George a surgeon? But it's all new to Brody. I'm not sure he understands the seriousness of the situation."

"I'm glad we're here for him and Ashley."

"I'm happy her parents finally showed up. I was worried they hadn't heard your voice mail."

"Do you think I should have continued to try to reach her parents?" Sally asked. "Ashley's mother has me feeling guilty about it."

"You did the right thing," John said. "They knew their daughter was in the hospital. So don't fret about it. That's their problem."

"Do you think I should call Mother and give her an update?"

"It probably wouldn't hurt since she's at home by herself."

Sally got the phone from her purse and called Geraldine's cellphone. When there wasn't an answer, she called the landline. She was about to end the call when Geraldine answered.

John watched as Sally talked to her mom, knowing Geraldine was likely giving her a hard time.

"I'm sorry, Mother," Sally said, letting out a light sigh. "I tried your cell first and you didn't answer. That's why I called the regular line."

After a short pause, she continued, "I'll remember that next time. But you shouldn't have your phone turned off."

Sally rolled her eyes. "I'm just calling to tell you that Ashley is still in the delivery room. I thought you would like to know. She's having a C-section so we may be here for a while longer. I'll let you know when she has the baby and when we'll be heading home. Is there anything you need for us to get?"

"Yes, Mother, I'll remind John to pick up a sandwich for you."

John whispered, "Ask her if she's let Whiskers out to potty."

Sally relayed the message. "Thanks, Mother. And don't forget to feed him and refresh his water bowl."

Sally closed her eyes for a moment, sighing again as her mother talked. "I need to go, Mother. We're waiting to hear from a nurse about Ashley's condition. We'll talk later. Love you."

"Interesting conversation?" John asked.

"You could say so," Sally said. "I wonder if I should call Wendell and Libby and have them check in on her?"

"You may want to give that some more thought," John said about contacting her brother and his wife. "You know how she feels about someone watching over her."

"You're right. It'd probably be easier for one of us to go back and check in on her."

"I can do that after we get an update about Ashley," John said as they walked back to her room.

"And you can pick up her sandwich."

"Of course," John said with a chuckle. "How could I forget? We have to set our priorities here."

"Now John, don't be so sarcastic. We both know how Mother can be."

When they returned, George and Donna were sitting quietly next to each other. Brody had unmuted the TV and was watching another tournament game. He had turned down the volume to where it wasn't too much of a distraction.

"Still no word?" John asked George.

"Nothing," he said, pressing his lips tightly.

"Hopefully, it won't be much longer," Donna said softly, reaching over and clutching George's hand. "I wish I could be with her."

"Ashley mentioned that you're a surgeon," John said to George.

"I was an orthopedic surgeon," he said. "While obstetrics isn't my specialty, I understand the seriousness of the procedure."

"Do you know Dr. Palmer?" Sally asked.

"Not personally but I checked into her background, and she has excellent qualifications and recommendations. Ashley is in good hands."

John and Sally walked to the large window, glancing at the long shadow from the building stretching across the courtyard from the fading sunlight. The only sound in the room came from the TV, which seemed to remove some of the gloominess of the moment, lulling them into a numbness from the endless chatter and crowd noise.

A nurse in blue scrubs clutching a computer tablet entered the room. They all turned and stared at her with frozen expressions. The nurse managed a tiny smile and said, "You have a baby girl."

Everyone's shoulders dropped with the news, and they smiled broadly as they looked at each other. John and Sally hugged, as did George and Donna. Brody flashed a grin, then John pulled him over. Sally embraced her son for a few seconds then kissed him on the cheek.

"How's our daughter?" George asked.

"She's lost some blood, but that was expected and is under control," the nurse said. "She's sedated right now."

"When can we see her and the baby?" Donna asked.

"They're getting the baby cleaned and doing a few tests. It shouldn't be long. As for the mother, it may take a while longer, but I'll let you know when you can be with her. As I said, she lost blood, so it will take a while. But she appears to be recovering from everything."

"Thank God," Donna said, wiping her eyes with a tissue.

Nine

"I wonder how long it will be until we can be with Ashley?" Brody said after the nurse had given them the update. "And I want to see the baby. This is taking forever."

"It takes time," Sally said. "They have to clean her and do a few assessments to make sure everything is okay."

"I'm still concerned about Ashley," Donna said. "First pregnancies can be difficult. I know from experience. I had a difficult time. Remember George?"

"I recall you being in labor for a long time," he said. "I didn't think it was ever going to end."

"But childbirth can be so beautiful," Donna said.

"I'm sure it is," George said with a warm smile. "Especially when it's over."

"Did you experience any problems with Brody?" Donna asked Sally. "And don't you have another child, too?"

"We have a daughter, Chloe, who is forty-one," Sally said." My pregnancies were rather routine. Brody's was easier. I think I was in labor for about an hour before he decided to enter the world." She smiled softly at her son.

There was a light knock on the door and the nurse stepped inside the room and grinned as she looked at everyone. "Your precious baby is in the nursery if you want to see her through the window."

Without hesitation, they followed her out the door and midway down the hall to the nursery, where several other dads, grandparents, and relatives were marveling at the newborns.

Brody was the first to the large rectangular glass, glancing over the small cribs before he saw "Baby Garcia" written on a note card. She was kicking her tiny legs back and forth. "There she is!" he gushed.

The grandparents surrounded him, all with beaming smiles, as they stared at the newborn. "She weighs six pounds and ten ounces," Brody said, excitedly. "And she's twenty inches long."

"It looks like she has all her fingers and toes," John said with a chuckle.

"Huh?" Brody uttered.

"That's a joke," John said, patting his son's shoulder.

"She's beautiful," Donna said. "I think she looks like Ashley."

"She is a little princess," George said, his hands on his wife's shoulders as he stood behind her.

"So precious," Sally said.

"And to think we were at the casino in New Albany when we read the message," George said. "We could have missed all this."

"I'm glad you checked your phone," Sally said, her brows gathered.

"We were attending a concert," Donna said. "We had tickets we purchased several months ago and didn't want to waste them."

John sensed Sally's uneasiness about Ashley's parents being at a concert rather than at their daughter's side. "I'm going back to the room," he said. "Maybe we'll hear some news about Ashley."

John took Sally's hand, giving it a light tug, and she walked with him to the room. Brody, George, and Donna remained at the nursery, ogling at the new addition to their families.

"I can't believe they went to a concert while her daughter was in labor," Sally said in the quiet of the room. "That's unbelievable."

"I'm surprised as well," John said. "Maybe she thought Ashley would be in labor for a long time."

"That's still no excuse. She's their daughter."

"You can't stop everything because of having a baby. The labor pains could have lasted for hours."

"Whose side are you on?" Sally asked, her eyes narrowed.

"Yours, honey. I was just sayin'—"

Sally ran a finger across his lips. John knew to keep his mouth closed.

Brody showed up a minute later, sitting next to Sally, while John stood by the window. The sun had already set, leaving the courtyard bathed in soft light from a row of lampposts.

"Ashley's parents are sure excited about the baby," Brody said. "Do you think she looks like Ashley?"

"I see you and Ashley in her," Sally said. "The best of both of you."

Brody grinned. "Good."

"I think all babies look about the same," John said. "Most of them are bald, puffy-faced, and skinny legs."

"You would think that," Sally said. "I think they're beautiful."

"I didn't say they were ugly," John said. "Although a few of them are." He chuckled.

"John, please keep your thoughts to yourself. You're already close to being in the doghouse."

George and Donna entered the room. Donna sat on the small recliner while George stood next to the bed.

"I'm really concerned about Ashley," George said quietly, his hands trembling. "It's been quite a while since we heard about her condition."

"Me, too," Brody said. "Something's not right."

Donna burst into tears. George hurried to console her, leaning down and holding her hands. He glared at Brody for a moment.

"I'm sorry," Brody said, pressing his lips. "I just meant that it's taking too damn long to hear anything. I'm going to the nurses' station and see what's going on."

"I'll go with you, son," John said.

"I'm going as well," George said as he followed John and Brody out of the room.

The men stood at the counter of the nurses' station while several nurses were seated in front of computers, seemingly unaware of the concerned visitors. The nurse who had been giving updates was not there. Finally, one looked up at them. "Yes?"

"Uh, we're checking on Ashley Garcia," Brody said. "We haven't heard anything in ages."

The nurse looked at the charts, then picked up the phone. Less than a minute later, the nurse who had been providing information about Ashley and the baby came out of an adjoining room and walked toward them, unsmiling.

"Can you tell us what's going on?" Brody asked, a touch of irritation in his voice.

"Mr. Ross, she's still sedated," the nurse replied. "She's undergone a difficult delivery, so it's going to take a while. I'll let you know as soon as I can. In the meantime, I'll try to get in touch with Dr. Palmer and she if she can stop by and talk to you."

"That would be much appreciated," George said.

"How long will that be?" John asked.

"I have to get in touch with her first," the nurse said. "She could be making rounds or delivering another baby. But I'll see what I can do. Please be patient."

"That's easy for you to say," Brody said.

George stepped toward the nurse. "I want to let you know I'm a doctor. I would appreciate that you be straight with us. Okay?"

"I am, sir," the nurse replied. "I can only tell you what I know."

"Thank you," George said.

The men walked silently back to Ashley's room.

"What did they say?" Sally asked.

"She's still sedated," John said. "They're going to try to get the doctor to come by and give us an update."

"I'm not holding my breath," Brody said.

"Just be patient, son," John said. "We know she's in recovery and being cared for. That's what matters right now."

"You sound like the nurse."

"She's right," George said. "You don't rush these things."

Ten

The men watched a basketball game on the TV as if in a self-induced trance while the women conversed quietly in the corner of the room as they waited for an update on Ashley's condition. John walked to the open door periodically, glancing down the hall both ways as if to conjure a nurse or doctor into the room. On his last venture, he nearly bumped into a person coming into the room.

"Excuse me," the woman said. She was wearing a white coat with a stethoscope draped around her neck.

John stepped back, red-faced from the unexpected encounter. She walked to the foot of the bed, holding an iPad and letting out a light sigh. Brody muted the TV sound as everyone stood and gathered around her.

"I'm Dr. Anne Palmer," she said. "I apologize for not getting with you sooner, but we've had several emergencies this afternoon. It's been a long day-."

George interrupted her. "Please, Doctor, what is the condition of my daughter?"

Dr. Palmer cleared her throat. "She is coming out of the sedation, so you should be able to see her soon. Her condition is stable, but we're monitoring her recovery. Because of the blood loss and trauma from childbirth, we've been concerned about possible clots. We're monitoring her condition and hope to prevent any complications."

"Is she out of the woods now?" Brody asked.

"I'm not sure if I would use that phrase," the doctor said. "But she is gradually showing signs of recovery. We'll continue to monitor her condition until we feel it's safe to return her to her room."

"Has she seen the baby?" Donna asked.

"Only for a moment after the delivery," Dr. Palmer said. "A nurse held the baby for her to see. I can tell you that your daughter smiled before she drifted to sleep. Is there anything else?"

"Just let us know when we can see her," George said.

"Doctor, my husband is a doctor as well," Donna said, as if it would persuade Dr. Palmer to give them priority attention.

"Ma'am, there's not anything else I can tell you right now," Dr. Palmer said, a slight smile crossing her mouth.

"We just want to let you know we realize the seriousness of her condition," George said.

"It shouldn't be much longer." Dr. Palmer glanced at each person, then turned and left.

"Well, that's certainly good news," Sally said. "Ashley is recovering and getting better."

"I suppose our prayers have been answered," Donna said, dabbing her teary eyes with a tissue.

"What do you think, Dr. Garcia?" John asked. "Do you think she was encouraging?"

"I sure hope she was. And you can call me George. I'm not doctoring right now. I'm a concerned parent, just like you and Sally."

"I'm glad she got to see the baby," Brody said. "That has to be something she can looking forward to when she's better."

"Hopefully, she'll have her in her arms soon," Donna said without looking at Brody. "They need to be bonding right now. That's so important. Right, George?"

"Yes, dear," he said.

"I'm going back to the nursery to see her again," Brody said. "I sure wish they'd let us hold her, at least for a few minutes."

"I'm sure they will in due time," Sally said. "Probably after Ashley returns to the room. They'll probably set up a bassinette in here."

"I think it's more important for Ashley to be with the baby," Donna said. "Before any of us holds her."

"But I'd at least like to touch her," Brody said. "I *am* her father."

Donna glanced smugly at her husband.

John felt unexpected tension fill the room like a heavy vapor. He ambled over to Brody and clutched his forearm. "I'll go with you to see the baby again," and he led him out of the room.

The nursery window was smudged with finger and nose prints. Another new dad was at the other end, in a world of his as he observed his tiny son.

"Why doesn't Ashley's mother want me or anyone else to hold the baby?" Brody asked, staring at his sleeping baby. "I've been with Ashley throughout the pregnancy. I feel connected to the baby. Maybe not as much as Ashley, but gee, I've felt her kick and move around in Ashley's tummy. I've helped choose clothes and furniture. Her mom acts like I don't count for anything."

"Don't take it personally. She's stressed, son," John said in a calming tone. "I guess we all are. She just wants the best for her daughter right now. That's understandable. Don't you think?"

"But I'm the father, and I want the best for her, too. Ashley wouldn't mind if we held the baby. She'd understand."

Sally walked up behind them, surprising them for a moment. She squeezed between them to see her granddaughter. "Isn't she a beauty?"

Brody turned toward her. "Do you know why Ashley's mom said that about holding the baby?"

"I don't know, sweetie. Maybe she's being protective and wants Ashley to be the first to spend time with the baby."

"I wouldn't try to read her mind," John said.

"Let's not discuss her right now," Sally said. "There are more important things, such as Ashley and the baby. They need our attention."

"Well, her parents never cared that much for me," Brody said in a sulking tone.

"Now why would you say that?" John asked.

"You don't know?"

"That's why I asked."

"Because they see their daughter as a high achiever and me as a dropout and former druggie. You know they had high hopes for her until I came along."

"Have they ever said anything to you about it?" Sally asked.

"No, but they've never acted comfortable around me. I've never felt I was part of their family."

"George seems cordial," John said. "At least to some extent."

"It's more Donna," Brody said, taking a deep breath. "I've about had it with that woman!"

"Donna and I were having a pleasant conversation when Dr. Palmer showed up in the room," Sally said. "We talked about having babies, raising kids, and her job as an educator. I suppose we had some things in common, since I was a teacher."

"She probably said more to you than she's ever said to me," Brody said, grim-faced.

"She brought it up about George giving up his practice as a surgeon and becoming a professor at the medical school. Did you know he has Parkinson's disease?"

"I noticed his right hand sometimes quivers, but I didn't know it was Parkinson's," John said. "I didn't give it any thought.

I can get that way when I'm nervous or apprehensive about something."

"This is the first time I've heard it," Brody said. "Ashley never mentioned it to me."

"Maybe it was recently diagnosed, and they kept it from her and others," Sally said. "I don't know."

"I thought he had the shakes because of a drinking problem," Brody said. "Maybe too many tequilas." Brody laughed at his comment, but John and Sally frowned.

"That's not nice," Sally said.

"I was only joking."

"I can understand why he quit being a surgeon," John said. "You certainly need a steady hand."

"Anyway, Donna also told me she hates being in the car with him especially when he hasn't taken his medicine," Sally said. "She said it can be nerve-wracking to see his shaky hands on the steering wheel. She added that was one reason they were late getting here. His hands tremble more when he is upset about something."

"I've learned more about them from you than anytime with Ashley," Brody said. "That's odd because I thought she had shared a lot of stuff with me."

"You'll discover you share more the longer you're with someone," John said. "Right, Sally?"

"Let's talk about this later," Sally said with a tender smile. "Let's just think about Ashley and the beautiful baby you and she produced. We have a lot to be thankful for right now."

"I'll try to," Brody said, placing his hand to the glass as if trying to touch the baby.

A nurse noticed the gesture, walked over and picked up the baby. She went to the window, holding the newborn close so they could get a closer look. The baby twisted a little and appeared to smile.

"Ah man, did you see that?" Brody said with a big grin.

"She's a sweetheart, that's for sure," John said.

After a minute, the nurse smiled at them and placed the baby back in the crib. John mouthed "thank you" to her.

"Let's go back to the room," Sally said. "Maybe there'll be another update about Ashley."

"Speaking of updates, have you called Geraldine?" John asked. "She's probably wondering what's going on here."

"I'll go to the waiting room and call while you and Brody go to the room. I shouldn't be long."

George and Donna weren't in the room when they returned. "I wonder where they are?" John said.

"Beats me," Brody said, shrugging. "Maybe they went to get something to eat."

"Perhaps. But you'd think they'd let us know."

"Not really."

Sally returned to the room about five minutes later. "Where's Donna and George?"

"No clue," John said. "They weren't here when we got here."

"Maybe they went back to the casino for another concert," Brody said with a light laugh. "It wouldn't surprise me."

"Now, don't be that way," John said.

"Oh well, Mother seems to be okay," Sally said. "I told her about Ashley and that we hoped we wouldn't be here much longer."

"And she reminded you to tell me to pick up the sandwich," John said.

"How did you guess?" Sally laughed.

The conversation abruptly ended when they noticed George at the doorway, looking as if he were in shock. And perhaps he was.

"What's the matter?" John asked.

"Ashley's gone."

<h1 style="text-align:center">Eleven</h1>

"What are you talking about?" John asked. "Has she been moved to another room?"

"She died." George's body faltered, his knees bending as John rushed toward him, grabbing him a moment before he was about to collapse on the gray tile floor. Brody followed, placing an arm around George's back, and they pulled him to a chair inside the room. George bowed his head, sobbing.

"Where's Donna?" Sally asked.

"She's with Ashley," George said, his voice cracking. "She didn't want to leave her."

Sally glanced at John. "I'm going to be with her." She hurried out of the room toward the nurses' station.

Brody walked to the window, stared up at the murky and cloudless sky, and wept. John stepped away from George, gently tapping Brody on the back, and moved to comfort his son. Brody turned and buried his face against John's shoulder as his crying grew louder and body trembled.

"I can't believe this," Brody said. He sniffled several times. "How could this happen? I thought she was going to be all right. Isn't that what the doctor said?"

"I don't know, son," John said quietly as he continued to hold Brody. "Some things happen that doctors have no control over."

George remained slumped in the chair, his face buried in his hands. Silent.

John guided Brody toward the small recliner, then picked up the remote and turned off the television. The only light in the room emanated from the fluorescent light strip behind Ashley's empty bed. John walked to the doorway, waiting for Sally and Donna to return.

After several minutes, he took out his phone and called Geraldine and told her the heartbreaking news. To his surprise, Geraldine was almost at loss for words, only expressing sympathy for Brody and Ashley in their short exchange.

He then called Chloe, who said she had just put Whitney to bed, and was relaxing in her apartment in New York reading a book. She cried when told what had happened, telling her father she wanted to come down and be with the family.

John urged her to stay at home. "We'll call if we need you here," he said. "I think we've got everything under control."

"That's beside the point," Chloe said. "I need to be with the family right now. I hope you understand, Daddy."

"Please wait a bit. Maybe discuss it with Mom prior to making any plans. Everything's happened in the past hour."

"Tell me about the baby," Chloe said.

"She's beautiful and healthy. That's another decision we must make in the next few days."

"What decision? Isn't she Brody's daughter? He's not going to give her up, is he?"

John stepped out of the room and walked several feet down the hall, wanting to be out of earshot of Brody and George.

"I haven't discussed any of this with Brody," he said. "I assume he plans to keep his daughter. But there may have to be some kind of arrangement with her parents since he and Ashley weren't married. I don't know what can happen. I really haven't thought about it. I don't know how these things work."

"Are you sure you don't want me to come down now?" she said. "I can probably book a flight for tomorrow morning. It won't be a problem. And I want to be there for Brody."

"Sweetheart, talk to your mother first and we'll go from there. Okay?"

"Promise you'll have her call me," Chloe said. "I'll be up until I hear from her."

John glanced toward the nurses' station and saw Sally and Donna, followed by Dr. Palmer coming in his direction. Sally had her arm around Donna's shoulders while Dr. Palmer was rigid in her stride, as if lost in thought about what had transpired. He opened the door and followed them into the room.

"First of all, I'm so sorry about what happened," Dr. Palmer said, making brief eye contact with everyone. "We were concerned about clotting, as we are with any surgery, and we thought she had stabilized with the proper medications. But she had a venous thromboembolism, which causes a clot to go to the lungs. Again, I'm so sorry about what happened."

Her lips pressed as if she were thinking of something else to say, then she turned and quickly left the room. She appeared to wipe her eyes.

"My sweet baby," Donna moaned. "I can't believe she's gone."

George rose from his chair, reaching out and taking his wife's hand and leading her to a chair.

John eased next to Sally, motioning his head for her to go with him outside the room.

"What is it?" she asked as they stood in the hallway.

"I talked to Chloe and told her what happened," he said.

"That's good. I was going to call her after everything settled down."

"That's not all. She wants to come here and be with us."

"What did you tell her?"

"That you would discuss it with her."

Sally paused for a few seconds. "I think she should come if she wants to. This is a family tragedy."

"Are you going to call her?"

"I will after I talk to Brody."

"I also called your mother. She handled it well."

"That's a relief. I sure didn't want to have any words with her over this."

"Oh, one more thing, Chloe asked about the baby."

"And?"

"Well, uh, what is going to happen to her?"

"I haven't had time to think about it, John. That hasn't even crossed my mind. Besides, she's Brody's daughter."

"Don't you think George and Donna are going to have some thoughts about custody?"

Sally gave a meditative look, wrapping her arms across her chest. "Let's deal with that later. There's so much going on right now."

"Such as a funeral?"

Twelve

When John and Sally stepped back into the room, George and Donna were sitting next to each other, holding hands and talking quietly. Brody was still gazing out the window, appearing mentally drained and physically spent from the long and emotional day. John walked over to him, placing a hand on his shoulder.

"Let's go back to the house," John said calmly. "It's almost midnight."

"I can't right now," Brody said. "I can't leave Ashley and the baby."

George turned his head toward them. "Go get some rest, young man. Donna and I will be here a little while longer, then we're going to a motel."

"I need to stay a little while longer," Brody said. "I hope you understand."

"Okay, then," John said. "You can stay at the house tonight if you want to."

"Thanks, but I'm going back to the apartment. I'll give you and Mom a call in the morning. Dr. Garcia, you and your wife are welcome to stay at the apartment. We've, I mean, I've got plenty of room."

George glanced at Donna, and she was already shaking her head "no."

"Let us know if you need anything," John said to Ashley's parents. "We live only ten minutes or so from here."

"Thank you for the offer," George said, "but I think we'll be fine. We'll see you later."

John picked up a napkin from a bed tray, wrote down his phone number, and handed it to George. "Here's my number."

George glanced at it and smiled.

John tapped Brody on the shoulder one more time. Sally walked over to Brody and gave him a lengthy hug. She followed John out the door in tears. John wrapped his arms around her outside the room as she buried her head in his shoulder and sobbed. An elderly couple walked past them, lowering their heads to give them a small degree of privacy in their sadness.

"I hate leaving Brody here," Sally said between sobs. "He seems so helpless and lost."

"I know," John said as he gently rubbed her back. "But he'll be fine. We've got to let him work through this on his own terms. He knows we'll be there for him if he needs us."

They didn't speak as they left the hospital, walking across the shadowy parking lot as a chilly breeze swept over them. John turned the ignition on the car, and they sat silently for a minute, then he pulled out of the parking space.

"What a horrible day," Sally said on the way home. She began sobbing again. "It seems like a nightmare. I wish it were a nightmare and I would wake up and everything would be all right. I can't imagine what Ashley's parents are going through right now. My heart is aching."

"Like you said, it's a nightmare — every parent's nightmare to lose a child," John said, as Sally wiped away tears with her fingertips. "And it's a dreadful nightmare for Brody."

"I wish there were something we could do," Sally said. "I feel powerless."

"All we can do is be there for him."

"And what about that precious baby?" Sally asked.

"I think she'll be taken care of," John said.

"Do you think Brody can raise a child?"

"We'll be there for him and the baby."

"Don't forget Ashley's parents."

"I know," John bobbed his head. "We'll see what happens. I don't believe they'll let us forget about them. And we won't forget about Brody and the baby. There's so much going on right now."

"And everything will work out in the end," Sally said softly. "It always does."

"Only time will tell."

The lights were still on in the house when John pulled into the driveway. When they went through the front door, Geraldine was sleeping on the couch under a throw blanket instead of her regular spot on the recliner in the den. Whiskers was eager to go outside, so John held open the door so the pooch could do his stuff.

When Geraldine didn't wake up, Sally tip-toed up to her and gently touched her arm. Geraldine blinked for a couple seconds before realizing what was going on. Sally held her hand as she carefully rose to a sitting position.

"We're finally home," Sally said quietly, sitting next to her and continuing to hold her hand.

"I see," Geraldine said in a low rasp. "How's Brody?"

"He's getting through it all, but it's been difficult. He's still at the hospital with Ashley's parents. He'll be going to his apartment later."

"That poor boy. I feel so sorry for him. I wish I could give him a big hug."

"I'm sure he'll stop by here tomorrow."

"Tell me about the baby."

"She's a precious little thing. I can see Brody and Ashley in her. I can't wait for you to see her."

"Is she more black or more white?"

"Mother, she has a lovely light complexion. Just perfect."

"I suppose that's good," Geraldine said. "Where's John?"

Sally motioned toward the open door.

"He's not taking the mutt for a walk at this time of the night, is he?"

"No, it was potty time for Whiskers."

John stepped back into the house, following Whiskers, who scurried to the kitchen for water.

"I talked to Chloe this evening," Geraldine said. "She asked about Brody."

"I had talked to her earlier," Sally said. "I was going to call her back, but it slipped my mind."

"She's going to be getting here around noon tomorrow," Geraldine said.

"She's flying in?" John asked, his head tilted.

"Well, she's certainly not driving or taking a train or bus. What did you think?"

"Please, Geraldine, this has been a long day. She had mentioned coming in, but we didn't know she had already decided to do it. She was going to discuss it with Sally."

"Is she bringing Whitney with her?" Sally asked.

"She says she's going to leave her with Sam."

"That's good to know. I'm not sure if Whitney needs to be exposed to everything that will be going on the next few days."

"It might be better than being with Sam."

"Samantha has been a good parent to her," John said.

"I've been glad ever since Chloe got out of that lezbun relationship," Geraldine said. "It's not healthy for Whitney to be around."

"It's lesbian, not lezbun," John said.

"Whatever!"

"Mother, it's been a long day for all of us," Sally said with a sigh. "I think I'm going to get undressed and go to bed."

"I'm bushed as well," John said, stretching out his arms. 'Tomorrow is going to be another long day. I'll text Chloe and see what time I need to be at the airport."

"Can I go with you?" Geraldine asked, sheepishly.

"I don't see why not," John said. "I'm sure Chloe would love to see you there. It would be a pleasant surprise."

"I think I'm going to bed, too," Geraldine said. John held out his hand to help her up from the couch. "I was hungry but that was a long time ago. I figured you didn't stop and get me a sandwich."

"It's late and the place was closed," John said. "We can do that tomorrow when we go pick up Chloe."

"Promise?"

"Yes, Geraldine, I promise. But you might have to remind me."

"I will," she said with an elfish grin.

"I'm glad you didn't starve while we were away. I assume you found something to eat."

Geraldine looked at Sally. "I hope you don't mind but I ate the rest of your veggie sandwich. It was good."

"I'm happy you liked it," Sally said.

"I think it was because I was so hungry. But I still prefer turkey slices or some kind of meat."

"We know," John said. "At least you didn't starve to death."

"What's that supposed to mean?"

"Nothing. I think it's time we all go to bed."

John turned off the lights as Sally and Geraldine headed to the bedrooms. He took a few minutes to give Whiskers some attention, holding and petting him. The comforted dog then dashed to his padded bed in the den.

Sally was under the covers when John got to the bedroom. He took off his shirt and pants, letting them fall to the floor, and flung his socks toward the dresser, then slipped into the bed next to her. He kissed the back of her neck.

"Are you going to be able to sleep?" John whispered next to her ear.

"If you let me," Sally mumbled. "I was almost asleep."

"You're beginning to sound like your mother."

"Why do you say that?".

"You're being a smart aleck accusing me of keeping you awake," he said.

"I didn't mean to," she said, turning over and kissing him gently on the cheek. "John, I'm just tired and sleepy. Totally mentally and physically exhausted. Do you understand?"

"I understand."

"Oh, one more thing, honey," Sally said after she turned back over.

"What?"

"Don't forget to buy Mother a sandwich tomorrow." She giggled.

He chuckled and gently poked her side, causing her to recoil. "Now, you're being a smart aleck again."

Within a few minutes, Sally was snoring lightly. John wasn't far behind.

Thirteen

John was surprised when he entered the kitchen the next morning to see Geraldine sitting at the counter, a cup of coffee and a long john on a paper plate in front of her. He glanced at the clock and saw it was nearly seven o'clock.

"I can't believe I overslept," he said as he took a cup from the cabinet. "How long have you been up?"

"I came down around six," she said. "I thought you might be sleeping. Either that or back at the hospital."

"It was a long day for us yesterday. It's still hard to imagine everything that happened."

"We all must deal with people dying. It's part of living. That's something you accept if you live as long as I have."

"I agree." John sat across from her. "It's never easy to lose someone. I feel especially sad for Brody. They were so excited about having the baby. Then the difficulty and everything that happened yesterday. I hope he's doing okay this morning."

"He seems to be doing okay," Geraldine said.

"How do you know?" John asked, taking a sip of coffee.

"Because I called him this morning."

"And he was already up?"

"I may have awakened him. I don't know. I didn't ask, but he sounded like he'd been awake for some time."

"What did he have to say?"

"Nothing much, other than he couldn't believe it happened and that he was mentally and physically tired. He even started crying. I told him he'd get over it in time."

"Really?"

"Don't we all? You've lost your parents, my husband passed, and we've both had friends, relatives, and loved ones die. Like I said, it's part of living. And do you know what?"

"What?"

"It doesn't get any easier to deal with the older you get. It may even hurt a little bit more."

"You're right about that," John said. He walked to the kitchen and refilled his cup.

"You?" he asked, holding up his cup.

"Please," she said.

"Was Brody surprised you called?" John asked as he sat down.

"I don't think so. I am his grandmother, you know."

"Do you still want to go with me to the airport later to pick up Chloe?"

"Of course. Why wouldn't I?"

"Just making sure, Geraldine," John said. "Excuse me for a few minutes. I need to let Whiskers out."

"I've already done that. I also fed him. He's downstairs sleeping now."

"You're way ahead of me."

"That's what happens when you oversleep."

"Maybe I should do that more often." John snickered.

"I can take care of myself, but I must admit it's nice to have breakfast waiting for me when I get out of bed. You've spoiled me." Neither of them could suppress smiles.

John got off the stool. "I need to get the newspaper. Unless you did?"

"I didn't see it."

"With our paper carrier, it's a hide 'n' seek game every morning. I'll be back in a minute."

When John returned, Sally was seated in her pink robe at the counter next to Geraldine. "Coffee?" John asked.

"Please," Sally groaned. She hadn't taken the time to run a brush over her short hair, something she always tried to do before making her morning appearance. She almost looked fashionable with it being partially spiked.

"Sleep well?"

"I barely remember putting my head on the pillow," she said. "I was out like a light. All I remember is something about a sandwich."

"You reminded me to buy Geraldine a sandwich today."

"I did?" Sally furrowed her brows.

"And then you were sound asleep."

"How about you?"

"I overslept. This sweet lady was waiting for me at the counter when I came down." He pointed toward Geraldine.

"I'm not sure I was waiting for you," Geraldine said, looking upward with a sigh.

"That's a figure of speech. And she also called Brody."

"You did?" Sally arched back her head as she looked at Geraldine.

"Yes, I did," Geraldine said, irritated by the comment. "What's the big deal. He is my grandson, you know."

"It's nothing, Mother. I just don't recall you ever calling him."

"Then you have a short memory. And you don't know what I do during the day."

"I'm glad to hear that," Sally said. "What did he have to say?"

"I've already told John," Geraldine said, turning toward him.

John cleared his throat. "Uh, Brody told her he was tired and couldn't believe what happened,"

"Did he say he'd come by here today?" Sally asked.

"I don't have a clue," Geraldine said. "Why don't you call and ask him? And John, could you warm my cup?"

"I'll call him after I finish my coffee and get a bite for breakfast," Sally said.

John walked over to the counter and picked up the coffee pot. He warmed Geraldine's cup and refilled Sally's. He took the newspaper and headed toward the den.

"You don't like our company?" Geraldine asked.

"You know better than that," John said, stopping at the steps leading to the den. "I don't want to interfere with the pleasant conversation between you and your daughter."

"I think you're being a smart aleck."

John sat on the loveseat and opened the newspaper, glanced over the front-page headlines, and then turned to the obituary page. He smiled after not recognizing any names of the deceased. Then it occurred to him that Ashley's obit would probably be listed in the next day or so. He pursed his mouth and closed the paper. His eyes watered as he thought about the previous day in the hospital.

Geraldine broke the silence when she sat on the recliner and turned on the television to a talk show. John waited a few minutes before getting up, not wanting her to think he was leaving because she was there.

"Care to read the newspaper?" he asked.

"Just leave it there," she said, her eyes aimed at the TV. "I'll look at it later."

"I'm going to get cleaned up before we go to the airport."

"Let me know what time we're leaving."

John went back to the kitchen and sat next to Sally.

"Is everything okay," he asked.

"I'm just heartbroken for Brody," she said as her eyes began to tear. "I hope he can handle it."

"You mean you're worried he could have a relapse on drugs?'

"I hope he's strong enough now. Ashley gave him so much support and strength. Now that she's gone, I hope he doesn't go back to his old ways."

"We'll give him our support and help him get through this. These will be new days for him to adjust."

"He also needs our love," she said, wiping away a tear on her cheek with her napkin.

"I agree with you." John put an arm around her shoulders.

"I hope that's enough."

He softly kissed her cheek. "We'll see as time goes on."

Fourteen

A re you ready to leave?" John bellowed at the top of the steps leading to the den.

"What are you talking about?" Geraldine shouted as she turned her head to look at him.

"Aren't you going with me to the airport to pick up Chloe?"

Seconds later, after turning down the volume on the TV, Geraldine stood at the bottom of the steps, bracing herself on her cane. She grumbled, "I thought you were going to let me know when we'd be leaving."

"That's what I'm doing now."

"But I'm not even dressed."

"We've got time," he said contritely. "She won't be arriving for another hour."

Geraldine walked up the six steps, faced him, and shook her head. "Men!"

John backed away from her a couple of steps. "Take your time, Geraldine. It's only a ten-minute drive to the airport."

Geraldine turned the corner and went up the next six steps in the tri-level to her bedroom. She looked back at him. "Don't leave without me."

"Don't worry. I'll take Whiskers out, and when I get back, we'll leave."

John hooked the leash to Whiskers' collar, and they headed down the street for a short stroll. A chill filled the air despite a bright sun and cloudless sky. Whiskers was up for a walk, longer than John wanted to take, leading John all the way to Shipley Park at the far end of the street. John glanced at his watch and realized they'd been gone for nearly fifteen minutes. He knew Geraldine would have some harsh words for him if they didn't get back soon. When Whiskers lingered on the way back, John picked him up and carried him the rest of the way to the house.

Geraldine was standing at the front door, dressed and ready to go, when he crossed the lawn with Whiskers in his arms. He flashed a smile she didn't return.

As he stepped inside the house, Geraldine scowled. "Did you walk to town and back? And has your little mutt forgot how to walk?"

"Sorry 'bout that," he said as kneeled to unleash Whiskers. "Time got away from us."

"Oh, really!"

"Let me wash up and we'll be ready to go."

Geraldine, grim-faced, stomped over to the couch and sat. "I'm not holding my breath. I'll be waiting here when you're ready to leave."

After washing his hands and running a brush over his thinning hair and bushy beard, John returned to the living room. Sally was sitting next to Geraldine, chatting about getting Brody's old room ready for Chloe's visit.

"Have you heard from Brody?" John asked as he stood in front of them, hands in pockets.

"He called right after you left and said he was on his way to the hospital," Sally said. "Apparently it had something to do with the disposition of Ashley's body. He was going to meet her parents there."

"I hope there are not any problems," John said.

"What do you mean?" Sally asked, her eyes crinkled.

"Nothing in particular."

"Then why did you say something?" Geraldine asked.

John took a short breath. "I was just saying I hope everything goes well because Ashley's parents are there. I'm sure they have plans for their daughter."

"Then why didn't you say that?"

John took another short breath and pursed his mouth for a moment. "Geraldine, are you ready to leave?"

"What do you think?" She grasped her cane and eased off the couch. John offered a hand, but she flicked it away.

John looked at Sally. "Call me if anything comes up."

Sally pressed her lips for a few seconds. "Do you think I should go to the hospital and be with Brody?"

"That's up to you."

"Some help you are," Geraldine piped in.

"Please, Geraldine," John said. "Sally and I are trying to discuss something, if you don't mind."

"Well, you're not doing a very good job at it."

John turned toward the front door. "Come on, let's get to the airport."

"It's about time," she said as John held open the front door for her. "Poor little Chloe is probably wandering all over the airport looking for us. Maybe even wondering if we forgot about her."

"Let's not get carried away," John said. "And even if that were the case, she'd know how to get here by herself. She's done it before."

"You never know."

John looked back at Sally, then put his hands in a prayer. She covered her mouth, making sure she didn't let out a laugh her mother would hear. "We'll be back as soon as we can," John said. "And call me if you need me for anything. Let's hit the road, Geraldine."

"It's about time!"

Geraldine didn't talk during the drive to Blue Grass Airport, content listening to the soft rock music playing on the radio. He dropped her off at the main entrance to the terminal, telling her he was going to park in the short-term parking lot.

When John entered the terminal ten minutes later, he noticed her sitting by herself in a row of seats near the TSA entry.

"We need to go to the baggage-claim area," he said. "She'll be coming down through that exit after she arrives."

"I wish you had said something earlier," Geraldine said. "I could have been waiting there for you."

"I thought you knew," John said, regretting the words the moment they left his mouth.

"How would I know?" she snarled. "I never come here."

"You're right," he said calmly. "My fault." He could have reminded Geraldine that she had arrived at the airport when she came in from Arizona for Christmas more than two years ago— and hadn't left. He knew it wasn't worth it.

They walked to the baggage area, sitting across from the conveyor against the wall. Various pieces of luggage began streaming onto the rectangular belt as travelers gradually gathered to pick up their belongings. Chloe suddenly appeared from around the exit, her eyes wide and gleaming as soon as she saw John and Geraldine.

Chloe hurried to them as they rose from their seats. She picked up on John nodding for her to go first to Geraldine. She hugged her grandmother, kissing her cheek, then did the same to John. "It's so great to see you," she said, reaching over and holding Geraldine's hand. Geraldine blushed.

"I insisted on being here," Geraldine said with a glowing smile. "You don't realize how much I've missed you. It's a shame you couldn't bring Whitney."

"She's in good hands with Sam."

Geraldine pushed out her lower lip and didn't respond.

"You look great, Grandma." Chloe continued, knowing her grandmother wasn't fond of her former partner.

Geraldine's petite chest swelled. "I try to take care of myself and get enough exercise and eat well."

John gave her an incredulous look. "It's all in the family, beginning with you, Geraldine."

"Oh, hush John. You're being silly, as usual, and embarrassing me."

Chloe pointed at the conveyor. "There're my two bags. The green ones."

John hurried over and grabbed them before they moved to the other side. They walked to the main entrance, where John continued to his car with the luggage while Chloe and Geraldine waited inside the automated door.

Minutes later, John pulled over into the passenger loading zone to let them in. "Ready to go home?" he asked, grinning.

"It sure took you long enough," Geraldine said.

Fifteen

Sally was standing at the front door when John pulled into the driveway and stepped out onto the porch when Chloe and Geraldine got out of the back seat. Chloe walked slowly arm-in-arm with her grandmother while John opened the trunk to remove her luggage.

"It's so wonderful to see you," Sally said teary-eyed, giving Chloe a prolonged hug while Geraldine sauntered into the house. Whiskers yapped and jumped against Chloe's leg, apparently remembering her from previous visits. She picked up the pup and rubbed under his chin for a few seconds; he responded with a quick lick on her cheek.

Sally held open the door for John. After he set the luggage on the floor, they went to the kitchen to join Chloe and Geraldine at the bar, which had served as the family meeting place since John's retirement.

"How's Brody?" Chloe asked. "I can't wait to see him."

"He called about thirty minutes ago," Sally said. "He was about to go to the hospital. He broke down and cried while we spoke. It broke my heart." Her eyes welled.

"I hate to hear that but what can you expect? He loved her so much, and they were so good for each other." Chloe's eyes watered.

"How would you know?" Geraldine asked. "You haven't lived here in years."

"Now, Grandma, you don't know everything. Brody and I talk on the phone now and then. He used to check on me when I was going through my chemo treatments. After he told me when Ashley got pregnant, he'd call and give me updates on her progress."

"Oh, I didn't know that."

"There's probably a lot you don't know," John said as he stood at the end of the counter.

"Now what is that supposed to mean?"

"It means we don't know what others are doing all the time," he said. "If it makes you feel better, I didn't know Chloe and Brody talked often on the phone. But it's not surprising since they're brother and sister. I'm happy to find out they have that kind of relationship."

"Well, I don't see Sally and Wendell talking all the time," Geraldine said.

"We would if we had a need to," Sally said. "After you fractured your hip, I got in touch with him and let him know how you were doing."

"That's nice to know," Geraldine said. "Speaking of Wendell, have you told him about Brody?"

"I haven't but I will," Sally said. "I'm sure he'll want to know about his nephew."

"You never know with Wendell."

"Are you guys hungry?" John asked. He glanced at Chloe. "I'm sure you must be."

"I suppose a bit," Chloe said.

"How about if I order a pizza?"

"That would be nice," Geraldine said.

"Well, I'd like to see Brody first," Chloe said. Geraldine lowered her head as if disappointed her granddaughter chose Brody over pizza.

"That's fine," John said. "We can pick up one later in the afternoon."

"If it's all right, I'd like to get cleaned up, change my clothes and get freshened up," Chloe said as she eased off the stool and headed upstairs. "I always feel a little grimy after going through airports and sitting on a plane for several hours."

John picked up on Geraldine's concern about missing an early meal, especially it being her favorite. "How about if I go ahead and place an order for you since I'm not sure how long we'll be at the hospital," he said to Geraldine.

Geraldine's face brightened. "Don't go to all that trouble for me."

"It won't be any trouble at all. Let me know what you want on it."

"How about one of those meat lovers' pizzas?"

"Not a problem," John said as he took his cell phone from his pocket. He placed the order. "It should be here in about thirty minutes."

Geraldine got off the stool, grabbed her cane, and went to the den. "Let me know when it arrives. My favorite soap is coming on."

"What did Brody have to say?" John asked Sally after Geraldine got settled into the recliner and increased the volume on the television. Now they could talk in private.

"I think he's having problems with Ashley's parents," Sally said. "Especially her mother."

"About the funeral?"

"No, about the baby."

"How so?"

"She believes the baby should live with her and George."

"And Brody wants the baby?" John said.

"Honey, she is his daughter," Sally said. "What do you think?"

"I'm not arguing with you. I feel the same way."

"She's apparently mentioned that the baby would receive better care with them."

"I hope it doesn't turn ugly between them."

"I hope not either," Sally said with a sigh. "But I'm not counting on it."

"Let's just get through the funeral. That's going to be hard enough on Brody."

"We'll be there for him."

Chloe returned to the kitchen, wearing black leggings and a light blue sweater.

"I'm ready to leave when you are," she said.

"Let's wait a few more minutes until the pizza arrives," John said.

"You went ahead and ordered a pizza?" Chloe asked, her brows furrowed.

"For your grandmother. We'll order another one or pick up something later after we go to the hospital."

"That's fine. I forgot about Grandma."

"How could you forget about her?" John said with a snort.

Chloe gave them an update on Whitney and her progress in the second grade while they waited for the pizza to arrive.

"It's a shame she couldn't have come with you," Sally said. "I've missed her so much, especially after spending so much time with her last year while you were undergoing chemo. She's such a sweetie."

"She still talks about the good time she had with you. Maybe after school's out in a few weeks we can make a special trip back here."

"Or maybe we can take another trip to New York," John said. "I enjoy going to the Big Apple."

"We'll see what happens," Sally said. "It's difficult to make plans anymore with everything going on."

"Grandma seems to be doing well," Chloe said. "As feisty as ever."

"She's as fit as a fiddle."

"And as sharp as a whip," John added with a grin.

"I can see that," Chloe said. "I hope that never changes."

Their conversation was interrupted by a knock on the front door. Whiskers let out a sharp bark and dashed to see who was there. John pulled out his wallet and followed the pooch, knowing it was about time for the delivery.

To his surprise, it was his neighbor Bert Reliford, his longtime friend from several doors down the street.

John opened the door and Bert stepped into the living room. "What's up? I noticed a little activity here the past couple of days and want to make sure everything's okay. You know, being neighborly."

"We had some bad news," John said. "Brody's girlfriend passed away after giving birth to a precious girl yesterday."

Chloe came around the corner and smiled at Bert, who had been her math teacher in high school. "Hi, Mr. Reliford," she said. "It's so nice to see you." She walked over and gave him a big hug.

"Wow, I didn't know you were here," Bert said. "It's great to see you, too, Chloe. What brings you to Lexington?"

"Did Dad tell you about Brody's girlfriend?"

Bert blushed. "I'm sorry. I didn't put two and two together."

Seconds later, Geraldine ambled into the room. "Oh, it's only you," she said to Bert with a long face. "I thought it was the pizza delivery."

Bert blushed again. "I guess I need to get back home. It's nice seeing you, Chloe. If you get a chance, come down and visit me and Wilma for a while. I know she'd love to see you."

"I'll do that, Mr. Reliford," she said. "Tell her I said hi."

"I'll see you folks later," Bert said and added with a wink, "You too, Geraldine."

"What's that supposed to mean?" Geraldine said with knitted brows.

As Bert stepped out of the house, the pizza delivery arrived. John paid the woman and carried the pizza to the kitchen, where Geraldine was already seated at the bar. Sally took a can of soft drink from the refrigerator.

"Are you going to be all right, Mother?" Sally asked as she placed the beverage in front of her. "We shouldn't be gone too long, at least I hope not."

"I can take care of myself," Geraldine said as she took a slice of pizza from the box.

"I know you can," Sally said sweetly.

Geraldine didn't say a word and took a bite of the pizza, seemingly oblivious to the others around her.

They shrugged and grinned, then John followed Sally and Chloe out of the room and left to go to the hospital.

Sixteen

John led the way through the maze of hallways and elevators to Ashley's room. When he opened the door, the room was dark and the bed linens changed, and nothing to hint she had been there. It was sanitized and colorless. And cold.

"Where in the world could they be?" John asked.

"Let's go to the nurses' station and get some answers," Chloe said.

"It's down this way," Sally said, pointing toward the opposite end of the hall they had entered. "About midway and to the right."

They gathered at the desk where three nurses were busy charting patients on desktop computers. John noticed two nurses down one corridor pushing carts and apparently making their required rounds of the patients.

"Excuse me," Sally asked. "Can you give us some information on Ashley Garcia?"

"She passed away yesterday," a nurse replied, barely making eye contact.

"We know that," Sally said. "We came here to be with our son and her parents. And the baby."

"Oh, I'm sorry," the nurse said with a light blush. "They're in the conference room making final arrangements about the deceased's body."

"Okay, then," John said. "Where's the conference room?"

"It's down on the first floor, off from the entrance, and near the admission area. You can't miss it."

"Is the baby still here?" Sally asked.

"I believe the baby is in the nursery. Do you know where that is?" the nurse said, letting out a sigh.

"Yes," Sally said. "Thank you."

The nurse turned her attention to the computer without another word while Sally strode toward the nursery with John and Chloe a step behind. When they peeked through the window, Sally located their new granddaughter in the second row of acrylic cribs. A pink ribbon was attached to the nameplate.

"She's so precious," Chloe cooed. "I can't wait to hold her."

"She's sure tiny," John said.

Sally began to weep.

"What is it, honey?" John asked, gently placing a hand on her lower back.

"I was thinking about Ashley and all she suffered to bring this little one into the world. And that she's not here to hold her and feed her and be her mother. It's so sad."

Chloe turned her head and wiped away tears from her cheek.

"Let's find Brody," John said. "I bet he needs us now."

Sally blew a soft kiss at the beloved baby before they backed away and searched for the conference room.

John pointed toward it when they reached the admissions desk, off to the left. He looked through a small glass window on the door and saw Brody sitting at a table with Ashley's parents and another person who was writing on a tablet. John knocked softly on the door and eased it open.

"I'm sorry, we're in a meeting," the man said coldly.

Brody rose from his seat. "It's okay. They're my parents and sister."

George turned to the man and gestured that Brody was telling the truth. Donna sat stone-faced, looking straight ahead as if in a trance.

John, Sally, and Chloe sat in the chairs nearest to Brody. The man cleared his throat twice, then resumed his questions.

John sensed friction in the room among all parties. The man rose with a tight smile. "I must go and speak to the supervisor of my department. I'll return as soon as I can so we can get this resolved and move on." He gathered the paperwork in a folder and left the room.

"What's the problem?" John asked, looking at Brody and then George for an answer.

"Well, uh, it's about the baby," Brody said.

"Mr. Ross, my wife and I believe we should be given custody of Ashley's baby girl," George said in a forceful tone he had not used in their previous conversations.

"What do you think, Brody?" John said.

"I'm the father."

"But you have little means of support for her," George said, a slight tremor in his hands. "We can provide for all of her needs and more."

"I believe Ashley would have wanted for us to have the baby," Donna said sharply.

"You don't know that," Brody said, anger rising in his voice. "Ashley and I discussed everything about the baby. We knew it would be difficult for a while, but we would make it happen."

"You can't even support yourself," Donna said. "Ashley was the breadwinner. All you've been in a short-order cook in a greasy spoon." She hesitated for a few seconds, then blurted, "And a recovering junkie."

"Now Donna," George said, lowering his voice and tapping her hand. "There's no need for that."

"But it's the truth," she said. "He can't take of himself without Ashley, so how in the heaven's name can he care for a baby."

"That was a long time ago," Brody said. "I'm okay now. And I can care for the baby."

"It wasn't that long ago that you were in rehab. If I remember correctly, you're still in rehab."

"I'm in a support group. It's something Ashley recommended. Most former users are in support groups. It's part of the long-time therapy."

"Yes, long term," Donna said sarcastically.

"We'll help Brody support the baby," Sally chimed in. "And we have the means to do it."

Brody smiled. "I'll do everything I have to do to provide for my daughter."

"What's that? Sell drugs?" Donna snarled.

George took a deep breath. "That's enough, Donna."

"So that's what the young man is doing right now?" John asked. "Deciding who gets custody of the baby?"

"For now, it's temporary custody," George said.

"I see." John crossed his arms over his chest.

Chloe rose from her chair and walked over to Brody, giving him a hug from behind his back. She whispered, "I hope you're doing okay."

"Thanks for coming in," Brody said. "You didn't have to."

"Yes, I did. You're my brother. I know you'd do the same for me."

John listened to their quiet exchange but remembered that Brody didn't go to Chloe's side when she was undergoing chemo after her ovarian cancer diagnosis. At the time Brody was in the throes of counseling for his addiction, a valid excuse. That was where he had first met Ashley, who was working as a counselor at the rehab facility.

"It's sure taking Mr. Rogan long enough," Brody said after Chloe returned to her seat.

"I'm sure it's complicated," John said.

"That it is," George said while Donna looked away from the others." Unfortunately."

"Do you mind if I ask about funeral arrangements?" John asked George. "I understand if this isn't the appropriate time."

"We're going to the funeral home after this meeting," George said, his eyes beginning to well." All I can say is that she'll be buried in our family plot in Louisville. I'll let you know when everything is finalized." Donna remained silent.

John responded with an awkward smile.

Donna began sobbing, taking a tissue from her purse and dabbing her eyes. George gently rubbed the back of her neck. "It's going to be all right," he said.

"We're so sorry," John said, letting out a short breath. "I hope you know we were very fond of Ashley and thought the world of her."

"She spoke highly of you and Mrs. Ross," George said.

Mr. Rogan returned to the room, standing behind the chair he had used. They stared at him, all holding their breaths awaiting his announcement.

"I've discussed this with my supervisor and our legal office," he said. "It's been decided that, in accordance with Kentucky statute, temporary custody will be awarded to Brody Ross, the baby's father."

Brody practically melted in his seat with the decision.

"You can't be serious," Donna exclaimed wide-eyed. George clutched her forearm, attempting to control her anger.

"But let me add," Mr. Rogan said. "We recommend that a judge make the final determination. I'll provide you with further information in the next day or so."

Seventeen

Everyone filed out of the room except the Garcias. John gazed at them as he left, sitting grim-faced and tight-lipped. Absolute disappointment written on their faces.

"I can't believe what happened," Brody said as they stood in the large foyer. "I don't know what to do next."

"We need to find out when you can take the baby home," Sally said. "Let's go back to the maternity ward now."

As they turned to go to the nursery, the Garcias came out of the conference room, stopping when they saw the Ross family. After a few tense seconds, they continued to the front exit without saying a word.

"Have you decided on a name for her?" Chloe asked Brody as they stepped into an elevator.

Brody sighed. "Ashley and I came up with several names but couldn't decide on anything we really liked. I supposed I should give it some more thought."

"This is just a thought, but you might want to discuss it with her parents," Sally said.

"Not a bad idea," John said. "It might help patch up things a little."

"I don't know," Brody said as they stepped quickly off the elevator. "You heard what her mother said back there."

"I know it was hurtful," Sally said. "I didn't like it either. But she's distraught over losing her daughter."

"Give her a little slack," John said.

"Yeah, and she might want to give me a little slack, too. I'll think about it."

The charge nurse looked sideways for a moment when Brody asked about when he could take the baby home with him. They were told the baby needed a few more tests and a sign off by the doctor prior to being released. John wondered if the nurse was simply buying time to make sure Brody had been granted custody. He also contemplated if Mr. Rogan had spoken to her.

Brody sighed. "When is a good time for me to return?"

"She should be ready around noon tomorrow," the nurse said in a less-than-pleasant demeanor. "You should probably call first." She turned and began a conversation with another nurse.

"I wonder what that was all about?" Chloe asked as they headed back to the elevator.

"She must be having a bad day," Sally said, shrugging.

"Maybe the Garcias have brainwashed her," Brody said with a half-laugh.

"If I didn't know better, I'd think some folks here are taking sides," Chloe said.

"My thoughts, too," Sally said. "But I hope not."

"So, what are the plans right now?" John asked.

"I was thinking about going back to the apartment and getting things ready when we left for the hospital," Brody said. "We have a crib and stuff. Ashley was getting things ready when she started having labor pains." His voice cracked. "Seems like ages ago."

"I'll go with you," Chloe said. "It shouldn't take us long."

"We'll go on home," Sally said. "Let us know when you're finished, and we'll get something ready to eat."

"I'm sure your grandmother would like to see you," John said to Brody. "She's been concerned about you."

"Really?" Brody said.

"Didn't she call you?"

"Yeah, but it was brief. She didn't say a whole lot."

"Maybe because she knew you were hurting," Sally said.

"I guess you're right. I wasn't in the mood for talking, either."

They parted ways in the parking lot. John wandered around the cluster of vehicles for several minutes. He finally stopped and looked around in confusion.

"Do you have any clue where we parked?" John asked.

"You're getting as bad as me in forgetting where I put things," Sally said.

"I could have sworn we parked in this direction from the entrance."

"You didn't write it down anywhere?"

John shook his head. "Apparently I didn't."

Seconds later, Brody pulled his car up to them and rolled down the window.

"Your mother forgot where we parked," John said.

"John! You know better," Sally said, lightly tapping his shoulder.

Chloe leaned over toward the driver's window. "It's in section C. You're in section E."

"How do you know that?"

"Easy. The first letter of my name. I noticed that right off."

"That's a good way to remember something," Sally said. "It's something like mnemonics."

"I suppose," Chloe said. "That's how I remember stuff. If I think I'll forget, I take a photo on my smartphone."

"That's another good idea. You should try that, John."

"If you remind me the next time," John said.

Brody offered to drive them to section C, but they declined. A minute later, they were in Sally's SUV and on their way home.

John was about to pull into the driveway when he noticed a familiar Escort station wagon in the spot. "You've got to be kidding me," he said. "Wendell and Libby are here."

"I bet Mother called them and told them about Brody and Ashley," Sally said as he backed slightly, then parked on the street.

They expected to see everyone in the living room when they entered the house, but instead, they were downstairs in the den watching television. Wendell waved at John from the loveseat, then rose and came up the steps toward the dining room.

"There was a soap opera on television Mama wanted to watch," Wendell said with an embarrassed look. John glanced into the den and Libby appeared engaged in the program as well.

Sally gave her brother a light hug. "It's so nice of you and Libby to come over. It'll mean so much to Brody." She led the way to the kitchen bar.

"We were just in the neighborhood and decided to drop by." Wendell pulled out a stool and sat. "I hope it's not an inconvenience."

"Of course not," John said. "Can I get you something to drink?"

"I'm good," Wendell said. "Why does Brody care if we visit?"

"You haven't heard?"

"Heard what?" Wendell creased his brows.

"Uh, Brody's girlfriend Ashley died after giving birth yesterday," John said solemnly.

"My goodness," Wendell said. "This is the first I've heard about it."

"Mother said nothing to you?"

"She was busy watching one of her TV shows. She didn't want to talk until it was over. That's why we were in the den."

"For Christ's sakes!" John exclaimed. "You've got to be kidding me."

"Mama loves her soap operas," Wendell said sheepishly. "We didn't want to disturb her."

Libby came up to the kitchen bar and sat next to Wendell. "Geraldine will be here in a minute. You know how slow she moves with that cane."

"Please, Libby," Wendell said. "Mama's old. Give her a break. She can't move fast."

"I was just telling Wendell about Brody's girlfriend," John said. "She passed away last night after having a baby girl."

"Oh, that's terrible," Libby said, pushing out her lower lip. "Wasn't she a Black girl?"

"What's terrible?" Geraldine asked as he ambled into the room.

"I was telling them about Brody's girlfriend," John said.

"Oh. That was simply awful."

"Awful and terrible," Libby said. "Was she Black?"

"Her mother is Black, and her father is Hispanic," Sally said. "She was a beautiful daughter."

"I was just asking," Libby said. "I didn't mean anything about it."

"Brody and Chloe will be coming over a little later to eat," Sally said, looking at her brother. "I hope you can stay."

"Are you sure we won't be imposing on your hospitality?" Libby asked, tilting her head.

"That's never bothered you before," Geraldine said. "I've never seen you turn down a free meal."

"Now, Mama, that was uncalled for," Wendell said.

"Well, it's the truth. And the same goes for you."

Libby began fighting back tears as she squinted her eyes.

"Libby, can I get you something to drink?" John asked in a consolatory tone.

"Do you have any diet soda?" she asked. "You know I like diet soda."

"I know. We try to keep a few here just for you."

"That's so sweet of you to do that."

John opened the refrigerator, took out a can of Diet Pepsi, and handed it to her. "Anyone want something to drink?" he asked the others.

"Any regular soda?" Wendell asked.

John went back to the refrigerator and took out a Pepsi.

"You don't have Coke?"

"Only Pepsi."

"Well, I guess I'll take one," Wendell said as he took the can from John. "But I really prefer Coke."

"I'll try to remember the next time I go to the grocery," John said.

"This is silly," Geraldine said. "They taste the same."

"No, they don't," Wendell said. "Pepsi is sweeter, and Coke has more carbonation. Right Sally? Right John?"

"I'm not getting involved in this debate," Sally said.

"Me either," John said.

"And I'm going back to the den and watch TV," Geraldine said. "This is silly! I hear more intelligent conversation on my soaps."

John leaned over and whispered in Sally's ear. "I think she's right."

"I believe she watches *Days of Our Lives*," Sally said.

"That's appropriate."

Eighteen

Everything slightly settled down when Geraldine returned to the den to watch another of her soaps. Wendell and Libby remained in the kitchen, sipping their soft drinks at the counter, while John opted to escape by taking Whiskers for a walk.

Sally followed him to the front door. "Do you think I should call Chloe or Brody and tell them we have company?" she asked quietly.

John looked up while fastening the leash to Whiskers' collar. "It probably wouldn't hurt to give them a heads up, although I'm sure Chloe would like to see her aunt and uncle. I'm not so sure about Brody in his state of mind."

"Should or shouldn't? I want your opinion."

"Oh, go ahead." John opened the front door. "Let them decide if they want to come over or not. They're adults. If they decide not to, come up with a good excuse for them."

"Oh, thanks a lot, John. So, you want me to come up with a lie?"

"I didn't say that. Tell them whatever."

"You're a big help."

Whiskers tugged at the leash to go out. "Let me know what you decide. I should be back in thirty minutes or so."

"Don't be in such a hurry." Sally closed the door.

Whiskers practically pulled John across the front yard. "Whoa, little buddy! We're not supposed to be in a hurry."

They ended up at their usual place, a bench next to the large pond at Shipley Park. It was one of John's favorite spots, where he could sit and contemplate what was going on in his life, or nothing at all. Usually, he would be content to sit and enjoy the peace and tranquility, listening to birdsong and watching waterfowl gliding across the water. Occasionally, he'd see a jogger or walker on one of the asphalt paths that circled the pond and crossed the park. Whiskers liked it as well, since he could tease the ducks and geese who frequented the pond.

John was half paying attention to Whiskers and thinking about Brody when someone came up behind him and tapped him on the shoulder.

"Hey, you gotta light, old man?"

"Sorry, I don't smoke," John said with a smirk for the remark.

"Got any money?" the man asked as he moved to the side of the bench.

"I beg your pardon?" John said with a twisted grin. He guessed the scruffy-looking man to be in his early twenties. His hair was long and stringy to his shoulders, and he had a series of tattoos crawling up the side of his neck like a spiderweb.

"You heard me."

"How much do you need?"

"Uh, like everything you have."

Whiskers stopped chasing after the fowl and began barking at John's intruder, slowly moving toward the bench. John wasn't sure if Whiskers was simply barking at a stranger or sensed something bad was happening.

"You might want to tell your mangy mutt to shut the fuck up," the man said, his right hand stuffed in a bulging pocket on his brown bomber jacket. John thought it might be a concealed gun and didn't want to take any chances, especially with Whiskers getting riled up.

"Hush, Whiskers," John said. The pooch scrambled up to him, jumping up on the bench. He glared and growled at the man.

"Did you hear me?" the man demanded, raising his voice and looking in different directions to make sure he wasn't being watched. "Hand over your dough, old man!"

John reached behind and take out his wallet. "Hold it," the man said. "You better not try anything, or I'll shoot your dog. Understand?"

John held up his hands in front of him. "I'm getting my billfold," he said with measured composure. "That's where I keep my money. Okay, young man?'

"Go ahead."

John pulled out the wallet and opened it. Before he could remove any cash, the man yanked it from him.

"Take the money," John said. "But I'd appreciate it if you leave my driver's license and everything else."

"I'll take whatever I want, old man." The punk yanked the cash from the wallet and began counting it. "Fifty-six dollars. Is this all you have?"

"I may have some change in my pocket."

"Funny," the man snarled, then tossed the wallet toward the pond. John breathed a sigh of relief when it landed inches short of the water.

John's cellphone vibrated. He acted as if nothing was happening and hoping the two-bit bandit didn't hear the faint buzz either. Without another word, the man turned and sprinted in the opposite direction from where John had come to the park.

Whiskers let out several more barks and lunged in the thief's direction before John tenderly placed him on the ground. "It's okay, little buddy. Just settle down."

John walked toward the pond and retrieved his wallet, thankful it was only money that was taken from him. Counting your blessings can come in different ways, especially when it comes to money, he thought, knowing replacing driver's license, credit cards, and other items can be a pain in the butt.

His phone vibrated again, and he answered.

"I thought you'd be home by now," Sally asked. "Brody and Chloe are on their way here."

"Sorry, I got held up."

"Do you think you can go to KFC or some place and pick up something for everyone to eat?" she asked.

"That shouldn't be a problem," he said. "Whiskers and I will be back in ten or fifteen minutes. If there's anything else you need, call or text me."

"Aren't you going to come in the house with Whiskers?"

"I forgot about Whiskers. I'll do that."

"Didn't you walk to the park?"

"Of course, I did," John said. "You saw me leave the house."

"You might want to come home and get the car before going to KFC."

"What in the world are you talking about? Were you expecting me to walk to KFC?"

"I wasn't thinking," she said. "Sorry."

"You're sounding more like your mother."

"Those are fighting words, mister!" she said with a laugh.

"I've got something to tell you in a little bit. I'll be home in about fifteen minutes."

"I'll ask the others what they'd like."

"Do that but don't get carried away because you'll have me going to different places. Let's keep it short and simple, like a kiss."

"A kiss? What are you talking about?"

"I'll explain it later. Bye."

When John got back to the house, it took an extra ten minutes because he stopped and chatted with neighbor Rufus Martin. Everyone except Brody and Chloe were sitting at the dining room table.

"I thought you had already gone to KFC since it took you so long," Sally said to John, standing at the entryway with Whiskers still on the leash.

"I stopped and talked to Rufus for a few minutes. I also had to bring Whiskers back to the house."

"He's gone with you in the past," Geraldine said.

"Well, not this time." John said. "So, it's KFC?"

"Try to get mostly white meat," Wendell said.

"And white gravy for the mashed potatoes," Sally said.

"I'd prefer fried potatoes instead of mashed potatoes," Libby said.

"I'll get both," John said.

"Anything else?" John asked. "Desserts? Drinks?"

"You might get a pitcher of sweet tea," Sally said.

"I'd like some cheesecake," Geraldine said.

"I'm not sure if they have that."

"Then get whatever they have," Geraldine said. "Just go. I'm getting hungry. A person could starve around here."

"I hear ya, Geraldine," John said. "We're a third-world family."

"What's that supposed to mean? Are you being a smart aleck?"

John ignored her and glanced at the others. "Anything else?"

"Oh, John," Libby said.

"I know, you like diet soda."

"How did you know that?"

"Oh, almost forgot," John said.

"About the diet soda?"

"No, Libby. I had an interesting encounter at the park."

"Can't it wait?" Geraldine asked. "It can't be that interesting. Can't you see we're starving here?"

"Let's not get carried away," John said with an eye roll.

"Honey, you'd better go before there's a revolt," Sally said with a smile and wink.

"I can see the natives are growing restless."

John shook his head in amusement and left. After encountering rush-hour traffic and a long line at the drive-thru, he returned nearly forty-five minutes later. They were still sitting at the table, including Brody and Chloe, this time with paper plates and silverware in front of them. They were listening as Brody tearfully explained what had transpired at the hospital.

"What took you so long?" Geraldine asked, interrupting Brody and turning her attention to John. "Did you walk?"

John forced a tight smile and took a deep breath as he placed two buckets of chicken and a large bag of sides and drinks on the bar counter that separated the dining room from the kitchen. Sally walked over and opened the containers for everyone to take what they wanted.

"They didn't have any white gravy?" Sally asked.

"Only brown."

"Where's my diet soda?" Libby asked.

John handed her a drink with diet punched on the lid. She grinned. "Bless you, John. I'm glad you remembered."

"I think we still have some in the fridge," John said.

"Oh, I forgot," Libby said.

"No coleslaw?" Sally asked.

"I don't recall anyone asking for coleslaw."

After everyone loaded their plates, they returned to the dining room table. There was little sound except for the chewing of the food. John looked around to see if anyone was licking their fingers. Only Libby.

"Did they have any cheesecake?" Libby asked after she cleaned her plate.

"Nope," John said. "Chocolate chip cookies."

"I suppose that'll be okay."

"I've never seen you turn down any dessert," Geraldine said, glancing at Libby while taking a nibble off a chicken leg. "Although it wouldn't hurt you do to do it occasionally."

"Now Mama," Wendell said with a frown.

"It's the truth."

"Mom said you went to the park this afternoon," Chloe said, changing the conversation. "I bet it's getting pretty this time of the year."

"It's certainly not Central Park, but it's a nice neighborhood park. Whiskers and I like our walks there several times a week."

"Did you see anything interesting today?"

"Well, I got robbed."

"What?" Sally exclaimed, twisting her head. "Why didn't you tell me?"

"I tried to."

"What happened?"

"Some young punk took my cash," John said casually, taking a bite of a fried potato.

"Why didn't you say something when you got home?"

"Everyone seemed more interested in getting something to eat, so I didn't have time to say anything about it. I didn't want anyone to starve to death." He glanced at Geraldine, but she was occupied stripping meat off a chicken leg.

"How much did he take?" Brody asked.

"According to the punk, it was fifty-six dollars. He didn't want the change."

"Was he Black or white?" Wendell asked.

"Would it make any difference," John replied with an agitated gaze. "But for the record, he was white."

"Oh, I see. Just curious."

"Did you report it to the police?" Chloe asked.

"I didn't have time. And furthermore, they will not do anything over a petty robbery."

"Maybe they'll be on the lookout for people like him at the parks," Libby said. "It's a shame. You just don't feel safe anymore. Life was so much safer when we were young."

"I plan to go back to the park," John said. "It's a rare occurrence for that to happen."

"Maybe take a gun with you next time," Wendell said.

"I don't think so."

"You'd better be prepared." Wendell pointed his index finger like a gun. "You never know what might happen the next time you go there. It's better to be safe than sorry."

John ignored him, turning his attention to Sally. "I may give a call to the police later on," John said. "I have a few friends there. I also have a good description of him."

"Didn't you say you bought chocolate chip cookies?" Geraldine said, abruptly ending the conversation about the park robbery.

"Yes, Geraldine. After what I've been through, I decided to let everyone have a cookie."

"And eat it, too," Sally said, smiling.

John gathered a few scraps of meat from everyone's plates and put it in Whiskers' bowl. The pooch scarfed down in no time, almost as if he were on the verge of starving to death. After a few laps of water, and his belly full, Whiskers scuttled to his pad in the den.

Nineteen

Everyone except for Geraldine went to the living room after dinner. She headed to the den to watch *Jeopardy*, a program she seldom missed. Sometimes while watching she could be heard shouting correct, and a few incorrect answers before the contestants. Whiskers seemed unfazed by it all, snoozing away unless Geraldine got too loud with her answers.

Wendell, Libby, Sally, and Brody squeezed next to each other on the couch. Chloe sat cross-legged on the floor, next to John on the easy chair. Brody scooted from his place to the floor, his back against the couch.

"We can't wait to see our new great-niece," Libby said, patting Brody on the shoulder. "It's so exciting."

"I'll be going to the hospital tomorrow to pick her up," Brody said, tilting his head back to smile at her. "It's going to be interesting. I've never taken care of a baby."

"I was hoping we'd have her today," Sally said. "She's so precious."

"Some red tape at the hospital, courtesy of the Garcias," Chloe said. "I can't believe them."

"I guess you have to look at both sides," John said. "They have their reasons."

"Whose side are you on?" Sally asked, crinkling her forehead. "It's Brody's daughter and our granddaughter."

"I'm just trying to be fair. It must be the news-paperman inside of me, trying to get both sides of a story."

"But this isn't a newspaper story," Sally said.

"Okay, okay," John said with a laugh. "I plead the fifth."

"Daddy does have a point," Chloe said. "I think it's good to consider the other side. I don't think it diminishes what we want for the baby. If anything, it gives us some empathy for the Garcias. Don't forget, they lost their daughter tragically."

"Thanks, Chloe," John said, reaching over and patting her on the back. "I couldn't have said it any better."

"You're a smart girl," Wendell said.

"Yes," Libby added. "Just like your mother."

"Let's change the subject," John said.

"Yes, let's talk about bringing the baby home," Sally said.

"It gave me a little more time to prepare for her," Brody said. "I'm still a little nervous. This is all new to me."

"We'll be there to assist you," Chloe said, beaming.

"I'm glad I've got you and Mom," Brody said.

"You'll get the hang of it in no time. It's mostly instinct."

"But don't you think it's mostly that way for mothers?" Libby asked. "It's kind of a natural state for mothers. You know, maternal instinct. What do you think, Sally?"

"Brody isn't the first single father to raise a child. Brody won't be the first to do it. It's a lot of common sense and TLC."

"TLC?" Brody asked. "What's that?"

"Tender loving care."

"I've got plenty of that," he said with a soft smile.

"Anyway, you've got mothers here to give you a hand," Libby said.

"Don't your girlfriend's parents want to have anything to do with the baby?" Wendell asked.

John noticed Brody's uneasiness with the question.

"That's what I was referring to earlier," John said, who then explained that the custody would be determined later in court.

"I hope it doesn't get nasty," Wendell said, dryly.

"We'll see," Brody said, raising his brows. "It's out of my hands."

"When will there be a funeral for your girlfriend?" Libby asked.

"First of all, my girlfriend's name was Ashley," Brody said.

"I didn't mean to upset you. I just couldn't remember her name. I've been wracking my brain about it."

"That's okay," Brody said, glancing at her. "I'm sorry. I'm still a bit stressed. I apologize."

"You're going to feel that way for quite a while, son," John said. Sally turned and gave Brody a comforting tap on his shoulder.

"That could last for a long time," Wendell said. "Every time you look in that baby's face, you'll think of her."

"But you'll get over it," Libby said.

"I really don't want to get over it," Brody said. "I have good memories I want to keep about Ashley."

"That's the right attitude, Brody," Chloe said with a tender smile. "I didn't really know her, but I know she had such an amazing impact on your life. That'll be something special you can always share with your new daughter. From now on."

"Didn't she help you get past the drugs?" Wendell asked.

"Yes, she did," Brody said. "For that, I'll be forever thankful she came into my life." He fought back tears. "But I wish she was still in my life. I still can't believe she's gone."

Sally placed hands on Brody's quivering shoulders and squeezed. Chloe began wiping tears from her face. Wendall sat tight-lipped. Libby looked around the room, her eyes welling.

"It's okay, son," John said. "We understand what you're experiencing."

"Maybe it was God's will," Libby blurted. "You know, maybe He was working in mysterious ways to take her up to heaven. That should give you comfort, Brody. Maybe it was a blessing in disguise. She's in heaven now with the Lord."

"What?" Brody glared at her. "God's will? A blessing? Are you serious, Aunt Libby?"

Libby, at a loss for words, puckered up. Silence engulfed the room for a few seconds.

Brody shot up from the couch. "I'm sorry, folks, but I've got to go back to the apartment and get things ready for tomorrow."

Chloe stood. "Do you want me to go with you?"

"I'm good, Chloe," he said as he headed to the front door. "I'll call you later this evening or in the morning. Good night, everyone."

Libby remained dumbstruck. She glanced around at everyone.

"It's okay," Wendell said, patting her leg. "He's just upset. He'll get over it."

"I didn't mean to hurt him," she said in a high-pitched voice. "I was trying to give him some comfort. I didn't think he'd react that way."

"Well, Libby, it's only been two days," John said. "I'm sure he knows you meant well, but it's too soon. He'll be grieving for quite a while."

Sally rose from the couch. "Does anyone care for coffee or anything?"

"I think we'd better be leaving," Wendell said as he slowly pushed up from the couch. He put out his hand to help Libby get up. "Let us know if you need us for anything."

"Please tell Brody I'm so sorry," Libby said. "I really didn't mean to upset him. I hope he forgives me."

"We will," John said. "It's a difficult time for all of us."

Geraldine stood at the top of the steps to the den. "What's all the commotion about? And where's Brody?"

"He's tired and went back to his apartment, Grandma,' Chloe said as she walked toward her.

Geraldine turned toward Wendell. "You and Libby leaving too?"

"Yes, Mama. It's been a long day for us as well."

"I guess you got your bellies full. Any cookies left?"

"A few," Sally said. "Let's go get one."

Libby seemed to chew on her lower lip after hearing there were more cookies. Wendell took her by the arm. "Let's get on home, hon."

John grinned as he opened the door, letting Wendell know it was a good decision.

Twenty

John was up early the next morning getting the coffee started and taking Whiskers outside for a few minutes. The dawn sky was clear, the air crisp and fresh and a full moon faded through the treetops in the west. He sat on the top step of the porch, savoring the solitude of the moment. Even Whiskers seemed to enjoy the brief serenity, coming up to the steps and lying next to John's feet.

John heard a creak at the door and turned around. Chloe, wearing her mother's pink robe, poked her head outside. "Daddy, what are you doing?" she asked.

"Just sitting here and taking in the quiet," he said.

"Oh, I won't bother you then."

"No, don't run off. If you can stand the cool air, come out and sit with me for a few minutes. Coffee should be ready soon."

Chloe slipped out the door and sat next to her father. She wrapped her arms around her elevated knees. Whiskers licked her bare toes a few times.

"What's on your mind?" she asked. "Brody?"

"Oh, I suppose so," John said. "He's been through a lot, and he's got some difficult days ahead."

"We'll all be there for him," Chloe said.

"I know we will, but I hope that's enough."

"What do you mean?"

"Brody's not strong like you. You meet obstacles head on, like you did with cancer. He tends to retreat and looks for excuses. He's not nearly as strong-willed and determined as you."

"I guess you're worried he'll have a relapse with the drugs."

"That's my biggest concern. Ashley was there during his rehab and afterward to keep him on the straight and narrow. Now he doesn't have her to turn to or lean on."

"Let's hope that she gave him the strength to move on past the drugs. Isn't that what the rehab support group is all about? Kinda like Alcoholics Anonymous?"

"We can only hope."

"He'll have more responsibility now with the baby. I don't think he understands what it involves. A child changes everything. I learned that myself with Whitney. I was fortunate to have Sam to help raise her."

"That's my other big concern," John said, looking solemnly into the distance. "He's never raised a child and he doesn't have the finances to do it. I'm being honest with you. I don't know what he can do."

"I'll be happy to take leave from work and come here and help him," Chloe said.

"That'd be nice, but that's a short-term solution."

"Could he move back in here with you and Mom while he gets back on his feet?"

"I suppose we could accommodate that if he's willing. You know how stubborn he can be at times. He likes his independence, even though he's dependent on others."

"Do you think he can find a decent job? He has an accounting degree and had a good position in Chicago before he got involved in drugs."

"Let's hope he can. Maybe this will motivate him to find something better."

"I think I'm going to have to go back inside," she said. "It's getting too chilly out here for me."

"I'll join you. The coffee should be ready." He stood and took her hand to help her up. Whiskers was the first through the door, scrambling ahead of them to the kitchen for his water and kibble.

Chloe filled their coffee cups and sat at the bar while John took care of Whiskers' needs.

"Aunt Libby sure upset Brody last night," Chloe said after John pulled out a stool and sat across from her.

"She meant well," John said. "Brody shouldn't have reacted the way he did. He knows how she can be. For her, anything bad that happens is 'God's will.' That's always been her rationale. Unless, of course, it's something that has happened to her. Then it's the 'devil's doings.'"

Chloe laughed lightly. "I never thought about it, but you're right. That's her way of explaining events."

"It's interesting that for people like her, and there are many, God always takes a hit when bad things happen. They can't seem to accept that it's simply part of life, the good, the bad and the ordinary."

"I've always tried to go with the flow."

"We might as well, because there's little we can do to control what happens in our lives, for the most part."

"Kind of like God's will?"

John chuckled. "Probably so."

"Have you and Mom been doing okay?"

"We can't complain. Ever since that high school reunion you conned me into going to last year, nothing much has been going on."

"Now, Daddy, the reunion couldn't have been that bad. Mom said you guys had a good time, except for a few things. Didn't you enjoy seeing some of your old high school friends?"

"A few. But we've all gone down separate paths since we graduated. We're not the same people we were fifty years ago. Other than that, I admit it was interesting to see how some people changed and how others kind of stayed the same to some extent. And I wouldn't mind reconnecting with a few of them."

"I promise I won't do it again," Chloe said, easing off the stool. "Want some more coffee?"

John raised his cup. "Sure."

"I think I'll give Brody a call a little later and see if he wants me to go to the hospital with him," she said.

"Why don't you and Mom go? He could probably use all the help he can get. I can't see him doing it by himself."

"His apartment is already set up for the baby. He and Ashley did a great job getting everything ready for her arrival."

"That's good to hear. Would you believe that your Mom and I were never over there?"

"That is strange," Chloe said. "I wonder why?"

"You'll have to ask Brody. My guess is he didn't want us prying into his private life. Of course, maybe they were too busy, with her working and completing her doctorate studies. He came over now and then. Never for a long time. He's difficult to read at times."

"I don't know what to say," Chloe said with a shrug. "I guess that's Brody."

"Yep." John took a sip from his cup. "Unless he needed something."

"Money?"

"Yep."

Twenty-one

"Save any coffee for me?" Sally asked as she ambled into the kitchen barefoot, wearing black leggings and an oversized yellow sweatshirt.

"Take a seat, Mom, and I'll pour you a cup," Chloe said as she sidled off her stool. Sally sat next to John, placing her elbows on the counter for support as she twisted on the seat to move closer to the middle.

"Do we have any pastries?" Sally asked John. "I thought you bought some yesterday."

"I thought I did, too," he said. "But with Wendell and Libby here, along with Geraldine's passion for them, they wouldn't have lasted long. Would you like me to go out and buy some more?"

"No, I don't think so. We're eating too much of that sweet stuff. It's not good for our health."

"Tell that to Geraldine."

"Mother would laugh and say it hasn't harmed her in her ninety years. Maybe we can fix a regular breakfast this morning of eggs, bacon, and toast." Sally said. "Or maybe pancakes."

"That sounds great to me," Chloe said as she placed the coffee in front of Sally. "Want me to get it started?"

"Let's wait until Mother comes down."

"But she'll want long johns," John said. "She always does."

"Mother doesn't need them."

"You tell her that."

"I will."

"Oh, Chloe plans to call Brody a little later and meet him at the hospital," John said, indicating their daughter. "She's going to give him a hand with the new baby. Why don't you go with them?"

"I'll be happy too if Brody wants me there."

"You know he will," Chloe said.

"You're the one with the most experience," John said.

"We'll see," Sally said, taking a swallow from the cup. "That was a long time ago. I've probably forgotten more than I remember."

"Don't forget that maternal instinct Libby was talking about."

"We'll see."

Chloe sat across from her. "What would you think about me taking time off from work and coming down here and giving Brody a hand?"

"And bringing Whitney with you?"

"I was thinking about asking Sam if she would keep her."

"Doesn't she have a busy schedule?"

"Busier than mine, but we could hire a babysitter to make things work out. I don't think it'd be a problem."

"That'd be great," Sally said. "Just run it past Brody. I don't know why he'd object."

"How's Sam these days?" John asked. "You haven't said much about her lately."

"Well, uh, she's going through some hormone therapy now."

"Therapy?" Sally tilted her head. "For what?"

"She's decided she wants to be a man."

"What?" John said, wide-eyed. "Are you serious? I mean, is she serious?"

"Very much so," Chloe said. "She told me a few weeks ago that she was unhappy with being a woman and decided to get a sex change. She's undergone psychiatric evaluations and has started hormone treatments to make the transition."

"And that involves surgery?"

"That's the idea, Daddy." Chloe couldn't stifle a laugh.

"Wow!"

"That was kind of my feeling when she first told me."

"Are you okay with it?" Sally asked sincerely. "I mean, you and Samantha were partners for a long time."

"I respect her wishes. We broke up a while ago but have remained friends. I still feel for her because we shared so much. And that includes Whitney. Regardless, I told her she has my full support. Don't forget she was there for me while I was going through the chemo."

"I hope it won't impact Whitney too much," John said.

"We'll bring her along slowly as Sam goes through everything. She knows we both love her, so I think that will help."

"I wonder how her parents are dealing with it?" John asked.

The conversation was interrupted by tapping on the floor near the steps, signaling Geraldine's approach.

"Good morning, everyone," she said brightly. "It looks like I'm the sleepyhead this morning."

"Let me get you some coffee, Granny," Chloe said as Geraldine sat on the stool next to her.

"That would be nice, sweetie."

"I forgot. Cream and sugar?"

"Please."

John gently nudged Sally, wondering if she was picking up on her mother's superficial remarks. Sally acknowledged by turning toward him and flicking her brows twice.

"Anyone ready for breakfast?' Chloe asked.

"I am," Geraldine said, cheerily. "What are we having?"

"How about eggs, bacon, and toast?"

"Mmm, that sounds delicious." Geraldine raised her brows. "I haven't had a decent breakfast around here in ages. It seems like all we have are pastries."

Sally rolled her eyes. John began coughing.

"How do you want your eggs, Granny?"

"I'll take them however way you want to fix them."

"Scrambled?"

"That suits me fine." Geraldine said with a broad smile. "I'm sure they'll be delicious."

"Let me give you a hand," Sally said as she eased off the stool. "Maybe you can give Brody a quick call and see what time he wants us at the hospital."

Sally placed bacon strips in the microwave while Chloe darted off to her bedroom to call Brody. Sally was cracking eggs in a large bowl when she returned.

Chloe had a puzzled expression.

"What's the matter?" Sally asked.

"Uh, he said he only wants me there to help him," Chloe said. "He said he didn't want a lot of commotion at the hospital."

"Commotion?" John asked, noticing Sally's wounded expression.

"That's okay," Sally said with a subdued smile. "It's not a big deal. I can do some other things."

"Maybe you could meet us at Brody's apartment?" Chloe asked.

"We'll see," Sally said, turning her back to them and pouring the whipped eggs from the bowl into a skillet. John rose from his seat and took out plates from silverware from the cabinet.

"Can I help?" Geraldine asked.

"You're fine, Granny," Chloe said with a quick smile. "I believe we've got everything under control."

John stood next to Sally as she stirred the eggs. "Don't worry, everything's going to be all right."

"I'm fine. Really I am."

"I'll make the toast," he said.

After everything was put on the plates, they sat quietly for a few minutes when Chloe's cell phone rang. She quickly answered, mouthing "Brody" to everyone.

After the call ended, she smiled and said to her mother, "Brody says it's okay for you to go to the hospital. Apparently, he had something on his mind when I first talked to him."

A soft smile came across Sally's face. "Are you sure?"

"He said to be there around ten," Chloe said.

"I wonder what that was all about?" Geraldine asked. "Changing his mind like that."

"I'm sure it was nothing," Chloe said. "He just wasn't thinking earlier."

"Maybe he was thinking about the Garcias," John said.

"No doubt they're on his mind."

After they finished eating, John told Sally and Chloe to go ahead and get dressed and he and Geraldine would clean up the kitchen. Geraldine gave him a bewildered look.

When Sally and Chloe went to their bedrooms, Geraldine rose from the bar and stared at John.

"What?" he asked.

"Do you think you can pick up some long johns for tomorrow?"

"No problem."

She smiled and headed to the den for her TV shows while John took care of the kitchen.

Twenty-two

"Are you sure you don't want to go with us?" Sally asked John as she put on a light coat.

"I think I'd be in the way," John said, who was sitting on the couch reading a nature magazine. "Anyway, I need to make a run to the grocery store. I may even drop by McDonald's for a cup of coffee with my old buddies and break the news about our granddaughter. But call me if you need me."

Chloe sprang down the steps, a puffer jacket draped over her arm, and wearing a happy grin. "I'm ready," she said to her mom.

"You might want to put that on," John said. "It's still a bit on the chilly side."

"I'll be fine," she said with a grin. "I'm New York tough."

"I won't argue with that."

After they left, John called for Whiskers and took him outside. As the pooch was laying natural fertilizer at the side of the house, John noticed next-door-neighbor Manny Patel rolling a garbage can out to the street.

"Mornin', Manny."

Manny waved and they met at John's driveway. "How's everything?" he asked.

"We have a new granddaughter," John said. "She arrived three days ago. Sally and Chloe left to go to the hospital a while ago to give Brody a hand with the new arrival."

"Well, congratulations! I know everyone in your family must be excited. There's nothing quite like a brand-new baby. How's the mother doing?"

John took a deep breath and frowned. "She didn't make it. There were complications before and after the birth. It's been a bittersweet time for everyone, especially Brody."

"I'm so sorry to hear that," Manny said, slightly lowering his head. "Please let Brody and everyone know they'll be in our thoughts. And don't hesitate to let us know if there's anything we can do."

"I appreciate that. I think we're okay right now."

"The missus has some chores for me to do, so I'd better be going."

"We call them honey-dos," John said with a grin.

"I've never heard that," Manny said, squinting. "Does it have something to do with honey?"

"Sort of. If there's something your wife wants done, she might say 'Honey do this and honey can you do that.'"

Manny laughed. "I get it. I've got a few of those honey-dos then. I'll be seeing you, my friend."

Whiskers was sitting on his hind legs on the front porch facing the door, his way of telling John that he was ready to go back into the house.

Geraldine was in the kitchen, pouring a glass of water from the refrigerator dispenser. "When do you expect Sally to return? She didn't say a word to me when she left."

"She didn't want to disturb you while you were watching your TV program."

"She knows it's okay to say something to me when I'm watching something."

"Uh, I'll remember that," John said, smiling.

"Why do you have that grin on your face?" she asked.

"Oh, it's nothing," he said. "I was just thinking about how nice it will be when we get the baby home."

"Did she say how long they'd be gone?"

"I'm sure they'll be gone for a couple of hours. After checking the baby out of the hospital, they'll go to Brody's apartment for a while."

"You would think they would stop by here so I could see the baby. I am her *great grandmother*, you know."

"Don't you think they need to get situated at Brody's place first? The baby is only three days old."

Geraldine appeared nonplused by the suggestion, responding with a quick shrug.

"I've got an idea," John said. "How about if I take you over there so you can see the baby?"

"Maybe," she said woefully. "I think if they wanted me to see and hold the baby, they would have said something."

"Now, Geraldine, you know they're busy with just getting the baby out of the hospital. Everything will settle down after they get to his apartment. It just takes time."

"I'll think about it." She grabbed her cane and ambled back to the den. Seconds later, the TV was blaring some kind of game show.

John glanced at his watch. Sally had been gone for about an hour. Going to McDonald's was out of the question. He went down to the den and told Geraldine he was going to make a quick run to buy a few groceries, including long johns, before she could remind him. Instead of napping in the den with the TV noise, Whiskers followed John to the bedroom, where he curled on his secondary pad in the corner. John reached down and rubbed the dog's belly for a few seconds. "I'll be back in a bit, little buddy."

John grabbed a small buggy at the supermarket, thinking he wouldn't be buying many groceries. Before he realized it, the top and bottom baskets were loaded. He stood in line at the self-checkout, the next to go to a register when he remembered to buy the pastry. He wheeled back out and hurried to the bakery section.

There were only two long johns behind the plastic display. He quickly took the pastries with a tong and placed them in a small white sack. Better than nothing, he thought. While he was contemplating what other pastries to buy, someone lightly tapped his shoulder. He turned and was greeted with a pleasant grin from Kate Washington, a police officer who had helped him set up a Neighborhood Watch program that curtailed crime as well as nabbed some thieves. She was in uniform, standing erect, and carrying a small basket of foodstuffs.

"It's been a long time, Kate," he said. "How in the world are you?"

"About the same, John," she said, relaxing her posture. "Still chasing down the bad guys and gals. I stay busy. How about yourself?"

"I'm boring as ever, just getting older and grumpier," he said with a chuckle, then told her about the new baby and the passing of Brody's girlfriend.

"I'm so sorry to hear that. I wish I could say or do something to ease the pain. But I know the baby must be a blessing."

"We think so. She's coming home today. I mean to her new home at Brody's place. Sally and my daughter are with them now."

She glanced at her watch. "John, I need to run. I promised the crew back at the precinct that I'd bring in some goodies." She raised her basket.

"Same here for my house, but they were about sold out of long johns," he said. "They only had two. My mother-in-law isn't going to be a happy camper."

"I've got a dozen here." Kate held up a large cardboard container. "You can have them."

"Are you sure?"

"The guys at the precinct will gobble up anything," she said with a laugh. "I'll give them a mix of pastries."

"How about if I give you these two in exchange for the dozen?"

"That works."

"I need to get out of here and back home," John said. "Thanks again, Kate. Oh, let's have coffee one of these days, like we used to, if you're up for it."

"I'd love that," she said with a soft smile. "It has been too long."

"By the way, if you don't mind me saying, you look great."

"I don't mind it coming from you," she said with a light blush. "I'll see you."

Kate turned and headed to the self-service checkout with a little bounce in her step. John wheeled his cart to the long checkout line, glancing over at Kate at the self-checkout as she finished her business and left the store.

Spending nearly ten minutes getting through the checkout, John fretted if he'd been too friendly with Kate. He pursed his mouth for a few seconds. "Oh, my goodness," he uttered.

"Is something the matter, sir?" an elderly man standing in front of him asked.

Slightly startled, John replied, "Uh, I was thinking there was something else I needed to buy."

"I'll hold your place in line."

"I'm fine," John said. "Just a senior moment."

"I know what you mean," the man said with a big grin. "Happens to me all the time."

After John got through the line, he drove home, only to find Wendell and Libby's car parked in the driveway.

"Unreal," he mouthed.

Twenty-three

John parked his car on the street, opened the trunk and removed the container of bakery sweets from the sack and left them before going into the house. Wendell and Libby were in the den but came up to the kitchen as he started putting food away in the cabinets and refrigerator.

"How are y'all doing today?" John asked as they sat at the bar with curious expressions.

"We're good," Wendell said. "We were on our way to Target but stopped here for a minute to see how the family is doing. Mama's watching one of her favorite shows on TV and told us to wait until it was finished."

"She doesn't mind being interrupted," John said.

"Are you serious?" Wendell asked.

John chuckled. "Just kidding. That sounds like her."

"We're going to buy a gift for the baby," Libby said with a wide grin.

"That's awfully nice of you."

"Do you have any idea what she needs?"

"Geez, I wish Chloe or Sally were here. They're with Brody right now. They'd have a better idea. I'm a clueless granddad."

"We also wanted to apologize to Brody for getting him so upset the other evening," Wendell said.

"I think he took what I said the wrong way," Libby said. "I didn't mean to hurt him. I'm sure you know that. God knows I'd never do anything like that."

"Brody is going through a difficult time," John said as he stood across from them. "And he's going to be grieving for quite a while. I know you understand."

"I just didn't want him to think I thought God killed his girlfriend," Libby said with a troubled look. "I just meant that there are some things we can't control. You know what I mean?"

"Pardon the expression, but you simply go with the flow," John said with a warm smile. "We don't have as much control over things as we like to think we have. In fact, some would say we don't have any control."

"You have to put your faith in God almighty because He controls everything."

"For the most part."

"It's everything, John," Wendell said firmly. "God controls everything."

John paused for a moment, knowing the conversation could go off the rails if he said anything else. But he couldn't resist.

"Don't you believe in free will?"

"Not when it comes to God. He knows everything. The past, present, and the future. The alpha and the omega."

"Many people believe we have free will to determine our own destiny. Some would even consider it one of God's gifts."

"I think they're wrong," Wendell said resolutely. "They need to look to the Bible for answers."

"So when a person commits a murder or robs a store, then it's really God's fault?"

Wendell's empty expression had John wondering if he were lost in thought or simply lost at the thought of putting the blame on God.

Geraldine saved the day for Wendell when she sauntered into the kitchen. "Did you buy anything good?" she asked John.

"Of course, I did. I only buy the best when it comes to you. The healthy foods."

"Quit being a smart aleck, John."

"You know I do my best when buying groceries. I always consult you and Sally."

"Did you buy any long johns?"

Libby's eyes sparkled, and Wendell appeared to snap out of his stupor with the mention of the chocolate-iced pastry.

John sighed lightly. "I knew there was something I forgot."

"I can't believe you, John. I thought that was one of the main reasons you went to the grocery store."

"I'll go back later. I promise."

"You'd better write it down or you'll forget," Geraldine said. "You're getting absent-minded as you grow older. You're about as bad as Sally."

"I won't deny that," he said. "I know you won't let me forget your favorite confection."

"You know darn right."

"I bought a cantaloupe. Does that make you happy?"

"There you go, trying to be cute," Geraldine said. "You know what makes me happy and it's not a cantaloupe."

"Do you think Sally will be back this afternoon?" Libby asked.

"God willing," John blurted, then looked bemused at Wendell. "A figure of speech."

"Maybe we'll go to Target a little later then. I'll give Sally a call and get her opinion."

"Why do you want to talk to Sally?" Geraldine asked as she sidled up to the bar.

"I want to know what I should buy for the baby."

"My goodness, Libby, you've had kids and grands. You should have an idea what to get for that baby. It's not that difficult. I'd say buy disposable diapers. You can never have enough of those. Right, John?"

"Sure, Geraldine. Babies are always pooping and peeing all the time."

"I wanted to get something more personal," Libby said.

"Whatever," Geraldine said. "She'll outgrow it in a matter of weeks. So go ahead and waste your money if it makes you feel better."

"I guess we should be going," Wendell said. "We have a few other places to go to this afternoon."

"I'm glad you stopped by," John said. "I'll let Sally and the others know."

"I'm so anxious to see the baby," Libby gushed. "Tell that to Brody."

John gave a thumbs up. "Will do."

Wendell and Libby rose from the bar, and John walked them to the front door. Whiskers scampered up from the den, slipping out the front door with the others.

John remained on the front porch while Whiskers dashed to the side. After Wendell and Libby got into their car, there was a rat-a-tat sound several times over. Wendell rolled down the window. "I think the battery is about shot. Do you have any jumper cables?"

"I think I have some in the trunk of my car," John said. "We'll need to push your car into the street to make the connection."

Libby got out of the car and helped John push their car backward while Wendell stayed behind the wheel. With the car against the curb, John got into his and drove to the nearest driveway, backed out, and parked facing Wendell's hood.

Libby stood on the sidewalk as John got out and opened the hoods on both vehicles, since Wendell was unable to slip his hand under to make the disconnection. "I've always had trouble doing that," Wendell said. "They need to make it easier."

Wendell followed John to the rear of his car to get the cables. As the trunk sprung open, there lay the white box of Geraldine's pastry. John felt Wendell's hard stare as he reached in for the cables.

"Oh, there's the long johns," John said in mock surprise. "I knew I had purchased some at the grocery. They must have fallen out of a sack on the way home."

"If you say so," Wendell said gravely.

"Well, let's get you jumped so you can be on your way," John said as he grabbed the cables. As he was about to connect the cables to the respective batteries, he noticed Wendell walking toward the house carrying the box of goodies. He opened the door, and a few seconds later, handed the container to Geraldine.

"I want to make sure you didn't forget them again," Wendell said as he got into the driver's side of his car. A couple of turns on the ignition and his vehicle sprang to life. Libby got into the car, and they waited until John removed the cables and closed the hood.

John smiled as Wendell backed his car several feet, smiled tersely, and drove away.

"God's speed," John said softly as he put the cables back in the trunk.

Geraldine was sitting at the bar, munching on a long john when he returned to the kitchen with Whiskers.

"So you bought some long johns after all," she said. "Wendell said they were in the trunk."

"Wendell's right," John said as he refreshed Whiskers' water bowl and tossed the pooch a small treat.

"I wonder how that happened?"

He looked at her and grinned. "God's will?"

Twenty-four

After gobbling two pastries, Geraldine wiped the chocolate icing off the corners of her thin lips and padded to the den while John went to the bedroom. His eyes were getting heavy. He decided to lie down for a few minutes to give them a little rest. Those few minutes turned into a few hours and the next thing he knew Sally was tapping him gently on the shoulder.

"Are you going to wake up?" she asked.

"I'm just resting my eyes," he mumbled.

"They should be rested now. I got home over an hour ago and you were sound asleep then."

John propped himself up with his elbows and blinked several times. After several seconds, he swung his legs over the side of the bed. Sally had already gone to the adjoining bathroom.

"Why didn't you wake me up when you got home?"

"You were sleeping so comfortably, and I didn't want to disturb you. Besides, I spent some time with Mother, telling her about Brody and the baby." The toilet flushed.

"Get me up to date," John said from the bed as Sally washed and dried her hands. Several seconds later, she stepped back into the bedroom.

"Oh, first of all, the baby is so precious and tiny," Sally said as she sat next to him. "I didn't want to put her down after rocking her. All five pounds and eight ounces."

"Everything is in working order for her? She's not going to break if I hold her?"

"She passed all her tests," Sally said as she sat next to John. "But she's still 'Baby Girl' on the release form."

"I forgot she doesn't have a name. Does Brody have any idea what to name her?"

"He plans to talk to Ashley's parents and see what they think. Brody said he and Ashley hadn't given it much thought. Kinda funny, isn't it? We had our babies named by the time I went to the hospital."

"Did you have any suggestions? You've always been good with names."

"No, not really," she said. "But I do think it's a good decision to ask her parents. For all we know, Ashley could have discussed it with her mother."

"You think so? For some reason, they didn't seem that close."

"I'm still shocked she left Ashley at the hospital so she could attend a concert at a casino. I'm sure that's going to be something she'll regret the rest of her life."

"How is Brody?"

"He's on cloud nine. Practically all he does is stare at the baby with dreamy eyes."

"Has he said anything about a possible custody battle?"

"That never came up. I think right now we all just want to focus on the baby. We'll deal with that when the time comes."

"Don't forget, we still have a funeral to attend."

"Dr. Garcia texted Brody he'd probably be getting in touch with him later this evening about the service."

"Where's Chloe? In the den with your mother?"

"She's with Brody. I think she'll be there for several days to give him a hand."

"That's a great decision. He needs someone like her to teach him the ropes."

"He's got a lot to learn about taking care of a baby."

John rose from the bed, steadying himself by grabbing a footpost.

"Are you okay?" Sally asked.

"Got up too fast."

"Are you still taking your blood pressure pills?"

"Yes, dear," he said. "Every single night before going to bed."

They went to the kitchen, met by Whiskers less than a minute later, looking up at John to let him know he wanted to go outside.

"Mother told me you had company while I was gone," Sally said.

As John was about to summarize Wendell and Libby's visit, Geraldine entered the kitchen. "I already told Sally everything that happened. Even the long johns."

John smiled. "Good, then I'll step outside for a few minutes with my best friend."

Geraldine sneered and eased up on a stool. "Are you telling me that little mutt of yours is more important than Sally?"

"I didn't say that, Geraldine. You're making assumptions."

"Then what do you mean, wise guy?"

"Sally is the most important person and the love of my life, but Whiskers provides unconditional love. There are times I get on Sally's bad side. I don't know if that's ever happened with Whiskers."

"He's right, Mother," Sally said with a laugh. "John has seen my bad side a few times. It's not pretty."

Geraldine didn't respond, looking first at Sally and then at John. "Sometimes you two are too hard to understand."

"We could probably say the same about you, Mother," Sally said.

"Hey, don't get me involved in this," John said with a wide grin. "I don't want to be on her bad side."

"Now what does that mean?" Geraldine asked. "Are you just being a smart aleck?"

"I'm not saying anything. Come on Whiskers, let's go because things could get dreadful here."

As John left the kitchen, he heard was Geraldine asking Sally, "Are there any long johns left? I'm starving!"

Twenty-five

While outside with Whiskers, John took out his cellphone and called Brody to see how he was doing with the newborn.

"I hope I didn't catch you at a bad time," John said.

"I'm sitting here on the couch watching a ballgame," Brody said. "Chloe's back in the nursery with the baby. Everything's cool."

John paused for a few seconds, trying to think of something to say since he didn't call Brody very often to chit-chat.

"Have you heard from Ashley's parents regarding the funeral?"

"Not yet. I hope they don't forget about me."

"I don't believe they will."

"I was only kidding, but you can never tell with them. I'm really surprised how Ashley's mother has been toward me the past few days. She was always somewhat civil, but never rude. I suppose I'm seeing her true feelings toward me."

"This is a difficult time for her, so I'd give her some slack. Sometimes people say things they don't really mean."

"I know," he said. "I just wish she'd give me some slack."

"It takes time."

"When are you going to come over and see the baby?"

"I may just do that tomorrow," John said. "I'll bring your grandmother along as well."

"That's great."

"Is there anything I can bring?"

"I can't think of anything now. I'll discuss it with Chloe."

"Text me if something comes to mind. I'm outside with Whiskers. I'll get back with you later."

"Thanks for calling, Dad."

"You have a great day, son," John said. "And one more thing."

"What's that?"

"Congratulations on being a new father. I know you'll do a great job."

"Uh, thanks, Dad. That means a lot. I'll do my best."

Whiskers was eager to head down the street, tugging slightly on the leash as they headed toward Shipley Park. When they reached the crosswalk to the park, John turned around to return home. He was still apprehensive after encountering the petty thief on his last trip there. Whiskers gave him a perplexed look, as if he expected to spend some time at the pond chasing the waterfowl and maybe a squirrel or two.

"Sorry 'bout that, little buddy," John said, reaching down to pet the pooch's head. "Maybe next time."

Sally greeted him at the door when he got home. "We had company while you were gone," she said.

He followed her to the dining room where there were containers of food and disposable diapers, baby bottles, and other items for newborns on the table. Geraldine was dawdling around the table, examining all the wrapped gifts.

"Wow," John said. "Where did all this come from?"

"Apparently the word got out about the baby and our neighbors brought all this over while you were out," she said with a smile. "I believe it was Manny Patel who told the neighbors."

"My goodness. I talked to Brody a little while ago and mentioned that I may come over tomorrow to see the baby, but it looks like we may have to load up the SUV and head on over there today. I don't think we have enough room in the refrigerator."

"Can I go with you?" Geraldine asked earnestly. "I'd love to see my great grandbaby."

"Of course you can," John said. "I even mentioned to Brody that I was going to bring you along with me."

"Without asking me first?" Geraldine said with knitted brows.

"You know, I would have asked you. I wasn't going to tie you up and drag you over there."

"You know better than to do that!"

"Don't worry," John said. "So you wouldn't have gone with me?"

"Would you two quit this silly conversation," Sally said. "Of course, Mother wants to go."

"Why don't you give Brody a call and tell him we'll be there in an hour or so," John said. "It'll give us a little time to get dressed and load the car."

Geraldine went to her room, changing her clothes from blue sweatshirt and baggy gray sweatpants to a white blouse and jeans. She also spent time fixing her hair and applying makeup while John and Sally put the items in the back of the SUV and waited for her in the living room.

"Aren't you going to wear something else?" Geraldine asked Sally. "Didn't you wear that earlier to the hospital?"

"Yes, Mother, but it's clean. I'll put on something else tomorrow."

"I already look good," John said, flashing a smile as they rose from the couch. "Right, Geraldine?"

Geraldine sighed.

~ * ~

Brody was sitting in the rocking chair holding the baby when they arrived at his apartment. They gathered around him for a minute to "ooh and aah" the newborn. Chloe came out of the kitchen holding a baby bottle.

"It must be mealtime," Sally said.

"Every couple of hours, just like clockwork," Chloe said as she handed the bottle to Brody.

Brody smiled at Geraldine for a moment. "Granny, would you like to hold and feed her?"

"Uh, I don't know," she said. "It's been a long time since I fed a baby. Probably when Wendell's were babies."

"She won't break," Chloe said.

Brody handed the bottle back to Chloe and eased up from the rocker for Geraldine to sit. She released her cane close to the floor and held out her slender arms for the baby, holding her close to her chest, smiling as if in a trance. She then took the bottle from Chloe.

"She's so sweet," Geraldine said softly as she put the nipple to the baby's mouth.

"We've got some things for you in the SUV," John said to Brody. "Why don't you come with me and help bring them up here?"

"We don't need anything right now," Brody said. "We're good."

"Wait until you see what we brought you."

When John opened the trunk, Brody's eyes widened at the items. John explained that the neighbors also contributed monetarily for him and the baby as he handed him an envelope stuffed with cash and checks.

"I don't know what to say," Brody said. "I was thinking about asking you for a small loan to tide me over for a few days, but I don't have to now."

"That's good to hear," John said with a chuckle. "It saved me a few dollars then."

"I may need some later."

"We'll discuss that later," John said as he loaded Brody's arms with several containers of food. "It looks like we'll have to make another trip."

"I hope this food is good."

"I'm sure it is, Brody. Don't forget, it's the thought that counts."

"Right, Dad," he replied as they walked back to the apartment with armloads of food and gifts.

"I hardly know many of these people," Brody said as he put some of the food in the refrigerator and on the kitchen counter.

"But they know your dad and me, and they want to share in the joy with us," Sally said.

"Believe it or not, but they've been supportive of you while you've been in rehab," John said. "They're always asking how you're coming along. You might not see them often, but some of them remember you growing up in the neighborhood."

"Please let them know how much I appreciate everything," Brody said.

"Maybe in a few weeks, when the weather is nicer, we can invite them over to the house to see her," Sally said.

John pointed to a stroller that was a gift. "Or may we can take her around the neighborhood to meet everyone?"

"We can do that," Brody said with a wide grin.

Twenty-six

John held the baby for ten minutes on the couch, clutching her firmly as if she might drop from his lap. He handed her carefully to Chloe when she whimpered.

"I suppose we should be going," John said as he scooted to the edge of the cushion. "It's been a long few days and I'm sure everyone's tired."

"I hope you bring the baby over to the house so I can spend more time with her," Geraldine said. "That would be so nice."

"I'm not sure she'd like listening to the television all day," Brody said.

"That's not a nice thing to say," Geraldine said. "You're becoming a smart aleck like your father."

"Oh, you know I'm only kidding. You take things too seriously, Grandma."

"And you don't?"

Brody didn't respond.

"We'll try to keep things quiet when you come over," Sally said to Brody. "In the meantime, let us know if you need anything."

"I think we're in good shape, Mom," Brody said. "We have the funeral coming up, whenever that is."

"Keep us informed about that," John said.

Sally rose from the couch, then extended her hand to help Geraldine and they followed John to the door. Brody hurried over and hugged and kissed his mother and grandmother and shook John's hand, then pulled him closer for a light embrace.

"Thanks for everything," he said. "I couldn't do it without all of you."

John gave Geraldine a beseeching glance not to say anything. She apparently got the message, leaving the apartment without making a caustic comment.

Sally wiped a tear from her eye as they stepped outside and walked to the SUV, Geraldine locking an arm into Sally's and holding the cane to keep her balance on the rutted concrete surface.

"When is he going to give that baby a name?" Geraldine asked from the back seat as John pulled out of the parking lot.

Sally explained Brody hadn't talked to Ashley's parents to give them an opportunity to suggest a name.

"Well, I hope they give her an American name." Geraldine exclaimed.

"What's that supposed to mean?" John asked.

"I mean like some of the wild names singers and actors are called. I have too much trouble pronouncing them."

"I'm sure everyone will decide on a name that fits her," Sally said, turning around to face her. "I wouldn't worry about it. Besides, Ashley and her parents have so-called proper names."

"How about if they name her Gerry?" John said with a grin.

"That's not funny," Geraldine said. "Besides, when I was a little girl, my father called me Gerry."

"Then how did you become Geraldine?"

"My mother thought it was more proper and professional sounding. She made me tell everyone it was Geraldine, and to correct them if they called me Gerry. So Geraldine stuck. My mother had the last word on it."

"Would you like me to call you Gerry?" John asked. "You know, for old time's sake?"

"It's a little too late for that," she said. "Maybe if you had done that when you first married Sally."

"But you introduced yourself as Geraldine to me."

"Oh, never mind, John. This conversation is getting silly." She turned her head toward Sally, effectively ending the chat with John. "What are we going to have for dinner tonight?"

"We probably should have gotten a bite to eat at Brody's," John said.

"Am I talking to you?" Geraldine asked.

"All I'm saying is that the food the neighbors brought over was for the entire family."

"How do you know that?"

"Well, I don't know for a fact."

"Then you shouldn't say anything."

"How about if we stop for a pizza?" Sally asked. "Are you in the mood for that.?"

"Eat in or carryout?" John asked.

"I'd prefer to go inside and eat, if that's okay," Geraldine said, taking the edge out of her voice. "Unless it's too loud."

John drove to a small pizza restaurant near their home. It wasn't crowded and they were seated in a booth away from other diners—at John's request and out of Geraldine's earshot.

John ordered a draft beer, and to his surprise, Geraldine ordered one as well. Sally followed suit.

"I was wondering if Wendell and Libby will come over with their gift for the baby later this afternoon?" John asked.

"No, they won't," Geraldine said decisively. "They'll make an excuse and then forget to do it. They're just like that commercial I hear on TV."

"What's that?" John asked.

"Talk is cheap," Geraldine said. "They talk about doing things but don't always do what they say."

"Oh, Mother, they may be busy. I'm sure they'll get something, especially since they brought it up. Give them some time."

"We'll see." Geraldine folded her arms on the table. Minutes later, the server came back with their mugs of beer and took the order for the pizza.

Geraldine took a small sip from her frosted mug. "This isn't bad. Harry wasn't much of a beer drinker. He didn't even want it in the house."

"You're right, Mother. I don't recall ever seeing any beer in the refrigerator when I was growing up."

"We lived in the Bible Belt and people just didn't have it around. People would sneak around and drink it. Just a bunch of hypocrites, if you ask me."

"Times have certainly changed," John said. "Now you see advertising about craft beers, wine, and bourbon. Kentucky even promotes Bardstown as the 'Bourbon Capital of the World.'"

"I'd like to visit some of those bourbon places one of these days," Geraldine said.

"Maybe we can do it later this spring or summer when the weather is a bit warmer," Sally said. "It'd be fun."

"Do you think they give samples?"

"I understand they do."

"That sounds like fun then," Geraldine said.

"Any other places you'd like to see?" John asked.

"Before I die?" Geraldine said with an unexpected laugh.

"I didn't mean it that way."

"Don't they call them kick-the-bucket lists? Places to see before you kick the bucket?"

"They're simply called bucket lists," Sally said. "And yes, they are places you'd like to visit before you die. John and I have a few places on ours."

"So where would you like to go?" John asked, taking a swallow from his mug.

"I always wanted to see the ocean," Geraldine said.

"You've never seen the ocean?" John asked with an incredulous look.

"Harry wasn't much for travel. He promised me we'd do it someday, but he died on me."

"We'll put that down for this year. That shouldn't be a problem."

"Unless I kick the bucket."

The server returned with their veggie pizza. Geraldine and John ordered another beer while Sally opted for ice water.

"This turned into a nice day," Geraldine said out of the blue. She finished off her mug and took a slice of pizza.

"I'll drink to that," John said, raising his mug.

"Me, too," Sally said. Geraldine grabbed her empty mug and grinned.

They tapped their mugs together, chuckled, and turned their attention to the pizza.

Twenty-seven

The following day Brody unexpectedly dropped by the house while John was outside with Whiskers. Chloe was at his apartment with the baby and Ashley's parents. Brody said he made an excuse to leave so they could spend some time with the baby.

"What's going on?" John asked as he held the front door open as Brody entered the living room while Whiskers scampered to the kitchen.

Brody sat on the easy chair, leaning forward with his elbows on his knees while John was on the couch. Whiskers returned to the room, going between John's feet to be picked up. John put him on his lap. Brody waited to talk until Whiskers was settled.

"Ashley's funeral's going to be on Saturday.," he said with a long sigh. "They decided to keep it private for some stupid reason."

"Are we invited?" John asked.

"I'm not sure. I'm not sure I'm even invited." Brody appeared bemused at his comment.

"I don't believe they'd go that far."

"We'll see. I told him they should invite people from the rehab center. She had such an impact as a counselor. Everyone respected her. And I'm sure there were others at the university who would like to show their respect. You know, her professors and other doctoral students."

"I would think so," John said.

"I think it's her mother's idea. Sometimes she'd make snide remarks about people with addictions."

"In front of you?"

"Yeah, I think some of it was aimed at me. Ashley would get irritated with her for doing it."

"Did she say anything to her mother?"

"Not really. More than anything, she'd try to change to the subject. Her mother usually got the hint. Afterward, Ashley would apologize to me, but I told her it was all right because I didn't want to create any conflict between her and Donna. I wanted to have a good relationship with her parents."

"Oh well, maybe they'll change their minds about the funeral," John said. "Anything else?"

"I asked them about some names for the baby. They said they'd give me a list later this week. We didn't talk for long. George broke down and started crying again. He does that a lot."

"Understandable."

"How about Ashley's mom?"

"She left the room. That's when I left. Chloe does a better job dealing with them than I do."

"Have you thought of any names?"

"Chloe and I talked about it last night. We came up with Ashlyn, Leigh; you know, plays off her name."

Sally came into the room, holding a dust cloth and spray. "I thought I heard your voice," she said to Brody. "I was tidying up Chloe's room."

Brody explained why he stopped at the house and updated her on the funeral and baby names.

"Where's Grandma?" Brody asked.

"She's asleep in the den. I think she's exhausted from all the activity yesterday."

"I'll bring the baby over next week after we get her settled. She's been doing good so far. It helps that Chloe gets up with her during the night to feed her. I'm even getting the hang of it, giving her a bottle and changing her diaper. She's got a follow up with the doctor, so I'll stop by then."

"Your grandmother will like that."

Brody took a deep breath and clenched his jaws.

"What's on your mind?" John asked as Sally sat next to him. "Is there something else you want to tell us?"

"I'm getting some real bad vibes from Ashley's parents."

"How so?"

"I still think they're going to try to gain full custody of the baby."

"What makes you think that?" Sally asked.

"They've haven't outright said they will, but it's just the way George talked about her, like doing things together and stuff like that."

"They are her grandparents, too, so they want to have a part in her future like we do," Sally said.

"But I think it's much more than that, like I don't exist." Brody sat back and paused. "I think they're really serious about wanting full custody."

"Son, I wouldn't read too much into it right now," John said in a comforting tone. "Let's get through the funeral and see how things go."

"Uh, will you help me if this ends up in a custody battle?"

"Of course," Sally said. "She's your daughter, and she belongs with you. And she's our granddaughter. We want the best for you and her."

"I mean, I'll have to hire a lawyer and they aren't cheap. And I don't have a lot of money right now."

"We'll deal with that later," John said. "We'll do what we can financially if it comes to that."

"I hope you can work out some kind of amicable arrangement with them," Sally said. "That would be the best for everyone."

"But that will still involve the courts," Brody said with a shrug. "Her parents have money, and I don't."

"Maybe it's time you start looking for a good job," John said. "You've got the skills. You had a good accounting job in Chicago until you had your personal problems."

"I'll look into it," Brody said. "Maybe I should look for a job in Louisville since her parents live there. It'd make things easier."

"I don't think that's a good idea," John said. "There are plenty of jobs here in Lexington. Furthermore, you have your support groups here. You don't have them in Louisville."

"I could find some. It wouldn't be difficult. There are support groups all over the place. It's not a problem."

"Let's cross that bridge when we get to it. You always make things more difficult than they have to be."

"We're here to give you and the baby support," Sally said. "You wouldn't have that in Louisville."

"I would from her parents."

"Don't they both work?" John asked.

"Yes."

"So they don't have the time to keep the baby?"

"They would pay for daycare."

"How do you know that?"

"Well, uh, George sorta mentioned it."

"Really?"

"It was nothing definite. It was something he said in passing."

"Do you think they'd go for paying for daycare and you maintaining some custody?"

"Whatever works, Dad. I have limited funds. I'd be willing to compromise."

"But would they?"

"I don't know," Brody said. "It's all confusing to me right now."

"You seem to be wavering about it."

"I know I go back and forth. I guess it's because I think Ashley's dad would be somewhat agreeable to some kind of joint custody, while her mom would be totally against it."

"Let's discuss this later," John said, rising from the couch while Whiskers leaped to the floor. "You've got me confused about what you want."

"I guess you don't want to help me then," Brody said as he got up from the chair. "Be that way."

"What in the hell are you talking about? We've been with you every step of the way, whether we liked it or not."

"John, calm down," Sally said, taking hold of his hand.

John turned and looked at her. "Calm down? Did you just hear what he said?"

John could feel Brody's cold, hard stare as he turned and left the house without another word. Seconds later, they heard Brody's car start up.

"Well, I hope you're satisfied," Sally said, letting out a deep breath.

"There you go again. Always the enabler."

John stomped to the kitchen, poured himself a glass of water at the sink, and stared out the window to the shaded backyard.

"What's going on out here?" Geraldine said as she appeared in the room. "What's all the racket about?"

John turned toward her. "I'm sorry we disturbed your nap. We were having a family discussion."

"It's okay, Mother," Sally said as she went into the room and stood next to her. "We just had a little disagreement."

"A little?" John asked. "Are you serious?"

"Please, John. Let's discuss this later."

"This has to be about Brody," Geraldine said as she sat on a stool. "All your arguments are about him."

"Good guess," John said as he set the glass in the sink.

"He's not even here."

"He was."

"He was? Why didn't you tell me?"

"Because you were asleep, Geraldine."

"Oh, I guess I was."

"Mother, do you want something to eat?" Sally asked. "It's about time for lunch."

"Why was Brody here?" Geraldine asked. "And no, I'm not hungry."

"He came by to tell us about Ashley's funeral and a few other things," Sally said.

"I don't think you'd fuss about the funeral."

"There were some other things, Mother."

"I'm not part of the family anymore?"

"Yes, you are part of the family," John said, trying to temper his voice. "We just don't want you to get worried about things. We want to try to resolve things first."

"What don't you want me to get worried about?"

"It has to do with possible custody issues," Sally said.

"It has to be more than that."

"Oh, Geraldine, you are an inquisitive person," John said. "You should have been a news reporter."

"You still haven't answered my question. Why are you arguing with each other?"

"It's a parenting issue."

"I bet it has to do with money," Geraldine said. "Right, John?"

"Why are you asking me?"

"Because when it comes to money, you're always the one who gets mad."

John couldn't suppress an awkward smile, knowing he couldn't deny Geraldine's observation. "It's more than that."

"So Sally is giving in to Brody?"

"You know us too well."

"I knew it!"

"Mother, are you sure you don't want a bite to eat?" Sally asked.

"Are there any long johns left?"

"You've got to eat more than those things."

"How about if you order a pizza?

"We had pizza yesterday."

"I'm not hungry then." Geraldine pouted.

"Do you want me to order a pizza?" John asked.

"We don't need to eat pizza," Sally said. "We have other food here."

"What do we have?" Geraldine asked.

"I can fix you a sandwich," Sally said.

"How about if John went out and got us sandwiches at Subway?"

Sally opened the refrigerator and saw there wasn't anything to make a sandwich other than eggs and cheese slices. "John, aren't you buying anything for us to eat?"

"Huh?" he said. "I buy what you two want me to. Don't put the blame on me."

"Maybe I need to go with you next time. There's nothing here to eat."

"You're welcome to go with me anytime," John said. "In fact, you can go by yourself if you so desire."

"I may just do that."

"Just remember where you park the car."

"What is that supposed to mean?"

"Never mind," John said, deciding not to remind Sally about the time he had to go to the supermarket and help her locate her SUV.

Geraldine appeared to be enjoying the back and forth, sitting back with a sly smile.

Sally noticed a white box at the end of the counter, opened it to reveal three oblong treats. "Here's your lunch," as she placed it in front of her mother.

"But I was counting on a sandwich," Geraldine sulked.

"Later!" Sally said as she left the room in a huff.

Geraldine looked at John with her mouth half-open at her daughter's rare outburst. "I think you and her need to make up."

"I believe you're right," John said as he headed to the bedroom.

 Sally was standing in front of the medicine cabinet mirror, applying light makeup on her face.

"I come in peace," John said as he walked up behind her, placing his hands on her shoulders.

She picked up a brush and ran it across her head a few times without saying a word.

John stared at their reflection in the mirror as he gently squeezed her upper arms. He flicked his brows playfully. "I forgive you."

She turned around quickly with fire in her eyes. "You forgive me?"

"Just kidding, sweetheart." He pecked her on the cheek. "Let's not argue."

A small smile crossed her lips. "I don't want to argue either."

They kissed lightly.

"It's my fault," he said. "I shouldn't have lost my temper with Brody. Do you forgive me?"

"Yes, hon," she said. "And I shouldn't take up for him all the time. Do you forgive me?

"Yes, sweetheart."

They kissed again.

"I thought I'd go out," Sally said as she left the bathroom and went to the dresser.

"Where to?"

"The grocery store."

"Uh, mind if I go with you?"

"Of course not," she said. "I'll even let you drive."

Twenty-eight

The private funeral for Ashley Garcia was a somber affair, conducted in a small chapel outside Louisville where the family owned several grave plots. Miles Davis's "Blue in Green" elegantly filled the air as mourners sat quietly, many with heads bowed.

George, Donna and two of their children, George Jr. and Evie, sat in the front row. Brody, John, and Sally sat midway in the chapel. The closed casket was covered in yellow and pink roses. Several tall floral arrangements were positioned on each side including one from the Rosses.

The minister recalled Ashley's short but productive life, eliciting loud sobs from Donna as George pulled her close to his side to console her. Brody, sitting between John and Sally, wept and trembled slightly throughout much of the service. Albinoni's "Adagio in G Minor" played after the final prayer.

When the service concluded, Brody led the way to offer final condolences to Ashley's parents and siblings. John watched as George shook Brody's hand while Donna offered a tearful frown. He was almost hesitant about going up to the grieving parents, but took Sally's hand and faced them with a solemn expression.

"Our thoughts are with you and your family," John whispered as he gripped George's hand. Sally gave Donna a gentle hug and kiss on the cheek before they joined Brody in the foyer of the chapel.

"I'm glad that's over," Brody said quietly as they stepped toward the exit. "Let's get out of here."

"I thought they were having a reception afterward," Sally said.

"I think it's more for family."

"You're family," John said.

"They don't think so."

"How about the burial?"

"I was told it was only for immediate family."

"Then you should attend," Sally said.

"I'll visit her gravesite later," Brody said as his shoulders sagged. "I'd prefer that than being around them. At least I can be alone in my thoughts with Ashley."

"But Brody—" John said.

"Forget it, Dad," Brody said without making eye contact. "I've made up my mind."

"Okay, it's your decision."

"I know."

As they departed, John glanced back and saw George with his arm around his slumping wife as they stood alone at the casket. Their children sat with their heads bowed in the pew.

Brody walked between John and Sally in silence to the SUV. Brody pulled out his cellphone when he got in the back seat and called Chloe to check on the baby. "She's sleeping," he said after ending the call.

"How about we stop and get a bite to eat on the way back to Lexington?" John suggested as a light rain fell. "There's several Cracker Barrels along the way. Unless you're in a hurry to get back."

"That's fine, although I'm not sure I feel like eating," Brody said.

They stopped at the restaurant off Blankenbaker Parkway. John let Sally and Brody out at the front entrance and parked the car. He found them seated in the far corner of the crowded dining room.

"It's still hard to believe Ashley's gone," Brody said after the waitress took their orders. "Sometimes I feel like it's a nightmare and I'm going to wake up with her next to me and everything's going to be okay again."

"It's never easy losing someone, especially a person you love," Sally said.

"She believed in me. She's the big reason I got over the drugs. There were times early on when I was tempted to use them, but she was always there to encourage and support me. It was unconditional. This may sound crazy, but I never wanted to disappoint her."

"That's probably something that drives a lot of us in our lives," John said. "I think we're all tempted now and then to do foolish things, but when we think about those who are important to us, we're able to withstand those temptations, whatever they may be." He smiled at Sally.

"Believe it or not," John continued, "but I never wanted to disappoint your mom, you, or Chloe. That was somewhat of a guiding light for me. I never wanted to bring any disgrace because I felt it was something that might taint the rest of the family."

"I suppose I did that," Brody said.

"You didn't," John said. "It was something we kept in the family and didn't publicize to others. And with drugs being so prevalent now, I'm not sure if people give it a lot of thought unless it involves a celebrity."

The waitress returned with their drink orders, pausing the conversation for a few seconds.

"George and Donna sure didn't have much to say at the funeral," Brody said.

"That's to be expected," John said. "They're grieving parents."

"But what about me?"

"We were there for you," Sally said, gently tapping the top of his hand. "We know you're suffering. Grandma knows. Chloe knows. We all are."

"Her mother just doesn't care for me. You would've thought they'd ask me to sit with them."

"Come on, Brody," John said. "Give them a little slack. All this will pass in a few weeks as we all come to terms with Ashley's passing."

"I'm not sure I'm even going to ask them again for name suggestions for the baby. I'm fed up with them."

"Please don't be that way," Sally said. "You want to have a good relationship and be on decent terms with them, especially for the baby. Don't make any rash decisions."

Brody smirked. "I'll think about it."

The waitress came back with their food. They ate in silence except for occasional comments from Brody about living adjustments with a newborn.

"I don't know what I'd do without Chloe," he said.

"I'm sure she loves taking care of the baby and giving you a helping hand," Sally said.

"How is her cancer?"

"She's in remission. She was fortunate it was discovered early."

"That's good to know. I wanted to ask her about it, but didn't want to make her feel uncomfortable."

"That's considerate, although I believe she'd be okay with letting you know how she is doing. She's open about it."

As they drove back to Lexington, John avoided asking Brody about his plans to support his daughter, knowing it would probably set off a heated argument or sulking from his son—or both. Instead, he listened to Sally give her son a few tips on raising a baby while soft rock on the radio played softly in the background.

Chloe was sitting in the rocking chair, feeding the baby when they entered Brody's apartment. That the apartment was spotless didn't go unnoticed.

"How do you do it?" Sally asked, looking around the area. "Looking after the baby is a full-time job."

"I do a few things while the baby is sleeping, like putting things away and doing the laundry."

"She's also rearranged everything in the cabinets and closets," Brody said. "I can hardly get her to sit down and relax. She's a non-stop whirling dervish around here."

"Don't get carried away," Chloe said. "Ashley kept things nice and tidy."

John recalled when Chloe did the same on her last visit to Lexington, even doing the same thing at her apartment when they stopped back on their return from Budapest. She had to have everything so-so and orderly.

"She's up to any challenge," John said.

"A person with obsessive-compulsive disorder never rests," Chloe said with a laugh. "Others just have to get used to it. We're in our own little world."

"I guess that's a bonus when it comes to cleaning," Sally said with a tender smile. "But, like Brody, I wish you'd take it easy and relax once in a while."

"Amen," John said.

"How was the funeral?" Chloe asked after Brody went to the bathroom.

"Sad," Sally said quietly. "Very solemn."

"How was Brody?" Chloe whispered.

"I think he did all right," John said. "But please don't bring it up. At least while we're here."

"Why?"

"He felt snubbed by the family."

Brody stepped out of the bathroom. "Did I hear my name?"

"I asked about the funeral," Chloe said. "Was it a nice service?"

"It sucked."

"Oh," Chloe said, glancing at their parents.

Brody walked to the rocker, leaned over and kissed the top of the baby's head.

"How was she?" he asked.

"Just perfect," Chloe said with a bright smile.

"We should be going home, but I want to hold the baby for a few minutes after you finish feeding her," Sally said to Chloe.

"Speaking of home, I'd better give Geraldine a call and see how she's doing," John said as he rose from the couch. He punched in her number on his cellphone and moseyed toward the adjoining small kitchen. He spoke for about a minute.

"Is Mother okay?" Sally asked.

"There's no need to hurry back," John said. "She has visitors."

"It must be Wendell and Libby."

"That means one thing. I have to pick up some more you-know-what on the way home."

Sally chuckled. "You might want to buy some diet soda, too."

"Why's that?" Chloe asked. "I didn't think you drank diet drinks."

"It's a family thing," John said.

"Huh?"

"For Libby."

"Oh!" She grinned.

Twenty-nine

Wendell and Libby had left by the time John and Sally returned home with a six-pack of diet soda and twelve cream sticks. The neighborhood was darker and quieter, with streetlights sputtering on and a few porch lights turned on.

"Let's leave the long johns in the backseat," John said as they got out of the SUV.

"Why?" Sally asked.

"Just a little game."

"You need to quit teasing Mother."

"Oh, she likes it," John said. "It's our little game. She likes to aggravate me and for me to give it right back."

"Maybe so, but don't get carried away. You know how easy it is to hurt her feelings."

"You know I wouldn't intentionally do that to her."

"But you might accidentally do it, so be careful."

"I will," John said.

"Now, about those pastries," she said. "Are you sure you want to leave them overnight?"

"We don't need them now anyway. I'll get them out in the morning for breakfast."

Sally sighed. "If you say so."

After they got out of the car and walked toward the house, John took hold of Sally's hand.

"I'm glad we have each other," he said. "It sure makes it easier going through difficult times."

"I know what you mean." She leaned over and kissed his cheek when they reached the porch.

"You just missed them," Geraldine said as they entered the house. She was standing next to the stairway to the den, wearing a light blue-checkered housecoat and navy-blue slippers.

"That's too bad," John said, holding up the soft drinks.

"Did you pick up any pastries for breakfast?"

"Sorry," John said as he headed to the kitchen. "I think we're eating too many of those sugary concoctions. We need to start eating healthy foods for breakfast."

"I don't think so." Geraldine said defiantly as she followed him. Her cane tapped the floor louder than usual.

"I bet I've gained nearly ten pounds over the winter."

"Maybe if you'd get out more, you wouldn't be getting fat. Have you considered joining a gym?"

"Fat? Isn't that kind of a stretch, Geraldine?"

"Have you looked at yourself in the mirror, John? Apparently not."

"Now, Geraldine, are you trying to give me a complex about my body?"

Sally, sitting at the counter, laughed.

"What's so funny?" John asked, grinning. "Your mother is body-shaming me!"

"Maybe you should start drinking those diet sodas," she said.

"Now you're doing it!"

"Those diet sodas sure haven't helped Libby," Geraldine said as she sat next to Sally.

"I'll try to remember to get some pastries the next time I'm out," John said. "Or maybe I should get them every time I'm out."

"Now that's a good idea," Geraldine said with a big smile. "And make it my favorite."

"As if I could forget."

"And if they don't have long johns, get chocolate-iced donuts."

"You're not asking for much."

"Don't you think I deserve it?"

"Oh, you are most deserving!"

"Would you two cut it out?" Sally said with a laugh. "You'll be back at each other before you know it."

"Hmm, I wonder if they make diet donuts?" John said.

"Don't even think about it if you know what's good for you," Geraldine said, her eyes playfully narrowed.

Whiskers had been at John's feet ever since they got home. He finally let out a several sharp yelps to get John's attention.

"I think someone wants to go outside," John said as he leaned down and patted the pooch on the head. "Excuse me for a few minutes." Whiskers led the way to the front door.

When they returned to the kitchen, Geraldine was back in the den, watching *Jeopardy!* John poured kibble and water in Whiskers' bowls and sat across from Sally at the bar.

"Are you hungry?" she asked.

"Not really. Maybe something a bit later. I'm still full from our lunch at Cracker Barrel."

"Same here," she said. "Mother will let me know if she wants something."

"No doubt."

"I have my book club tomorrow," she said. "I'm not sure if I'll go. I've hardly had time to read much of the book."

"Oh, go ahead. You need to go out with your friends. Maybe you can read some reviews or synopses online so you can be familiar with the book."

"That feels like cheating a little."

"Do you really believe everyone in your book club reads every single word of every single book?"

"I know a few that do but I agree there are some who haven't because they don't say much or make comments that show they haven't read the book."

"It's probably because they can't get into the book or because everyday life gets in the way. For you, life got in the way the past week or so."

"You always come up with wonderful excuses," Sally said.

"What is life without some excuses to overcome obstacles?"

"Okay, you sold me. I'll do a little research before we go to bed tonight and bone up on the book."

"What's the book?"

"*War and Peace.*"

"Are you serious?" John said as he arched back on the stool.

"No," she said. "I just wanted to get a reaction."

"You're getting more and more like your mother every day."

"Now those are fightin' words, mister!" she said, raising her hands in fists toward him in a mock boxing pose.

"Because you can't handle the truth," he said, grinning.

"What are you two fussing about?" Geraldine asked as she unexpectedly entered the kitchen.

"Just acting silly, Mother. It's been a long day."

"Do you plan to fix anything for dinner? People could starve around here."

"We're still stuffed after eating at Cracker Barrel this afternoon."

"Cracker Barrel? I like Cracker Barrel."

"You should have gone with us to the funeral," John said.

"I don't recall being invited." Geraldine eased on a stool next to Sally.

"My apology. You're right."

"We should have taken you over to Brody's apartment to spend the day with Chloe and the baby," Sally said.

"It's a little late to say that now," Geraldine said.

"You're right again," John said.

"Is there anything you'd like for dinner?" Sally asked.

"I hate to put you to any trouble," Geraldine said. "Plus, all the dishes are clean. I did them while you were gone."

"Why, thank you, Mother. You didn't have to do that."

"I know, but I like to contribute," she said with a huge smile. "I can't sit around all day and let you do everything."

"I see you've already put them away," Sally said, glancing at the kitchen sink.

"No, they're in the dishwasher," Geraldine said. "You can empty it later."

"How about if I run over to Subway and get you a sandwich?" John asked. "It wouldn't be too much trouble."

Geraldine's eyes brightened. "I would like that."

"Anything else while I'm out?" he said. "Chips. Cookie?"

"Chips would be nice. And maybe a few chocolate chip cookies. I also like those with macadamia nuts."

"How about one of each?"

"That would be sweet of you."

"I'm out of here," he said, easing off the stool.

"And maybe a soft drink," Geraldine shouted as he headed to the front door. "I don't like that diet stuff you buy for Libby."

"Sure thing."

He returned twenty minutes later.

Geraldine sat at the bar and ate her dinner while Sally drank a cup of decaf coffee and John opted for a beer. Geraldine offered a cookie to Sally, which she accepted, but broke in half to share with her mother.

After Geraldine finished eating and returned to the den to watch television, John picked up the morning newspaper he had hadn't a chance to read and retreated to the living room while Sally told him she was going to the bedroom to research *The Keeper of Lost Things* for her book club.

Later, after Geraldine retired for the evening and seeing Whiskers snoozing on his padded bed, John turned out the lights and headed to the bedroom. Sally was in her nightgown under the sheets, reading the novel.

"How's the book?" John asked as he stood in front of the dresser taking off his clothes.

"This is pretty good," she said. "I may finish it before the meeting tomorrow."

John stood in front of the mirror, viewing himself from different angles, sucking in his gut and flexing the muscles in her arms a few times.

"What are you doing?" Sally asked, sitting up.

"Uh, nothing," he said, feeling his face turn red.

"Yes, there's something. What is it?"

"Do you think I'm fat?"

Sally laughed. "Mother got to you!"

He tapped his belly. "I suppose she did. And she's right. I may have to join a gym or get back to the Y."

"It wouldn't hurt."

"What's that supposed to mean?" John asked. "You think I'm getting fat, too?"

"For your health, hon."

"Maybe you need to go as well."

"And what does that mean? Do I look fat?"

"For your health, sweetheart," John said as he slipped under the sheets. He leaned over and kissed her cheek.

He turned over and cradled the pillow while Sally picked up her book and continued to read. "Do you mind if I turn off the overhead light?" he asked after several minutes.

"I'm sorry," she said. "I forgot I was keeping you awake. I'll turn on the lamp."

John got up and flicked the light switch, and within a few minutes, he was out like a light.

Thirty

Sally spent the morning in bed finishing *The Keeper of Lost Things* for her book club meeting while John piddled about in the yard, picking up twigs and small branches that had fallen from the trees during winter. Whiskers was in the back yard trying to renew a relationship with a teasing squirrel, staring up at an old oak tree and letting out an occasional bark, but to no avail.

"Come on, little buddy, let's go out front," he said to the pooch, who gave out another yap and raced to catch up with John rounding the corner of the house.

While yanking wild onions from mulch next to the house, John was startled when neighbor Bert Reliford suddenly appeared like an apparition next to him holding a rake. "When did you get here?"

Bert ignored the question as he scrutinized the lawn. "Getting your yard ready for spring? Looks like you have lots of work to do."

"No doubt about that," John said. "I figured I'd be mowing it in a few days so decided to clean it up a bit."

"I mowed my lawn last week."

"I didn't know that," John said, glancing over at Bert's soon-to-be immaculate yard, one that his friend probably hoped would be the envy of the neighborhood.

For as long as John had known him, Bert always took pride in his yard, spending most of his waking hours mowing, trimming shrubs, pruning trees, putting down mulch, planting flowers, or whatever he deemed necessary to have the best-looking lawn in the neighborhood. It wasn't that difficult because hardly any of the residents, mostly the men, did much more than mow their yards on a semi-regular basis. A few women took time to transplant flowers from nurseries that usually wilted during the hot and humid Kentucky summer. Sally wasn't one of them. She was a minimalist landscaper like John.

"I've thought about getting with some neighbors about a gardening group to beautify the area," Bert said. "What do you think?"

"Good luck with that," John said.

"You don't think it's a good idea?"

"I think folks are too busy with other things."

"You wouldn't be interested?"

"What do you think?" John asked.

"You might enjoy it instead of sitting around and doing nothing all day."

John was taken aback by the biting remark, but still managed to grin in amusement at his grim neighbor. "What do you mean by that?"

"I never see you doing much since you retired," Bert said bluntly.

"Well, maybe some people do things in their homes and away from home. Have you ever thought about that? Some of us have lives beyond our lawns."

"John, please don't take offense, but your vehicles are parked around your house most of the time. Other than walking that little dog of yours to the park now and then, or maybe running some errands, you seem rather sedentary to me. Do you sit in the house watching TV all day, or napping?"

"I beg your pardon?" Stunned by Bert's cutting comment, John dropped several twigs. "You have no idea what I do."

"Now don't get angry," Bert said, raising both hands, palms out. "We've been friends and neighbors for a long, long time. It's just a simple observation."

John took several deep breaths, even counting to five, to regain composure. "I don't have to go outside everyday like someone I know to prove I'm doing something. And I'm not out to impress anyone either with something as shallow as a nice yard."

Bert's eyes narrowed, and jaws clenched. "So that's the way you feel? Some friend you are."

"Friend?" John said. "Have you considered what you said about me?"

"I was just trying to be helpful. It's apparent you can't take constructive criticism, John. I'm truly amazed. I thought I knew you better. I guess I was mistaken."

"And you can take criticism?" John could sense his head getting warm and took another deep breath.

Seconds later, Sally stepped out of the house holding her book, and headed toward her SUV.

"Good morning, Bert," she said brightly. "I see you're out working on your yard, too. You're a good influence on John." She winked at her husband. John closed his eyes and lowered his head.

"I've tried, but he's a lost cause, Sally. I hope you have a good day." Bert turned unexpectedly and marched toward his home.

"What was that all about?" Sally asked.

"Our longtime neighbor and former friend, Bert Reliford, believes I spend too much time on my ass," John declared sardonically.

"Why would he say something like that?"

"He didn't exactly say it that way, but certainly implied it."

"Why?"

"Why don't you ask him. Apparently, he must watch our every move while he wanders around his yard all day in a mindless daze planting petunias and plucking dandelions and trimming shrubs and mowing countless times and—"

"John, that's a terrible thing to say about your friend."

"Former friend."

"Now, you know better than that," she said, looking at her watch. "I need to go, or I'll be late. We'll discuss this later."

"Maybe." John left to check on Whiskers, kicking at a few twigs along the way. He found the pup back at the oak tree being taunted by a spirited squirrel.

When they returned to the house, Geraldine was at the kitchen bar eating a sandwich Sally had apparently made for her before she left. John took care of Whiskers' water bowl and tossed him a small treat.

"Are you going to do anything today?" Geraldine asked.

"What's that supposed to mean?" John snapped.

Geraldine gave him a curious look, bordering on hurt, as the corners of her mouth sagged. "I was hoping you could take me to Target if you're not too busy," she said meekly. "There are a few things I need to buy."

John forced a weary smile. "Of course, Geraldine. That won't be a problem. Give me some time to get a bite to eat and get cleaned up."

"I'm in no hurry, so let me know when we can go."

John remembered he had left pastries in the vehicle the previous evening. "I got something out in the car for you," he said. Her eyes beamed as he headed to the front door.

But when he opened the door, he realized the sweets were with Sally.

When he returned empty-handed, Geraldine asked, "Where is it?"

"I forgot it was in Sally's car," he said. "I'll get it later when she returns."

"What is it?"

"Let's let it be a surprise."

She gave a half-hearted smile. "If you say so."

John ate a peanut butter-and-jelly sandwich with a glass of milk, then washed off and changed his clothes. He went to the den where Geraldine was watching TV.

"Are you ready to go?" he asked.

"Can't you give me a little more notice?" she said. "This show will be over soon, then we can go."

"That's fine, Geraldine." He marched off to the living room.

Thirty minutes later, Geraldine showed up. John's head was angled against the back of the couch as he'd dozed off waiting for her. "Are we going or not?" she asked. "We don't' have all day."

John snapped out of his brief shuteye. "I'm ready," he said as he eased up and stretched his arms, then covered his mouth when he yawned.

"Are you sure?"

Whiskers dashed into the room as they were about to leave.

"You're not going to have to take your little mutt out now, are you?' Geraldine asked.

"No, he's fine," John said. "He's just sayin' goodbye to us."

"Sure," she said in a half-groan. "You and that dog."

John commanded Whiskers to go back to his pad in the den, which the pup dutifully obeyed. "Good boy."

After walking to his car parked on the street, Geraldine hesitated for a moment as he opened the passenger door for her.

"John?" she said, looking back at the house.

"What is it?"

"You need to do something about your yard. You and Sally should be ashamed." She then turned toward Bert's home, where he was edging along the sidewalk. "Look at your friend's lawn and see how nice it is. He takes pride in his yard."

John glanced over at Bert's house as she eased inside the passenger seat.

"Get a life," he mumbled.

"Did you say something?" Geraldine asked.

"Uh, I said it was a great yard," John said and closed the door. He looked down at his neighbor's yard once more as he walked around to the driver's side. He noticed Bert's disapproving face.

Thirty-one

Geraldine shopped for more than an hour while John sat in the small food court drinking coffee and reading news items on his smartphone.

"I'm ready to go, John," she said across the railing separating the two areas of the store. She held a small bag in one and clutched her cane in the other.

"Did you get everything you need?" John asked as he walked around to her. "It doesn't look like you bought very much."

"I got what I needed," she said as they left the store.

"Anywhere else you care to go?"

"I can't think of anyplace."

"Then how about we stop and get lunch?"

"That would be nice," she said with a perky smile.

"Let's go to Olive Garden."

John drove across Reynolds Road to the front of the Fayette Mall parking lot where Olive Garden was located. It was an off-busy period, so they parked near the entrance and were seated quickly. They both opted for glasses of red wine as they waited for their Italian dishes to arrive.

"I'm concerned about Brody," Geraldine said.

"To be honest, I am as well," John said. "There's so much uncertainty right now. I hope he can handle it all."

"Do you think he can raise a baby?"

"I guess we'll have to wait and see. He seems determined to try it."

"He hardly seems able to raise himself at times, if you ask me."

"I think he's grown up some in the past few months. We'll see how he handles being a father."

"Are you and Sally prepared to do it?"

"What? Raise a baby?" He took a sip of wine. "I haven't really given it that much thought."

"You should," she said. "If he fails, the responsibility will fall on you and Sally."

"You know Ashley's parents are contesting custody. I hope they can reach some kind of compromise. And I'm not sure they're capable of taking care of a baby, although I'm sure they have the financial means to hire a nanny and provide daycare."

"That's something Brody can't afford, can he?"

"You're right about that. He barely has enough to take care of himself."

"He'd have to depend on you and Sally to help him."

"I suppose so," he said with a shrug.

The server showed up with a basket of breadsticks, Caesar salads, and spaghetti dinners for each of them. John was thankful for the break in the conversation as he was feeling uncomfortable with her questions and observations about Brody being a parent.

"I love their breadsticks," Geraldine said as she reached into the basket.

"Sally does as well," John said. "I can't handle all the bread. It goes straight to my belly."

"I've noticed."

"Thanks, Geraldine. I didn't need to hear that."

"I'm just being honest. Isn't that what you liked as a newspaperman?"

He laughed softly. "Somewhat, but make that former newspaperman. Maybe now I prefer half-truths about my body. Would you like me doing that to you?"

"I guess not, but I know you wouldn't be so mean to your sweet ninety-year-old mother-in-law." She flashed a toothy grin.

"Since you put it that way, I suppose you're right. Just call me your respectful sixty-eight-year-old son-in-law."

They both snickered and clinked their wine glasses.

Seconds later, Geraldine's smartphone rang. She reached for her handbag and took it out, staring at the screen.

"Is something the matter?" John asked.

She slowly typed a note and hit the send button.

"I've never seen you use your phone outside the house," he said.

"Probably because I'm seldom out of the house," Geraldine said, focusing on the screen. She typed some more, hit the send button, and put the phone back in her handbag.

"I hope it wasn't anything important."

"That's for me to know and you to find out."

They finished their meals and drove home in a light shower. Sally was in the den reading a magazine on the love seat when they returned. Whiskers was snuggled next to her. Geraldine went directly to the recliner and turned on a soap opera on the television, apparently oblivious to Sally.

"I guess I got her back home just in time," John said, turning toward Geraldine.

John sat next to Whiskers, rubbing gently between his ears, and told Sally where they had been, and she told him about the book club discussion. Geraldine was too immersed in the soap to pay attention.

"Let's go upstairs," John said, tugging at her outstretched hand for assistance. Whiskers hopped off and dashed to the front door. Although it was still raining, Whiskers was persistent about relieving himself, but didn't waste any time in returning inside the house. John noticed Bert sitting on a front porch swing with his wife, Wilma, stiff and erect like concrete ornaments.

"Rained out?" he said to himself with a satisfied smile, then went to the kitchen.

"Your mother and I talked about Brody," John said at the bar while Sally prepared coffee for them.

"And?"

"Believe it or not, she brought up some valid points about him raising the baby."

"Such as?" she asked, placing the coffees on the bar and sitting across from John.

"If he has the financial wherewithal to do it."

"I think we know the answer to that."

"And if we're willing to provide the financial support."

"I suppose we can."

"And maybe Ashley's parents could do a better job, since they have the resources to do it."

'You're giving me a headache," Sally said, taking a sip from her mug. "Can we discuss this another time? I think you're looking for answers when we don't have all the questions."

"Don't you think we need to be prepared for whatever happens?"

"So, we may be raising another child?"

John frowned. "The future looks bleak. Are you ready at this time of your life for another child?"

"Now, John, don't say that. We'll do whatever we can to help our children and grandchildren."

"I don't disagree with that, but I try to be a realist. We don't have a money tree, and Brody's been more of a money pit the past couple of years."

"Can we change the subject? You're getting me upset."

"I don't mean to."

"I know you don't," she said with a dour expression. "It's just your nature."

"Now you're getting personal," he said with a lighthearted grin.

"Well, it's the truth."

"I can't help it."

"That's why I said it was just your nature."

"But you still love me?" he asked, pushing out his lips.

"You know I do," she said. "Maybe that's one reason I do. You always say what's on your mind. The only problem with that is that sometimes you should just keep it in your head instead of voicing your thoughts. Or at least pick a good time to express your opinions."

"This is getting deep," he said.

"Well, it's the truth."

"So that may be the key to a successful marriage?"

"I don't know about that because I've listened to you for over forty years. I've learned to adjust to what comes out of your mouth. Or at least tried to. It's not always easy."

"Oh, so that may be the key. Being adaptive?"

"Haven't you done the same with some of the stuff I say?" Sally asked.

"I try to let it go in one ear and out the other."

"Now that's not nice," she said, playfully sticking out her tongue.

"Not everything, sweetheart. Just those things I believe would be better by not responding."

"I guess that's fair."

Their discussion abruptly ended when Geraldine entered the kitchen and stood next to John.

"Didn't you say you had a surprise for me in Sally's car?" she asked, her head slightly tilted with a syrupy smile.

"I forgot, Geraldine," John said, sliding off the stool. "Thanks for reminding me." He hurried out the front door to Sally's SUV and returned a minute later empty-handed.

Geraldine was seated at the bar, taking the stool next to where John had been seated. "Where's the surprise for me?"

"Aren't you full of all the breadsticks and everything at Olive Garden?" John asked. "I know I'm stuffed."

"What's that supposed to mean?"

John turned to Sally with a pensive look. "Did you see a carton of pastries in the backseat?"

Her face reddened. "Well, uh, I thought you bought them for me to take to the book club meeting."

"That explains it all," John said with a light chuckle. "No long johns for us."

Sally got up from the counter and opened a cabinet door, taking out a rectangular white box. She carried it to the bar and opened it, revealing the dozen chocolate-iced sweets.

"So you didn't take them to the book club," John said.

"Fooled you," she said. "You wanted to tease Mother, so I brought them in when I got back from my meeting."

"And I knew about it, too," Geraldine said.

"How did you know?" John asked. "You were with me."

"I know how to use my phone. Sally texted me while we were out and told me."

"But how did you know we were at Olive Garden?" John asked Sally.

"Mother texted me. That's when I told her about the long johns."

"Now you found out," Geraldine said.

"Huh?"

"I told you at the restaurant that what I was doing on my phone was for me to know and you to find out. Now you know."

"Can we quit this silliness now?" Geraldine said as she reached for a long john.

"At least you know I bought some for you," John said.

"I knew you would."

"How so?"

"Mostly when you have a surprise for me it's going to be long johns or pizzas."

"You know me too well."

Thirty-two

Brody, Chloe, and the baby made a family visit several days later after taking the baby to a pediatrician for a checkup.

They went to the den and sat on the love seat. Sally took the baby and held her in the rocker while John sat on an ottoman. Whiskers raised up next to the rocker, took a few sniffs at the baby and went back to his pad. Geraldine remained in the recliner and surprisingly muted the television.

"She's in perfect health," Chloe said of the snoozing infant nestled in Sally's arms.

"We all knew she was perfect," Sally said, kissing the baby on the nose.

"Ashley's parents visited over the weekend," Brody said.

"How did it go?" John asked.

"Considering everything, I suppose it went okay. George was friendly enough, but Donna was her usual coldness toward me. She didn't have much to say and held the baby most of the time. That was fine with me because I didn't feel like carrying on a phony conversation with her."

"That's not the right attitude," Sally said.

"She's an odd woman, Mom," Chloe said in defense of Brody's remark. "She's bitter about something. I'm not sure what it is. She's difficult to read."

"They have a suggestion for the baby," Brody said.

"And that would be?" Sally asked, raising her brows.

"Sasha Malia."

"I kinda like it. It has a rhythmic sound." Sally looked at the baby and repeated the name slowly, "Sa-sha Ma-lia."

"Why can't people come up with regular names?" Geraldine chimed in. "What's wrong with something sweet like Mary, Teressa, and Cheryl, or cute, like Trudy?"

"Sasha Malia has a fresh sound," John said, looking at Brody and Chloe. "What do you guys think?"

"I love it," Chloe said. "I think it fits her."

"I hate to admit it, but I like it as well," Brody said. "I've been thinking about other names since she was born but couldn't come up with something I really liked. I think I may have to go with their suggestion."

"I'm sure they'll love that," Sally said.

"I don't think I want to give them that much satisfaction."

"That's no way to be, Brody," John said. "You need to learn to get along with her parents. In a sense, they're in-laws. And it's always good to try to keep peace with them."

"Like you and Grandma?" Brody asked with a grin.

"Uh, yeah," John said, glancing at Geraldine. "I think we've pretty much been on peaceful terms for nearly fifty years. What do you say, Geraldine?"

"Except when you're a smart aleck," she said.

"You dish it back."

Geraldine dismissed John's comment and turned her attention to Brody. "I still don't care that much for the name. But you're not going to listen to me. I'm too old. You're going to do what you want to do."

"Now Mother, she is his daughter, so he should name her what he wants to," Sally said.

"But he's not naming her. It's her parents doing it."

"What difference does it make?" John asked. "If it's a good name for her, it shouldn't make any difference who came up with it."

"Someday he may regret that name. She may not even like it when she grows up."

"Then she can legally change it," Chloe said with an annoyed look.

"No one listens to me," Geraldine said, shifting in the chair to face the television. John thought for a moment she'd turn on the sound to let others know she was unhappy with the conversation, but she didn't. She sulked.

There were several seconds of silence as everyone except for Geraldine looked at each other as if waiting for someone to say something.

Chloe did the honors. "I may have to be going back home soon."

"Is something the matter with Whitney?" Sally asked.

"No, it's Sam. She may have to go out of town for a few weeks for work."

Geraldine turned to Chloe. "That doesn't surprise me," then turned back to face the TV.

Chloe ignored the comment, knowing her grandmother's feelings about her former significant other. "She's going to try to find a nanny to watch Whitney. I hope to hear something from her later today or tomorrow. If not, I'll have to fly back and be with her."

"If that happens, Mom, I was wondering if you can help me with Sasha until she returns?" Brody asked.

"I'd love to," Sally said, then kissed the baby again on the forehead.

"That'd be great. I'll need all the help I can get after Chloe leaves." He flashed his sister a warm smile.

"Maybe Ashley's parents would want to lend a hand," John said. "Spread the love."

"I don't think so," Brody said with a sullen expression. "I don't want to get them started."

"Because they live in Louisville?"

"That's one reason. Another is that I don't want Donna to try to take over. She can be bossy about things. Even Ashley would agree."

"You just have to let her know who's the boss," John said. "Don't forget you're the father."

"Something she doesn't really accept. I'm surprised she hasn't requested a DNA test."

"Really?"

"Just kidding, Dad, but I wouldn't put it past her."

"Maybe you'll come up with a better name for the baby," Geraldine interrupted.

"She's Sasha Malia," Brody said, matter-of-factly.

"I think it's a cute name," Chloe said. "I like Sasha Malia."

"It fits her," Sally said with a sweet smile. "She looks like a Sasha Malia."

"Good decision," John said. "Our little Sasha Malia."

"Oh, good grief!" Geraldine groused, increasing the volume on the TV.

Thirty-three

Brody finalized the baby's name as Sasha Malia with the Kentucky Office of Vital Statistics. However, there was some contention as to whether her last name was Garcia or Ross. She ended up with Garcia-Ross as her surname.

A day later, George and Donna paid a half-day visit to Brody's apartment, seemingly pleased with the final names. Donna even cracked a smile, although it could have been a self-satisfied one instead of aimed at someone.

Brody and Chloe went to a restaurant in Hamburg Place to give the grandparents some alone time with Sasha and returned mid-afternoon. They spent a few minutes exchanging pleasantries about the baby. Then the Garcias got up and left.

But two days later, Brody was informed they had petitioned Family Court in Louisville to grant them full custody of the baby.

"I can't believe it," Brody told John on the phone. "I thought we had a good visit with them and now this. What in the world is going on with them?"

"Did they give you any clue why they're doing this?" John asked while leaving the kitchen where Sally and Geraldine were chattering about a TV show and heading to the living room for some semblance of quiet.

"Nothing," Brody said with exasperation. "I asked Chloe and she's as surprised as I am. Those people are truly nuts!"

"I don't know what to tell you."

"I think I'll need a lawyer."

"No doubt."

"Uh, can you help me on that? I'm not sure if I can afford one now."

"We'll give you a hand. You need to ask around and find an attorney who specializes in custody cases."

"I'll do that and get back with you," Brody said with a melancholy tone. "This is so unreal what they're doing. I let them name the baby, compromise on the surname, and now this shit. They want total control."

"Just be patient, son," John said. "You'll get through this."

"Did you know Chloe was flying back to New York in three days?"

"She told your mother," John said. "She's making plans to help you. Have you considered moving back in with us for a while? At least while Chloe's away?"

"Chloe said something to me about it, but I'd rather stay here. We've got a lease on the place."

"That doesn't mean you have to stay there."

"I know, but I like my privacy. Okay?"

"Whatever you think best."

"That's what I think."

Brody ended the call after telling John he'd get back with him when he'd located a lawyer. John returned to the kitchen, lost in thought, while Sally and Geraldine looked at him in silence, waiting for him to speak.

"Who was on the phone?" Geraldine asked. "I bet it was Brody."

"You guessed right," John said with a heavy sigh.

"What did he want?" Sally asked.

John sat at the bar while Sally warmed his coffee, then related the conversation to them.

"I thought everything was improving between Brody and them," Sally said.

"Brody thought so, too. I guess we all did."

"Brody needs to take that baby and leave the state," Geraldine said. "That would show them!"

"Now, Geraldine, let's not get carried away," John said. "And don't give him any ideas."

"Just sayin.'"

"I know. We're all frustrated and disappointed by what they're doing. Brody is going to look for a good family lawyer to represent him."

"I wonder what their motivation is for doing this?" Sally asked. "They both have busy careers. They can't take care of a baby."

"But they can afford a nanny and daycare."

"That's no way to raise a child," Geraldine said. "I was a stay-at-home mom for Sally and Wendell. That's the way it should be. America has not been the same since mothers started working. It's a crying shame."

"Those were different times," John said. "Even if Brody had Sasha, he'd have to rely on daycare and us to raise the baby."

"At least she'd have a loving home," Geraldine said. "She wouldn't be neglected and raised by strangers. I don't like that one bit."

"Let's just take this one step at a time." Sally moaned. "I wish we could sit down and talk to them and maybe work something out. This is getting so ugly."

"I assume we'll find out in a few weeks when the Family Court judge sets a date for a hearing."

"All I can say is that when I see them, I'm gonna give them a piece of my mind!" Geraldine said, banging her bony fist on the bar.

John smiled with a furtive wink to Sally.

"Well ladies, if there're no objections, I think I'm going to venture down to McDonald's for some coffee," John said.

"Can't you drink coffee here?" Geraldine asked.

"You're right, but I need to get out for a little while and clear my head."

"At McDonald's? You just want to sit around and gossip with those old geezer friends of yours," Geraldine said.

"Maybe so," John said as he got off the stool. "Friendship is good for the soul."

"Enjoy yourself," Sally said.

"Can I bring back anything?" he asked.

"You think you can bring me back a hamburger and fries?" Geraldine asked, an angry scowl transforming into a pleasant smile.

"No problem," John said.

"Maybe a fish sandwich for me," Sally said. "No cheese. And some fries."

"And make sure you come straight home with the food," Geraldine said. "I don't like cold fries."

"I wouldn't do that to you," John said. "But remember, we have a microwave you can use to reheat the fries. It works really well."

"There you go, being a smart aleck!"

Whiskers scampered up to John, scratching at his shoe. "Maybe I'll buy you a Happy Meal, little buddy."

"He doesn't need fries," Geraldine said.

"I'll eat the fries."

"Do you think you could get me a chocolate-chip cookie?" Sally asked, wide eyed.

"Me, too," Geraldine said, raising her hand.

"On one condition. You don't say anything about me letting Whiskers outside for a minute."

"You and that…" Geraldine said, placing her hand over her mouth.

John grinned and went to the front door, allowing Whiskers out to do his thing. He stepped out onto the porch, noticing several neighbors prepping their lawns for spring. He saw Bert spreading mulch with a rake along the foundation of his house. Bert turned and looked at him, as if he sensed John looking at him, then quickly resumed his yardwork.

Whiskers returned, leading John to the water bowl. Sally was washing the coffee cups while chatting with Geraldine about family matters with mention of Wendell and Libby that John ignored.

"I'll be back in a flash," John said, putting on a light jacket.

"Tell the guys I said 'hi,'" Sally said.

"And come straight home with the food," Geraldine said. "And don't forget the cookies."

"Yes ma'am," John said, giving her a quick military salute.

"You're being a smart aleck again!"

Thirty-four

John entered the side entrance to McDonald's in Palomar Center, waved to his buddies in the back, and proceeded to the counter to order coffee. As he stood in line glancing at the menu, a woman picked up her food at the register and headed toward the tables in the front of the building.

Moments later, she turned and squinted at him. "Are you John Ross?" she asked, slightly twisting her neck to get a better look at him.

"The one and only," he replied with a chuckle.

"You don't remember me, do you?"

"Give me a hint," he said, moving forward in the line.

"I can't believe you. Have I changed that much in twenty years?"

John turned and studied her face for a few seconds before being interrupted by the counter staff asking him for his order. He asked for a medium coffee and blueberry muffin and turned around toward the unfamiliar person.

The woman was slender, with red streaks in her gray hair that bobbled on her neck when she moved her head. She had lines in her face, nothing deep, a full mouth, and intense dark brown eyes.

"Twenty years? That was a long time ago." He took his tray and stepped out of the line and looked at her again with a frown. "I'm sorry, ma'am. I don't have a clue."

She rolled her eyes. "Never mind," she huffed, walking away.

John wondered why she was offended as he headed to the rear section to be with his old friends. They were discussing the University of Kentucky's recently concluded basketball season that ended in the Elite Eight with an upset loss in overtime to Southeastern Conference-rival Auburn.

"Aren't you old coots ready to move on from basketball?" John asked as he sat next to Curtis McKenzie. "It's baseball season."

"Never," Mel Schneider said. "And it's not just basketball. It's the Cats!"

"There's more to life than following a college basketball program."

"Maybe to you," Mel said. "But not to a lot of Kentuckians."

'I won't argue that with you." John took a bite of his muffin. "I had my fill of it while at the paper. Maybe that's why I'm a bit jaded when it comes to sports."

"What have you been up to?" Curtis asked. "You haven't been around in a few weeks."

John recounted Ashley's death, how the family was coping, the newborn, and the conflict with the other grandparents.

"That really takes the cake," Curtis said, puffing out his cheeks. "To go through all that tragedy and then try to take custody of the child. People have no shame these days."

"To be fair, I understand how they feel about their grandchild," John said. "But they seem to take it out on Brody.

The mother has been especially hard on him. We're hoping both sides will work things out, but I'm not counting on it. It's a bad situation all the way around, especially for the baby."

"Good luck with that," Mel said. "We've had some awkward times with how some of the other grandparents have tried to control the time with the grands. It can get awkward and unpleasant if you let it. You've got to stand your ground, or some will roll over you."

"How did you deal with it?"

"The best thing is to let things run their course. You'll discover those differences and disagreements will eventually fade away."

"And if they don't?"

"You just do your thing and hope for the best. And usually things improve over time."

"I sure hope so," John said.

"One more thing," Mel said.

"What's that?"

"Some of the problems are real, but most are imagined."

"Wow, that's deep, Mr. Schneider," Curtis said with a laugh.

"Gimme a break! It's the truth. Sometimes you can get so caught up in things you make them bigger than they are. And some are nonexistent."

"Makes sense to me," Curtis said, his thick brows gathered. "I think."

"I don't think what we're going through right now is imagined," John said. "They want custody. We're not imagining that."

"I hope things work out for Brody," Mel said.

John got distracted from the discussion when he saw the mystery woman taking her trash to a receptacle.

"What is it?" Mel asked, turning his head around to see what caught John's attention. Curtis leaned over and looked as well.

"My god!" Curtis said. "If it isn't Glory Belleau."

"Glory B," Mel exclaimed. "She still looks as insufferable as she did at the paper."

John rubbed his chin. "Oh, I remember her now. She was a general columnist a few years back. She approached me when I was at the counter and got peeved when I didn't remember her."

"That doesn't surprise me," Curtis said. "She was a legend in her own mind."

Glory looked at them, hesitated for a few seconds, then marched in their direction as if in an attack mode.

"Oh, shit," Curtis whispered and slightly hunkered his hulking six-foot-four frame.

"Hello guys," she said with a haughty smile. "You never know who you'll run into at Mickey D's."

"What have you been up to, Glory B, uh, Glory?" Mel asked, hesitantly.

She gave him a shrewd look, and to everyone's surprise, sat at the table. "Do you mind, John? Or should I ask, do you remember?"

"I apologize for not recognizing you," John said, a small smile creasing his lips. "But it has been a long time. People's looks change over the years."

"I suppose so," she said. "My hair was black and a lot shorter than it is now. And, if you haven't noticed, there's a few wrinkles. But men always notice those things."

"We all fit into that category of growing older," Curtis said. "What brings you here?"

"McDonald's?"

"Sorry. I mean Lexington. Didn't you leave about twenty years ago?"

"Good memory, Curtis." She gave John a dismissive glance. "Yes, I moved on to Kansas City, then Seattle, and finished up in Denver. I decided to come here and retire. I always enjoyed my time in Kentucky, especially the thoroughbred farms and racing at Keeneland."

"And the Cats?" Mel asked with an impish grin.

"You can't be serious. That may have been one reason I left. But I did a lot of research and found the city has made a lot of cultural advancements since I left. So here I am again. Doesn't that make you all happy?"

"Well, welcome back," John said. "It's always great to get to see former co-workers from the newspaper."

"Yeah, we meet here several times a week around ten o'clock to shoot the breeze about things," Mel said. "Nothing too serious. Just friends spending time with friends."

"I can't imagine it being too serious," she said, glancing around the table. "Are women allowed now?"

"Why not?" John said. "It's simply old friends getting together for breakfast."

"Yeah, it's not a men's club," Mel said.

"So I'd be welcome?"

"It's informal but drop by around ten and you're likely to see a few of us here," Curtis said. "No dues or anything. Come as you are. Tuesday is usually the first day."

"The only things off-limits are politics and religion," Mel said.

"That's no fun," she said.

"Politics do creep in once in a while," John said. "But we try not to let it get out of hand or personal."

"Yeah, we come here for the most part to get away from politics," Curtis said. "There's too much of that crap everywhere else, if you know what I mean."

"If you're free and there is nothing better to do, then drop by at ten," John said.

"I may just do that," Glory said as she rose from her seat. "Take care." She smiled and left through the rear exit.

"I remember her now," John said. "She was quite the character. She had huge, purple-framed glasses and wore those long dresses, I think they were called granny dresses, with white Converse basketball shoes. She sure doesn't look a thing like that now. That's why I didn't recognize her at first."

"She still looks eccentric," Mel said. "Those black tights and yellow poncho make her stand out in a crowd, especially with those skinny legs."

"I think they're called leggings," John said. "Sally and Chloe wear them."

"I bet they look a lot better in them than she does," Mel said. "She reminds me of an ostrich."

"Let's be nice," John said. "Even if she's not here."

"Well, it's the truth."

"I gather you weren't in her fan club," Curtis said to Mel with a chuckle.

"You got that right. She acted as if I didn't exist. She sucked up to the powers-that-be, like Clay Rawlings, our late, lamented editor."

"Glory threatened to sue the newspaper for equal pay," John said. "She contended she wasn't paid as much as Roland Gish, and after arbitration, she was granted a hefty pay raise. It upset a few folks because Roland had about eight years' seniority on her. But I guess the newspaper didn't want to drag it out in court."

"Don't you think the newspaper would lose in court?" Curtis asked.

"Without a doubt," John said. "In her defense, and don't get upset with me saying this. but she was deserving. Her output was greater than the other columnists on the paper. Another thing that upset people was that she kinda dragged the other columnists into the fray. They felt like they were innocent bystanders, but she had a point when you looked at her productivity."

"That doesn't make it right," Mel said. "She was taking advantage of the system."

"Don't we all?" Curtis said, raising his right brow." I think you just didn't like her, Melvin."

"She always had an insufferable attitude and had a chip on her shoulder," Mel said. "Most folks kept their distance from her. It seems like she left a year or so after that. She strutted around with her nose in the air like she was better than anyone else."

"I know she wasn't missed by a lot of folks," Curtis said. "The newsroom seemed a bit more at ease when she wasn't throwing her weight around, marching around with her unsolicited opinions."

"Yeah, there's enough stress in putting out a daily newspaper without having to deal with a prima donna," Mel said.

"She worked with the sports department on a horse-racing project," John said. "She wrote a few nice pieces but didn't want to take much direction. She didn't even want our copy editors to read her copy, insisting they weren't as good as those on the news side. As you can imagine, that didn't go over well. But we got through it all. I think she even won some kind of award for her stories."

"Now we can look forward to seeing her again," Curtis said. "Thank you, Melvin."

"Why me?" Mel said. "What did I do?"

"You told her we meet here at ten o'clock on most days."

Mel's face contorted. "I did? Sorry guys."

"I bet she doesn't show," Curtis said. "She wouldn't want to be associated with any lowlifes like us." They all laughed.

"Yeah, we mentioned friends meet here and she certainly wasn't a friend," Mel said. "Maybe she'll give that some thought."

"Don't count on it," Curtis said. "I thought she was giving you the eye."

Mel snorted. "Get out of here!"

"By the way, whatever happened to Roland?" John asked. "I haven't heard his name in ages."

"Last I heard, he was living in a senior home," Curtis said. "He'd occasionally show up at newspaper reunions. He was an old codger full of stories about some of the people he covered and probably a few he didn't. He was a natty dresser as well, except his clothes were about twenty years behind the times. Roland still had a distinguished look with that pencil-thin moustache and coal-black hair. Suave and debonair for his age."

"I bet he's ninety or so by now," Mel said. "Quite the contrast to Glory B."

"She certainly enlivened our morning," John said. "She's still quite a character, even in retirement."

"And I bet she enjoyed every single moment," Curtis said. "You know Glory still loves being the center of attention."

"Well friends, I need to head out," John said. "It's getting late, and Sally will wonder if I got lost. At least I know why I came here. Sometimes I go into a room in the house and forget why I went in."

"You're not alone," Curtis said. "Happens to me all the time."

"Why are we here?" Mel said with a hearty laugh.

"Oh, Glory B," Curtis said. "She's the reason."

"Hey, that's not funny," Mel said, scrunching his nose in amusement.

They rose in unison, carrying their trash to the bins and heading to their cars.

John was about to back out when his phone vibrated. He pulled back into the parking space and saw it was a message from Sally, reminding him to get their food.

"As if I would forget," he said to himself with a smile as backed out again and eased his car into the drive-thru line. "Thank goodness for modern technology."

Thirty-five

Two weeks later, Brody was accompanied by a young lawyer to the Family Court hearing in Louisville. John offered to go with him when Brody dropped off Sasha at the house for Sally to babysit. Brody insisted he could handle the situation without John's physical presence.

But that changed after Brody returned to Lexington.

"I can't believe what they told the judge," Brody said as they sat in the living room. "They practically made me out to be a homeless bum. They want full custody of Sasha. Believe me, that ain't gonna happen."

"What did they say?" John asked.

"They said stuff about me and Ashley not being married and how I didn't have a good job and adequate income to support Sasha. They also brought up my drug problems and how that could endanger the baby if I had a relapse. I couldn't believe it. I'm still dumbfounded by it all."

"Did your attorney say anything?" Sally asked.

"Not much. I think he was as surprised as I was. He said he was expecting them wanting visitation rights, and maybe some joint custody. The judge gave us fifteen days to respond."

"Did you say anything to the judge?" John asked.

"I told him I was searching for a better job and that you and Mom were going to help me with taking care of Sasha, and that maybe Chloe would be back to help."

"What was the judge's reaction?" John asked.

"She didn't say much," Brody said with a sigh. "She listened to both sides and took notes. It was over in fifteen minutes."

The baby began squalling in the makeshift nursery set up in Chloe's old bedroom. "It's feeding time," Sally said as she rose from the couch and left the room to care for the infant.

"At least you have some time to get everything together to plead your side," John said. "Have you sent out your resume to any accounting firms?"

"Not yet, but I will this week," Brody said.

"I wish you had done that months ago."

"But things were going fine back then. Everything fell apart when Ashley died."

"That's why you must make plans. You can't tell me you were satisfied working at that diner."

"Ashley didn't mind. She thought it helped me with rehab because it freed me up for counseling and the job wasn't very stressful."

"And I bet it pays minimum wage. You can't raise a child on minimum wage. You know that. A single person can barely survive on minimum wage nowadays."

"You don't need to keep preaching to me about it. I'll find something real soon. I promise."

"Can I ask you a personal question?" John asked.

Brody smirked. "Don't you always?"

John glared at him for a moment. "Did Ashley have a life insurance policy?"

"Yeah, so what?"

"Were you a beneficiary?"

"I wish," Brody said with a shrug. "Her parents are the beneficiaries. She was going to change it after the baby was born."

"I was just wondering."

"I wouldn't be in this mess if she had me as the beneficiary. But she didn't, so there's nothing I can do about it."

"You might want to discuss it with your lawyer. There might be some recourse since her passing was unexpected."

"I will, but I'm not counting on anything."

"It's your call."

"I almost forgot," Brody said. "They told the judge they've already set up a million-dollar trust fund for Sasha. I couldn't believe it. They've really piled it on."

"I think that's bound to impress the judge," John said.

"That had to be the reason. They must have done it the past few days because they've never mentioned it to me. I told you they were loaded."

Sally returned to the living room cradling Sasha in her arms. The baby was sound asleep, nestled against Sally's bosom as she sat next to John. He reached over and placed a finger on her tiny hand.

"I believe Chloe will be back next week," Brody said. "She said her friend is back from work assignment but has a few other things to do. I imagine it's her sex-change stuff."

"It's not a problem for us taking care of Sasha," Sally said as she gazed tenderly at the baby. "We love her company. And you know Mother loves it, too."

"Do you mind keeping her a few more hours? I have some calls to make."

"That's not a problem," Sally said. "Call me before you come back and I'll prepare dinner for us."

"Where's Grandma?" Brody asked. "I don't even hear the TV."

"Believe it or not, she's at the senior citizens center. She went there a week ago and apparently made a few friends while playing bridge."

"That's something she's missed since she moved here from Arizona," John said. "She would talk about sitting around and playing bridge with her friends back there."

"I think it's nice that Mother is getting out of the house and socializing with others," Sally said. "She had to be getting bored sitting around here most of the time."

"And we don't have to listen to that TV blaring in the den," John said.

"Now, John, that's not nice," Sally said with a lighthearted scowl. "She hasn't had that much to do around here except watch TV."

"I know," John said.

Brody, who had yawned during their back and forth, rose from the easy chair. "Well, I need to be going. I'll call or text when I'm coming back."

"Just let us know if there's anything else we can do," John said as he followed him to the front door.

"I'm okay right now, but I may be asking for a little help in a few days."

As Brody headed to his car, John knew his bank balance would likely take a hit when his son asked for help.

John closed the door and returned to the couch next to Sally, leaning over and gently touching the baby's tiny toes peeking through the blanket.

"Seems like old times," he said with a wistful smile.

"I miss those days," Sally said.

"Things seemed a lot simpler then, compared to what's going on now in our family."

"It was a long time ago but sometimes it seems like only yesterday when I look at Sasha and think about our babies."

"You might want to relish those memories as much as you can because I'm not sure how much longer we'll have Sasha. I don't think it looks good for Brody. Or us."

Thirty-six

Sally sat on the rocker in the den, feeding the baby, while John dared to venture to the recliner with the newspaper. He pulled the side lever to raise his feet and closed his eyes for a few minutes. He'd almost forgotten just how comfortable it was to sit back in the chair. Especially with the TV off.

His peaceful cat nap was interrupted when the front door opened, prompting Whiskers to let out several sharp yelps. That saved him from dozing off to sleep.

"I'm home," Geraldine said cheerily as she approached the den steps.

John bolted out of the recliner, creating the usual squeak, grabbed the newspaper and stood facing the steps as she made her way into the room. He wondered for a moment why he felt guilty using the chair, since it had been *his* before she took it over.

"Back so soon?" he said with a tight smile.

Geraldine strode to the recliner, eyeing it for a moment and sat warily. "You need to oil those springs," she said.

"How did you get home?" Sally asked. "I thought you were going to call me to pick you up?"

"I got a ride from a nice gentleman," she said, primly. "He was my bridge partner. And oh, he was so delightful. Such a gentleman."

"That's nice, Mother. I'm happy you're having a good time at the center."

"Oscar says he's willing to pick me up next week and take me there. I told him I'd think about it. I don't want to rush into things, you know."

"For him to give you a lift to play cards?" John asked as he sat on the loveseat.

"I don't want to give him any ideas. A woman needs to be careful these days."

"Uh, okay. What ideas? Oh, never mind."

"What's that supposed to mean?" Geraldine gave him a severe look.

"Well, er, I mean ideas about picking you up and bringing you home. I don't want it to be an inconvenience for your friend."

"You let me decide that. Oscar didn't seem to mind."

"That's fine, Mother," Sally said, stepping in as the family arbiter. "It's not a problem for me to take you every week and to pick you up. Just let me know."

"Same here," John said. "It's great to see you get out of the house once in a while."

"Thank you, John," Geraldine said. "I apologize for spending so much time here. Has it been an inconvenience to you?"

"That's not what I mean. You're twisting my words around like you always do. I'm just saying it's good to be out with others, kinda like Sally and her book club and me and my trips to McDonald's."

"That's fine then," she said haughtily. "Oh, were you sitting on the recliner while I was away?"

"For a few minutes. I hope that's okay."

"It just feels a little different," she said, shifting her rear side in the chair.

"Sorry about that. I guess it has your body shape for using it for so long."

"That's why I like to sit here. It forms to my body."

"I'll try to remember that the next time I come down and you're not here."

"That would be nice," she said. She turned toward Sally. "Are you going to be taking the baby upstairs soon?"

"I guess I can," Sally said. "How come?"

"One of my shows is coming on soon and I don't want to disturb her with the volume."

"That's awfully considerate of you," John said.

Geraldine looked indignantly at him for a moment. "What is that supposed to mean?"

"Nothing, Geraldine. Like you said, you didn't want to disturb Sasha while she's sleeping. I try to do the same."

Sally slowly rose from the rocker with the baby against her chest. "Mother, let me know when you're hungry and I'll prepare dinner. Brody will be here to pick up the baby and have dinner with us."

"I wish I had something to do," John said, sitting back in the loveseat.

"Unless you haven't noticed, the grass in getting high," Geraldine said. "It'll be a jungle out there before too long."

"Let's not get carried away," John said with a chuckle. "It's high because it's rained the past few days. But thanks for the suggestion. I think I'll start up the mower."

As he pushed the mower out of the garage, he noticed most of the neighbors had already trimmed their lawns. He pulled the rope multiple times with no success. He checked the gas tank and saw it was nearly full.

John heard a voice at the end of the driveway. "Can't get it started?" He recognized it as Bert.

John stood and turned toward him. "I think it's the spark plug."

"One of the first things I do in the off-season is to get a tune-up for the mower for spring."

"I bet you do," John said. "I should do the same."

"Want to borrow my mower?"

"I'm good," John said. "I'll run over to Lowe's and buy one. I probably should get some oil, too."

"That would be a good idea. You don't want to overheat or burn up your engine. That'd mean purchasing a new mower."

"You've got that right."

Bert ambled up to him with an unexpectedly earnest face. "John, I want to apologize."

"For what?" John asked.

"You know what I'm talking about, John. We had words a few weeks ago about our yards. You didn't take too well to my criticism. And to be honest, I didn't do the same with what you said."

"I appreciate it, Bert. We've been friends for a long time and been through a lot together. I didn't take what you said personally. And I hope you didn't take what I said personally. It was simply a misunderstanding between good friends."

They shook hands.

"The offer still stands about using my mower," Bert said with a pert grin.

Rather than deal with any awkwardness, John agreed to use Bert's mower. "I'll refill it with gas when I'm finished."

"Oh, no need for that," Bert said.

"I'll be up to your house in a few minutes to get it."

"I'll bring it down for you," Bert said. "It won't be a problem."

"Well, if you insist."

"Need to borrow any of my other yard tools, like an edger?"

"I think mine's in good working order, but thanks anyway."

"I always use my edger right after I mow. Makes everything look cleaner and sharper."

"That's a good idea, Bert. I'll try to do that."

Bert glanced around at the lawn. "You might want to pick up some twigs in the yard before you start mowing. They can damage a blade or throw everything off in the mower."

"I'll do that while you get the mower."

"Those shrubs could use a trimming as well," Bert said as he pointed at the bushes.

"I need to do that as well."

"I'll be back in a few minutes," Bert said as he turned toward his house. "You might want to change your shoes to something more heavy duty. You don't want to lose any toes in case a blade flies off the mower."

"Thanks for the advice," John said. "I have a good pair of work boots in the garage."

As Bert disappeared down the street, John let out a loud groan and headed to the garage, pushing his dead mower. Friendships can sure be demanding, he thought, while lacing up his work boots. Especially with Bert.

Thirty-seven

Sally spent the day babysitting Sasha in Brody's apartment while he was in Louisville for a Family Court hearing. John had his car in the shop getting a tune-up and arrived ten minutes before Brody.

Brody was visibly distraught when he walked into the apartment, flopping down on the couch, leaning back with legs sprawled out on the floor, and closing his eyes without saying a word. John and Sally looked at each other, shrugged, and waited for their son to break the silence. Brody seemed to thrive in drama, John thought.

Brody said the judge advised that custody of Sasha would be temporarily awarded to Ashley's parents. And his lawyer informed him that, even though Ashley had mentioned changing the beneficiary on her life insurance, it couldn't be changed because of her death.

"The judge said she would reconsider custody in six weeks," Brody said. "In the meantime, she said I can have weekend visitation rights. Can you believe that?"

"What do you have to do to regain custody?" John asked.

"I need to have a good job, show how I can cover the expenses of raising a child, and continue to attend rehab meetings," Brody said. "It's damn depressing. I can't seem to get a break."

"You should be able to find a decent-paying job in six weeks that should ease some of the problems."

"I'm not holding my breath. I'm damaged goods. You know that. And besides that, the job market isn't that good."

"Son, you're not the only person who's experienced addiction problems. A lot of people have overcome their addictions and got their lives back in order. You've done it for the most part."

"If you say so."

"Do you have health insurance right now?"

"I've got Obamacare. That's all I can afford."

"That's better than nothing."

"Have you received any bites from your resumes?"

Brody shrugged. "Nada."

"How much do you need?"

"What do you mean?"

"How much money do you need right now to get back on your feet?"

"I'm not sure. Maybe five thousand. That'd cover rent, food, and some other things for a couple of months."

"Will you promise me you'll get your act together and find a good job?"

"What do you mean by that?" Brody asked.

"I mean quit going through the motions of looking for a job and go out to firms and talk to people face-to-face. Sending out resumes is fine and filling out those forms on hiring sites is okay, but you've got to let people see you. You've got to sell yourself to others. It may seem old-fashioned but it works."

"It's kinda hard when you've got a kid."

"No more excuses, Brody," John said, trying to maintain a calm presence. "Your mother and I can watch Sasha. We've been doing that for quite some time. And Chloe should be back next weekend. That should free you to find something."

"I'll try," Brody said unconvincingly.

"We need to be going now," John said as he rose from the couch.

"I'll drop Sasha off at the house tomorrow, if that's okay," Brody said to Sally.

"I don't have any plans," Sally said as she handed the baby to him. "She's no trouble at all. The truth of the matter is, I enjoy my time with her."

"Oh, by the way, when are the Garcias coming to get Sasha?" John asked.

"They said they'd get her this weekend."

"Apparently they're not in a hurry."

"I think George said something about a medical convention they had to attend in Indianapolis."

As John and Sally put on light jackets, Brody asked, "So, are you going to write me a check?"

"I don't have my checkbook on me," John said. "I'll stop at the bank on the way home and transfer the money."

"Thanks, Dad. And you, Mom, for watching after Sasha. I really appreciate everything you do for us."

After getting into the car, John stared straight ahead for a few seconds before turning on the ignition.

"What's the matter?" Sally asked. "Something's on your mind."

"I hate to say it, but I still have my doubts about Brody. I'm not even sure if he's capable or responsible enough to take care of a baby. He has enough problems of his own trying to take care of himself."

"We'll help him," Sally said, tapping John on the forearm. "That's all we can do."

"That seems like all we've been doing since he came back from Chicago. At least there wasn't anything catastrophic in his life while he was with Ashley. I guess we hope that stays on the same course."

"Don't you think that's an encouraging sign?"

"I have to believe that."

They were disrupted when Brody approached the car. John pushed the button to lower the window.

"What's wrong?" Brody asked.

"Uh, we were just trying to decide what we need to pick up at the grocery on the way home," John said with a forced smile. "We have to make sure we get what your grandmother wants. You know how she is."

"Is that all?"

"Sure, son," John said. "Anything we can get for you?"

"I'm good." Brody smiled, waved, and jogged to his apartment.

"I guess we better go," John said as he backed out of the parking space. "We must look a little suspicious sitting here."

"At least to Brody."

"I'm still somewhat surprised Ashley's parents want custody of Sasha." John said as he pulled out onto the road.

"Do you think it might be because she's their final remembrance of their daughter?"

"And they can't let go?"

"Maybe so, but I think it's deeper than that, especially for Donna. Maybe it's a thing only mothers can truly understand. She gave birth to Ashley, and Ashley gave birth to Sasha, so it's a connection that forever links them."

"That's pretty insightful," John said.

"Like I said, it has to do with motherhood."

"And fatherhood isn't as strong?"

"As a mother, and don't misunderstand me, but unless you have the birth experience, there's a bonding that men will never understand."

"I see your point," John said as he pulled into the bank's parking lot. "But I still love my children and grandchildren."

"I know you do," Sally said carefully. "But a mother's love is pure and unconditional."

John smiled and touched her hand. "You're right."

Thirty-eight

Several days later, John decided to go to McDonald's for coffee with his friends. Geraldine had her new escort to the senior citizens center while Sally babysat Sasha at home.

To his surprise, and probably to his old buddies, Glory was sitting with them, regaling about some old story she had covered at the newspaper. John wasn't sure if they were befuddled, bemused or bored because their stony expressions were difficult to read. She appeared oblivious to their reactions, as if in her own little world. And she probably was, knowing her enormous ego.

"Good morning, John," she said with a welcoming smile. "We were wondering if you would show up."

Curtis, sitting out of Glory's view, looked up at the ceiling as if in prayer.

"Yeah, John, where have you been?" Mel asked, tapping the chair next to him for John to sit. "Glory has brought back some old memories for us."

"I believe my memories are sharper than anyone here," she said. "If I say so myself."

"I won't argue with you," John said as he sat next to Mel. "I've been meeting with these old codgers for a couple of years and their memories have definitely slipped into a deep pool of muddied water."

"You've got that right, Johnny boy," Curtis said. "And you're just as bad as the rest of us."

"I feel like I have a pretty clear recall of things," Glory said. "At times, it seems almost like yesterday."

"We all had different experiences at the paper," John said. "You had things on the news side that some folks didn't follow. And likewise, there were incidents you probably had little or no interest in."

"Could be," she said with a shrug. "I'd like to think any reporter at the paper would try to keep up with what was going on in every news department. I tried to go through every section of the paper. Now mind you, I didn't read every story, but I would glance at the headlines. Sometimes I would discover some gold nugget that might result in a column."

"You were a general columnist," Curtis said. "We weren't. We had our specific jobs."

"You weren't curious about stories in the paper?"

"I never said that. I simply said we had our work to do and that didn't mean to find so-called nuggets to expound on. There are only so many hours in the day. You do what you have to do and then move on to the next day. It's kinda like a never-ending cycle."

"Good point, Curtis," John said. "I think that led to some burnout for a few folks. I know when I finally called it quits, I was ready to move on, although I wasn't so sure at the time."

"Newspapering can be a grind," Curtis said.

"Now you don't have to be nasty about it, Curt," she said with a condescending glare.

"So how did you like your other jobs after leaving Lexington?" John asked. "You certainly worked in some interesting cities."

"Probably more interesting and diverse than Lexington," she said. "That's one reason I had to leave. I was getting bored out of my mind here. I think I'd reached the limit of what I could do or tolerate."

"That was good reason to leave."

"That borders on burnout," Curtis said.

"More like bored-out," Glory said. "There's a big difference."

"You never had any children, did you?" Mel asked.

"What does that have to do with my career?" she said.

"Just an innocent question. I didn't mean to offend you. Some people stay put because they're raising a family. It's difficult to uproot everyone and move across the country. Especially as many times as you did."

"Some people simply like where they live and don't want to move," Curtis said. "They have roots in the area and don't want to leave."

"And there are those who love adventure and travel and writing about different things," Glory said. "Maybe we're modern-day free spirits."

"To each their own," John said. "I had lots of sportswriters move on to greener pastures, so to speak. Some were glad they left, and some wished they had stayed."

"There are no guarantees out there," Glory said. "It takes a lot of guts to leave one's comfort zone."

"Did you feel this was a comfort zone for you?" Curtis asked.

"In some ways," she said. "I was established here, although I confess, I didn't leave on the best of terms."

"Why's that?" Mel asked.

"C'mon Mel, you weren't working in a cave back then," she said sharply. "You know what I was going through with management."

"Just wondering."

"Bullshit, Mel." She shook her head in disgust. "Don't play games with me. I didn't like it back then, and I certainly don't like it now."

"I'm sorry, Glory. I would rather hear it from your mouth than from any hearsay or office talk from back in the day."

"Believe it or not, there were some people who applauded what you did," John said, although he knew Mel wasn't one of them.

"I certainly didn't receive much support from my co-workers back then except from a few people," she said. "Most were silent. Only the union leaders stood up for me. That's something I'll never forget." She appeared on the verge of tears as her lips quivered.

"But you came back, so things weren't as bad as you imagined," Mel said, lifting his brows.

"I beg your pardon?"

"I'm just saying if things were so darn bad, why did you come back?'

"I've got my reasons that I don't care to share with you now. Furthermore, I don't appreciate some of your comments today. I thought this was a casual group that chatted about everything under the sun. I guess I was wrong."

"We talk about everything here," John said. "As I told you last time, we usually try to stay away from politics and religion, but other subject matter is open. We try not to make personal attacks. If someone crosses that line, it's unintentional, for the most part."

"I sure didn't mean to make you feel uncomfortable," Mel said. "I apologize if I did."

"We're just curious to learn more about you since you've been away for so long," Curtis said. "You know, trying to catch up on everything. I'm sure you'll have some questions about what we've been doing."

After pausing with a cautious gaze, Glory responded, "Okay, guys, your points are well taken, so I won't be so defensive in the future."

"Or offensive?" John said with a grin.

"That's a good one, John. But I'll take it as a friendly poke."

"As intended."

Near the front of the restaurant, a young man with stringy long hair wearing a bomber jacket and sunglasses called in their direction, "Mom, are you ready to go?"

Glory turned around in her seat and smiled as she recognized the voice. "Just a minute, Clayton. I'll meet you in the car." The man scowled and hurried out through the front entrance.

The guys looked at each other but didn't say a word as Glory gathered her coffee cup and food wrappers from the table.

"I assume we'll see you again," Curtis said. "At least I hope so."

"I'll be back," she said. "I appreciate lively conversation, even when it's at my expense."

"Again, no hard feelings," Mel said.

"Of course not." Glory smiled, headed to the trash receptacle near the front exit, and left.

"So she has a son," Mel said, tilting his head. "She was evasive about it when we brought it up about having children."

"My guess is the young man is around twenty or so," Curtis said.

"Yeah, probably about the time she left the newspaper," Mel said with a grin. "Surely a coincidence. Right, John?"

"I don't know what to say," John said. "But the kid sure looks familiar. I've seen him somewhere. I'm going to have to give it some thought."

"Didn't she call him Clayton?" Curtis asked.

"I think so," John said.

"Wasn't the managing editor at the time Clay Rawlings?" Mel asked.

"Interesting," Curtis said.

"Well, I'm not going to ask her about it," John said. "It's a private matter. If she wants to tell us, she will."

"My guess is that she won't," Mel said.

"It's really none of our business," John said.

"You're no fun, John!" Mel said with a big laugh.

"I don't blame him," Curtis said. "Do you want to incur the wrath of Glory B?"

"Now that you put it that way, I suppose not," Mel said as they nearly stood in unison to leave.

"Until the next time," John said as they left the restaurant.

While driving home, John couldn't get the image of Glory's son out of his head. It was when Chicago's "Saturday in the Park" played on the radio that it finally occurred to him where he'd seen him. The robbery of fifty-six dollars at Shipley Park.

He smiled to himself. "What a small world it is."

Then John wondered if he should bring it up with the others. Or to Glory. He'd have to give that a lot of thought before the next time.

Thirty-nine

Chloe informed John and Sally by text that she wouldn't be returning to Lexington until the second week of May, after Whitney's school was out for the summer. She was concerned that Brody would have problems taking care of Sasha, but Sally replied everything was under control and not to feel pressured about getting back.

One aspect they didn't tell her was that since she had returned to New York, Brody was taking more time away from the baby, claiming he was working overtime at his job and trying to find another position. Some days, he would drop the baby off at seven in the morning and wouldn't pick her up until seven or eight in the evening. A few times, he called late and asked if they would keep Sasha overnight. John and Sally always obliged, but John noticed Sally was getting exhausted from her new role as surrogate mother besides being a grandmother.

They moved the bassinet from Chloe's former room into their bedroom so Sally could get some sleep while the baby was asleep. John even stayed home to give her a hand since Geraldine wasn't much help around the house other than offering opinions about raising a child. Geraldine also had her new love interest, although she wouldn't divulge anything about their developing relationship. All they knew was his name was Oscar.

In two days, the Garcias would arrive at Brody's apartment to take custody of Sasha. They tried not to talk about it, although it was on their minds every time they looked at the infant. They wanted to make the most of the time with their grandchild before she left with the other grandparents.

After Sally put the baby down for a nap from an early afternoon feeding. John slipped quietly next to her in bed. Geraldine was in the den, wrapped up in a soap opera, so they had some alone time for themselves, although they were forced to whisper back and forth.

"I still have my concerns about Brody," John said. "We've been seeing less and less of him. I hope he's not taking advantage of the situation."

"He's under a lot of stress," Sally said. "Trying to find a good job, taking care of the baby when he can and everything else. And don't forget, this fatherhood thing is new for him as well as he's trying to adjust."

"I guess I worry about him falling into old habits. I hate to ask him about his job search because he gets so damn defensive about it and upset. But I wish he'd give us some kind of progress report."

"Maybe I'll ask him the next time I'm alone with him," she said. "He rarely gets angry with me; at least on the level he does with you."

"It's hard to believe he'll be giving up Sasha in a couple of days."

"Why couldn't there be an amicable arrangement with Ashley's parents?" she said. "I'm going to miss that precious little angel."

"I don't believe that's going to happen. Ever. Too much has been said by both sides."

"I think you're right."

There were several gentle knocks. Then the door opened slowly, and Brody tiptoed into the room. He went over to the bassinet to peek at Sasha for a few seconds, then turned toward John and Sally. "I've got some good news," he said softly.

"A new job?" John asked.

Brody flashed a big smile. "Almost. A job interview."

"That's wonderful," Sally said, her voice rising until she remembered Sasha sleeping a few feet away, then covered her mouth.

"That's a start," John said. "When is it?"

"Tomorrow morning," Brody said. "I'll let you know if it goes well."

John eased out of bed, motioning with his hand for Brody to go along with him out of the room and to the kitchen.

"Mom needs a little rest," John said as they sat at the bar.

"I thought she'd be an old hand at taking care of a baby," Brody said with a chuckle.

"You've almost got that right, but being older can zap some energy when you haven't done it in forty years."

"I see," Brody said, beaming, and without missing a beat added, "Can you guys keep her tonight? I want to be fresh when I go in for the interview."

"Sure we can. You certainly need to give a good first impression."

"Yeah, I don't want to mess this up," Brody said as he glanced at his cellphone and slipped off the stool. "I need to be going. Tell Mom I appreciate everything she's doing."

"Be sure and let us know how everything went," John said as he followed Brody to the front door. "Good luck, and let us know if you need anything."

"Oh, I will," Brody said, grinning. "I don't want to get my hopes up, but I feel good about this."

John sat in the easy chair after Brody left. He wasn't sure what to think about Brody's bright attitude and the job interview. He wanted to have positive vibes, but after all he'd been through with his son, it was more like lukewarm emotions. He didn't want to get his hopes up either.

Sally sauntered into the living room a few minutes later and sat on the couch, her legs tucked under her and arm resting against a pillow. She looked at John and said, "Well, what did he have to say?"

John told her everything he knew about Brody's job prospects, which wasn't much. "At least it's some positive news."

"I was beginning to worry a little," she said.

"I'd still be worried," John said. "It's only a job interview. It's not a job. We've been through these things a few times with him."

"I want to have good thoughts about it."

"I do as well, but I want to be realistic. We know his track record."

"Always the realist."

"Oh, one other thing."

"What's that?"

"We've got Sasha for another night," John said. "He wants to be refreshed and ready for his interview."

"That's a blessing because she's not a problem. I want to keep her for as long as we can."

"Enjoy her while you can, because time is almost up."

"Oh, John, don't say that!"

Forty

On the appointed day, George and Donna Garcia picked up Sasha Malia at Brody's apartment and took her to their home in Louisville. John and Sally were with Brody, providing moral support for their son and saying what they hoped would be a temporary separation from their granddaughter.

There wasn't much drama on the occasion. The Garcias had texted Brody that they would arrive at two in the afternoon and were punctual as they knocked on the door at precisely that hour. Sally was holding Sasha in the rocking chair; John sat on the couch while Brody had packed several boxes containing items for the infant.

When Brody offered to carry the boxes to their Cadillac Esplanade, Donna said coldly, "There's no need for that. We have everything she needs at our house."

"Really?" Brody said, taken aback.

"You keep it here for when she visits," George said, apparently trying to take the edge off Donna's caustic comment.

"Sure thing."

The Garcias were there for about ten minutes, with Donna taking Sasha from Sally and not offering Brody the opportunity to hold her one more time. Brody stood several feet away in disbelief, holding back tears.

"Let us know if we can ever be of assistance," John said, looking at George. "We're going to miss that little princess."

"We will," George said as he opened the door for Donna. She managed to put on a feeble smile as she left the apartment. George waved and followed her to their vehicle.

Brody fell back on the couch and sobbed. Sally went over to comfort him while John peered out the window and watched the Garcias leave the parking lot.

"It's not over yet," Brody said.

"We'll get things worked out," John said. "It's going to take time."

"The apartment already feels empty without her," Sally said. "I'm sure the house will be the same way."

"I plan to get her back," Brody said. "This isn't right. She's my daughter. We've got another hearing in Family Court coming up in a couple of weeks. I'm going to do everything I can to convince the judge that Sasha belongs with me."

Brody rose from the couch and went to the kitchen, where he took a canned soft drink from the refrigerator. He took two gulps as he returned to the living room and sat on the rocking chair.

"How did the job interview go?" John asked.

"I thought it went well," Brody said, taking another swallow from the can. "I think I'll know something on Monday."

"You seemed confident about your chances the other day. I was hoping to hear from you after the interview."

"I got busy and figured there was nothing new to tell you,"

"Still feel good about how it went?"

"I was, and still am. I was hoping to say something after the interview, but it'll have to wait. Kinda follows the course of my life. Always waiting, it seems."

"Don't be so hard on yourself," Sally said.

"I try not to, but it's hard." He began weeping again.

"What is it?" Sally said, scooting down the couch to reach over and pat his knee.

"I miss Sasha. I feel so empty without her. It hurts."

"We understand. We hurt, too."

"Why don't we go out and get a bite to eat? John said. "It may take our minds off everything for a little while."

"You go on," Brody said. "I want to stay here and gather my thoughts. I hope you understand."

"No problem," John said. "Just be sure and let us know if you need anything."

"Or just want to talk," Sally said.

Brody rose from the rocking chair and embraced his mother. When John touched his shoulder to give him a hug, Brody flinched.

"Are you okay?" John asked.

"I'm fine. I fell on the floor getting out of bed this morning. I probably bruised my shoulder."

"Let me see," Sally said as she was about to lift his sleeve.

Brody stepped away and smiled. "I'm good, Mom."

"If it continues to bother you, I want you to go to a medical treatment center. Promise?

"I promise."

John and Sally returned to their house, as neither was in the mood to stop and get a bite to eat.

"You know, I barely touched his shoulder," John said.

"I hope it's not serious," Sally said. "There seemed to be a slight swelling when I tried to look at it. I'm going to call him later this evening and check on him."

"Do you remember Glory Belleau?" John asked.

"That name sounds familiar."

"She used to be a columnist at the paper. She left about twenty years ago for another job."

"Okay."

"That's not the end of the story." John chuckled. "She's back in Lexington and retired. She showed up at McDonald's and is now part of our little group."

"That's interesting," Sally said. "I'm surprised your buddies would allow a woman to be in the group."

"Hey, give us a break!"

"I'm just kidding," she said. "I think it's nice a woman is in the group. She'll keep everyone honest."

"But that's not the end of the story."

"What else?"

"When she was at our last meeting, there was a young man there as well. It was her son."

"Okay."

"I'm not finished."

"Go on then."

John took a short breath. "Her son's name is Clayton."

"I can see where you're going with this. Clay Rawlings."

"Yep," John said. "You know, Clay was quite a womanizer. She apparently left the newspaper for another job. But it appears she left for another reason. To have a baby."

"My goodness."

"And there's more."

"Now what?"

"Remember when I got robbed at the park a month or so ago? I think it was her son who did it. Clayton looked like him."

"Are you sure?"

"Maybe not one hundred percent, but probably ninety-eight."

John pulled into the driveway and turned off the ignition.

"What are you going to do?" Sally asked. "Call the police. Tell Glory?"

"I don't know," John said. "That's why I'm telling you. I want to know what you think I should do."

"Hmm. I think I'd tell Glory."

"I'll do that."

As they walked to the house, the front door opened, and Whiskers bolted toward them. John reached down and petted the pooch several times.

"Did you finally decide to come home?" Geraldine asked as she stepped out onto the porch.

"We had to stay with Brody until the Garcias came for Sasha," Sally said. "Let's go inside and I'll tell you what happened."

Geraldine looked at John. "You didn't bring anything home to eat?"

Sally took her arm and led her into the house. "Mother, I'll fix us something to eat."

John breathed a sigh of relief and sat on the porch and waited for Whiskers to return.

"A person could starve around here," John said to himself, smiling.

When he went back inside, Geraldine and Sally were sitting at the bar eating grilled cheese sandwiches and potato chips.

"Do you want me to make you one?" Sally asked.

"Thanks, but I'm not hungry," he said, pouring kibble in the dog bowl. "I may eat a bowl of cereal later."

"I called Chloe and told her there was no hurry to return," Sally said. "She's sad about Brody losing Sasha."

"I still hope she visits this summer because I'd like to see Whitney."

"Me, too," Geraldine said. "She's probably forgotten about me."

"I doubt that. You'd be impossible to forget."

"What in the world is that supposed to mean?" Geraldine said with a scowl.

"I just mean that you make a positive impression on most people. It's a compliment, Geraldine."

"Okay then, since you put it that way. But I must admit, I hardly remember her, other than the photos we get from Chloe."

"She's growing like a weed," Sally said. "And she loves school. I want to see her again because she's such a delight to be with. So inquisitive and bright."

"Gee, maybe you should get back on the phone and tell Chloe to come on anyway," John said.

"I told her that before we got off the phone. She mentioned something about an arts camp she was going to enroll Whitney in. I think it lasts about two weeks. So maybe we'll see them in June."

"If you ladies don't mind, I think I'm going to take a walk around the neighborhood," John said. He glanced down at Whiskers, whose ears perked up when he heard the word, "walk." "Care to go with me, little buddy?"

"Going to the park?" Sally asked.

"I plan to skip the park this time," he said. "I think I'll talk to Glory before going there again."

"Who's Glory?" Geraldine asked.

"A gal who worked with me at the newspaper years ago."

"So why would you want to talk to her about going to the park? That doesn't make a lick of sense."

"It's a long story," John said.

"Oh, here we go again, trying to keep things from me."

"It's not a secret, Geraldine. Sally can tell you while I'm gone."

John put the leash on Whiskers, and they left without further comment from Geraldine. Instead of turning right and heading toward the park, they went left and took a leisurely walk with the usual marking stops for Whiskers along the way.

It was still late afternoon when they got back. Geraldine was in the den watching an old movie on TV while Sally was upstairs taking a nap. After Whiskers curled up in his pad, John went back outside and got into his car. He sat for a minute in silence, then turned the ignition and backed out of the driveway.

He wasn't sure where he was going. If anything, he wanted some more time to clear his mind. The walk was too short to do it. He thought about Sasha leaving with the Garcias. Brody's job prospects. Glory's son. Even Geraldine's mystery love life.

John finally pulled into the parking lot at O'Malley's Pub, a favorite watering hole when he was worked at the newspaper and a friendly place to dine with Sally.

When he stepped into the pub, the Eagles' "Long Road" was playing on the sound system. The waiter offered a table, but John decided to sit at the bar, where he ordered a tall draft beer.

"You haven't been here in a while," said Max Callahan, the bartender and part owner of the establishment. "Has the world been treating you okay?"

"I can't complain," John lied. "I suppose things could be better, but they could be worse."

"I know what you mean. Take every day as it comes and deal with it."

"It's about all anyone can do." John took a large swallow from his mug.

John finished his beer a few minutes later, and after giving some thought about going home, ordered another one since it seemed to take the edge off his anxiety. Max brought over a bowl of shelled peanuts with the beer.

"How's your boy doing these days?" Max asked.

"He's doing much better. He became a father a few weeks ago."

"That's great. I don't think anything settles a man down more than becoming a dad. I know it did with me."

"Same here," John said, raising his mug.

Before Max could ask any more questions, several customers sidled up to the bar for drinks. "I'll talk to you later," he said to John.

John drank the rest of his beer. He glanced at the large overhead Modelo clock and saw it was only seven-fifteen.

"Another one?" Max asked.

"Oh, why not," John said. "One for the road."

Max came back with the large mug and refilled the bowl with peanuts. "Want anything to eat?"

"These peanuts are kinda filling, but I wouldn't mind a veggie burger and fries."

"Coming right up, old friend," Max said.

When he returned fifteen minutes later with the food, John ordered another beer. He tapped his foot to The Knack's "My Sharona." The music seemed to get louder as the evening wore on and more people showed up for drinks and food.

After eating his burger and most of his fries, he turned around on the stool to watch the crowd and lost his balance. A young man standing close to John, waiting for a drink order, caught him as he almost toppled to the floor.

"You okay, old man?" the person asked.

"I'm good," John said. "Uh, my shoe got caught."

"Better be more careful." The man said as he took his drinks.

"Will do. Thanks."

"Is that you, John?"

John turned to his other side and grinned. "The one and only," he said, then realized it was Officer Kate Johnson. She was wearing tight jeans, a white blouse, and Western boots.

"What are you doing here?" she asked. "It's getting late."

"I just stopped by for a few beers," he slurred. "Can I buy you one? I was just going to get me another one."

"You're drunk, John," she said.

"I am?"

Kate couldn't suppress a smile and laughed. "I've never seen you like this. What's going on?"

"Everything's hunky-dory," he said. "Couldn't be better."

Kate gave him a hard, disbelieving stare.

"Anything for you folks?" Max asked.

"Nothing for him unless you have coffee," Kate said. "I'll take a Pepsi."

"Coming right up."

"We'll be sitting over there," Kate said, pointing to an empty table. She helped John off the stool and led him to the table. Max brought over their drinks.

"I'll put it on his tab," Max said and left.

"What's going on, John?" Kate asked. "I've never seen you this way."

"I've never seen you this way either," John said. "You're always in uniform."

"Be serious."

John groaned for a moment, took a sip of coffee, then recounted what had happened the past few weeks.

Kate spoke softly. "I understand what you're going through, but you know you're not going to find answers by getting drunk."

"Don't you ever feel that way?" John asked. "Don't you ever want to tie one on and escape from it all, even if only for a few hours?"

"I guess I have, but not in a long time."

"It's been a long time for me. Sometimes I feel so depressed about things but don't have anyone to talk to. Everyone seems to think I'm some tower of strength."

"Maybe you think that and you're unwilling to show your feelings to others for fear of being perceived as weak."

John took another swallow from his cup.

"You could be right," he said.

"Give it some thought."

"I suppose I should go home," John said. "It's getting late, and Sally is probably wondering where in the hell I am."

"I don't think so," Kate said.

"You don't think Sally's wondering about me?"

"I'm saying you're not driving home in your condition. I'd be derelict of my job as a police officer and as your friend to let you get behind the wheel. I'm going to take you home."

"What about my car? I don't want it towed."

"Don't worry about that right now. I'll put a sticker on it."

John waved at Max as they got up from the table. "Don't stay gone for so long," Max said with a big smile.

"Put it on my tab?" John muttered.

"You've got it, friend."

Kate led John to her sporty black Toyota pickup truck, opened the passenger door, helped get him situated and fastened his seat belt.

"You really smell nice," John said when she got into the driver's seat.

Kate laughed out loud. "I can't believe you're this way. You've got a lot of explaining to do with Sally."

When they arrived at his house, the porch light was on. Sally was at the door seconds after Kate rang the doorbell.

"Oh, my goodness," Sally said, opening the door in a robe and nightgown. "What in the world is going on?"

"Your husband has had too much to drink," Kate said. "I found him at O'Malley's."

Sally took John's arm and got him to the couch while Kate stood in the doorway.

"Where do I know you?" Sally asked, looking back at Kate.

"I'm Kate Washington. I met you a few years ago when John and his friends were setting up a Neighborhood Watch program."

"Oh, I remember now," Sally said with a friendly smile.

"Thank you so much for bringing him home. He's never done this."

"He mentioned some things that were bothering him. I guess he wanted to drown them in beer."

"How about my car?" John moaned from the couch.

"I told you your car is safe," Kate said. "You can get it tomorrow."

"Thank you," John said, slapping his hand on the arm of the couch. "You're the best!"

Kate shook her head. "I think I should be going. Let me know if there's anything I can do."

"Doesn't she smell nice, Sally?" John mumbled. "You need to buy some of that perfume."

"Good night, John," Kate said. "And good luck, Sally." She smiled and went to her truck.

"Oh, poor John," Sally said as she went back to the couch. "You're going to have one bad hangover tomorrow."

John snorted and turned over on the couch. Sally took a blanket from the closet and placed it over him.

She kissed him on the cheek. "Good night, sweetheart."

Forty-one

The following morning, John was shaken from his beer-induced sleep by Geraldine tapping on his shoulder with her cane.

He turned around, groggy-headed and blurry-eyed, letting out a groan. "What are you doing?"

"It's past seven," she said. "Are you going to sleep all day? The coffee isn't even on."

"Don't you know how to make coffee?" he muttered.

"Quit being a smart aleck, John. You always make the coffee around here."

"Gimme a minute."

"And what are you doing here on the couch in your clothes? You look a mess. Did you and Sally have a fight last night and she kicked you out of the bed?"

John turned and put his feet on the floor. He could feel his head swirling about so much that he wanted to fall back on the couch and cover his head with the blanket. The morning light coming through the curtain burned his eyes.

"Are you going to get up or not?" Geraldine asked impatiently.

John pushed himself up, putting a hand on the armrest to steady himself, then sauntered to the kitchen. Geraldine was a couple of steps behind as if making sure he wasn't going to turn around and return to the couch.

"I could use a couple Tylenol," he said as he prepared a pot of coffee.

"You have the flu or something?" Geraldine asked. "You don't look too good."

"I wish," he said. "I'm going to the bathroom and get something for this headache. I'll be back in a minute."

When John entered the bedroom, Sally rolled over in bed and looked at him. "Decide to come to bed?"

"I wish," he said. "Do we keep the Tylenol in the medicine cabinet?"

"There should be a bottle there."

John took two pills and then splashed cold water on his face. He brushed his teeth and gargle mouthwash to get the sour taste out of his mouth.

When he stepped out of the bathroom, Sally was still curled on the bed, her arm wrapped around his pillow.

"Your mother is downstairs if you care to join us for breakfast," John said.

"Do we have any long johns?"

"Funny, funny," he said.

Sally laughed. "I'll be down in a few minutes."

The coffee was almost finished when John returned to the kitchen.

"Sally will be down in a minute," he said to Geraldine. "I'm going to let Whiskers out and get the newspaper."

"John?"

"What is it?"

"Do we have any long johns?" she asked.

"Sorry." He turned and headed to the front door with Whiskers. The newspaper was on the porch instead of behind shrubs or underneath the car. "We must have a new carrier," he said to himself. As he glanced over the front page, Whiskers did his thing and returned, ready to eat.

Sally was seated at the kitchen bar and had already poured coffee for each of them. John joined them at the counter after feeding Whiskers.

"Feeling any better?" Sally asked him.

"Not really. I need to take a shower and put on some fresh clothes."

"Why did you sleep on the couch?" Geraldine asked. "Sally said you and her didn't have an argument or anything. I remember a few times when I sent Harry to the couch."

"For drinking?" John asked.

"He didn't drink. You know that. Were you drinking?"

"It's a long story."

"I've got time."

"Well, I don't right now. Maybe later. Or let Sally fill you in."

"Mother, why did you make Dad sleep on the couch?"

"Do you really want to know?"

"Yes, I'd like to know because I don't recall Dad ever sleeping on the couch when I was growing up. As a matter of fact, I don't remember anyone sleeping on the couch because you wouldn't allow it."

"Hmm, I didn't?"

"Yes, Mother, you didn't."

"Okay, I made him sleep on the floor, if you want to know the truth." She chuckled.

"Why?"

"Sometimes your father had indigestion from eating things and he would start farting in the bed. Big, long farts. "

John and Sally began laughing.

"You wouldn't think it was funny if you had been there," Geraldine said. "It was awful. He stunk up the whole bedroom!"

"That's something I never knew about Dad," Sally said. "I almost wish I didn't."

"We learn something about you all the time," John said. "That's a funny story. Thanks for sharing."

"It's your turn. Why did you sleep on the couch last night?" Geraldine asked.

"I'll make a deal with you," John said. "Let me take a shower and change clothes first. Then I'll make a run to the grocery and pick up some long johns. While I'm away, Sally can spill the beans on me."

"Beans," Geraldine said. "That always set off the fireworks with Harry."

"Is it a deal?" John asked.

"I guess so. But don't take too long. A person—"

"I know, could starve around here," John said as he got off the stool and headed to the bathroom.

Forty-two

After finishing breakfast and discussing John's crazy night at the pub, Geraldine went to the den to watch a game show on television. Sally and John remained in the kitchen, refilling their coffee cups and getting recharged for another day.

"Hon, I apologize for last night," John said. "I stopped at O'Malley's for a beer, then one beer led to another and another."

"I didn't even know you had left the house," she said.

"It was a spur-of-the-moment thing. I just wanted some alone time to clear my head. And for some reason I stopped for a beer."

"Is there anything you want to talk about?" she asked.

"Not really. We've discussed everything going on. I just had to get out of the house for a bit, and I guess I got carried away. I guess I don't know my limit anymore."

"I know what you mean," she said. "That's why I sometimes escape to the bedroom. We all need some time to ourselves."

"I promise I won't do it again," he said. "Unless, of course, you want to join me."

"Then it wouldn't be alone time."

"But we've learned through the years to give each other some mental space, even when there's not much physical space between us."

"I know what you mean."

"But we're always there for each other when we need to be."

"I'm glad your police friend was there to bring you home," Sally said. "You must have liked her perfume."

"Huh? What are you talking about?"

"You don't remember telling me about it?"

John crinkled his nose. "I did?"

"She's attractive."

"You think so?"

"Oh, come on John, you know she is. It's not a big deal to admit it."

John blushed. "Okay, I admit she's attractive. And I'm glad she was there to bring me home. Speaking of which, we need to go over there later and get my car."

"We can do that after I get dressed," she said. "I need to run a few errands while I'm out. Do you have any plans?"

"I think I'll mow the lawn. I don't want to hear from Bert that the grass is getting too tall."

"That's what good neighbors are for," she said with a laugh.

John showered and changed clothes, and as promised, went to the supermarket for long johns. Geraldine was waiting at the kitchen bar when he returned, taking two from the box.

"Sally told me about last night," she said. "That doesn't sound like you."

"I don't remember the last time I got that way," John said. "Maybe in college or while I was in the Army. I guess I can't hold liquor like I did in my younger days."

"Remember your class reunion last year and some of the people getting looped?" Sally said.

"How could I forget," John said. "Especially after one guy tried to pick a fight with me."

"You never told me about that," Geraldine said.

"It wasn't worth repeating, or remembering," John said.

"Did you win?"

"Not really, but I didn't lose either," John said.

"I'll tell you about it later," Sally said to her mother. "There were a few things that happened at his infamous reunion."

"Even on the dance floor," John said, glancing at Sally.

"I can't wait to hear about it," Geraldine said, a glint in her eyes. She finished her second long john and went back to the den.

"Thanks for bringing up the reunion," John said. "We'll never hear the end of it until you tell her about it."

"She'll probably forget."

"Don't count on it. She never forgets anything."

As they were clearing off the bar, Brody showed up and sat on a stool. "Any coffee left?" he asked as he placed his hands on the bar. "And maybe something to eat?"

"I can make you a cup with a pod," Sally said. "And I think there's a long john or two left."

"That works."

"What brings you here this time of the day?" John asked. "It's kinda early for you to be dropping in."

"If you want to know, I've got some news," Brody said, his eyes bright with excitement.

"Good or bad

"I think it's good."

"Is it about Sasha?" Sally asked.

"In a way," Brody said.

"What is it?" John asked. "Don't keep us in suspense."

Brody beamed. "I got a job!"

"Oh, that's wonderful," Sally said as she walked with outstretched arms to give him a hug. "I'm so happy for you."

"Tell us about it," John said with a wide smile.

"It's at the rehab center."

"As a counselor?"

"No, Dad," Brody said as he sat on a stool. "They had an opening for a bookkeeper, and I got the job. I'll be in training this week with the gal who is leaving. The pay isn't great, but it sure beats what I make at the diner."

"That's great."

"Because of my experience in Chicago, they want me to help with some of the marketing."

"Maybe getting this job will carry some weight in family court."

"I sure hope so," Brody said. "Maybe I won't look like such a flunky."

"What's all the commotion about?" Geraldine asked as she came into the kitchen. "I could hardly hear my TV show." Then she noticed Brody sitting at the bar. "What are you doing here at this time of the day?"

"He's got a job, Mother," Sally gushed.

"I thought you had a job at some greasy spoon," Geraldine said.

"I've got a position at the rehab center," Brody said.

"Rehab center? Do they have a restaurant there?"

Brody laughed. "No, Granny, I'm going to be their new bookkeeper. It's a full-time job with benefits."

"It's about time you got a decent job," she said, holding out her arms. "Come over here and let me give you a hug."

"We're hoping it will help him gain primary custody of Sasha," Sally said.

"Maybe you won't have to be asking for money all the time," Geraldine said. "You can get back on your own two feet."

Brody lowered his head for a moment at the biting remark. "That's what I want. I don't like being a sponge or a grifter. That's how the Garcias think of me. I want to prove them wrong."

"It's not being a sponge or grifter to us," John said. "It's a family matter of helping each other in time of need."

"I'm thankful you feel that way."

"Are you going to give notice at the diner that you're leaving?" John asked.

"Are you kidding me? I don't know anyone who gives notice for those jobs."

"You don't think it's the right thing to do?"

"You're saying I should go back there and work two more weeks, and possibly lose my new job?" Brody said.

"I'm just saying it would be the professional thing to do rather than to leave them without any notice so they could fill your spot."

"Dad, I don't understand you sometimes."

"You do what you think is right."

"Well, I gotta go," Brody said as he got up from the stool. "A busy day ahead of me." He walked over and gave Sally and Geraldine kisses on their cheeks. He smiled at John and left.

"Why did you put that kind of pressure on the boy?" Geraldine asked.

"I don't think it was pressure," John said. "Would you want someone walking out on you without saying a word?"

"Probably not, but it's just a low-level job."

"Perhaps it's not to the owner."

Geraldine gave him a thoughtful look but didn't say anything.

"I don't want to agree with you because I want the best for Brody," Sally said. "But I think you're right."

"It's Brody's decision," John said. "Any coffee left?"

Forty-three

Sally went upstairs to make up the beds and get dressed. Geraldine was back in the den, watching *Family Feud*, letting out an occasional laugh at the contestants' answers.

John took Whiskers out for a quick walk around the block since dark clouds threatened rain at any moment. Whiskers wasn't fond of rain, and thunder and lightning caused him to tremble with anxiety.

Moments after they returned, the clouds unleashed a torrential downpour, along with thunderous booms. Whiskers leaped up John's leg with fear in his eyes. John sat on the couch and cradled the frightened pooch in his arms until the storm eased a few minutes later.

When Whiskers appeared settled, John took him to the kitchen for a treat. Whiskers munched it quickly, then darted to his pad in the den, where Geraldine's loud TV masked any further thunder.

Sally returned to the kitchen and poured herself another cup of coffee and took out another pastry.

"Can I fix you anything?" she asked as she sat down.

"You can warm my coffee."

John picked up the newspaper and scanned the pages. A short item caught his attention—about a person arrested for robbery at Masterson Station Park. The police said the man was a suspect in a recent rash of robberies at other parks in the county. The person apprehended was Clayton Belleau.

"My goodness," he said to himself.

"What's the matter?" Sally asked as she returned to the kitchen, peering over this shoulder.

"Glory Belleau's son was arrested for a robbery yesterday at Masterson Station Park," John said. "The story said he's a suspect in other robberies around town."

"Does it mention her name?"

"Nope. Only that he's been lodged in the Fayette County Jail. He's going to be arraigned today."

"That should make some interesting conversation with your McDonald's buddies," Sally said.

"No doubt about that if they see it. They seem to only read the sports pages."

"I wonder if Glory will show up?"

"She's never been one to shy away from things."

"But this involves her son."

"Good point. We'll see."

As John was about to leave, Geraldine showed up in the kitchen.

"Where are you going?" she asked.

"Going to see my friends at McDonald's. Can I bring you back anything?"

"There's no need for that," Sally said. "I can prepare us something for lunch."

"I think he asked me," Geraldine said.

"I can stop somewhere else on the way back." John said.

"I feel like something Mexican. Can you go to one of those taco places?"

"No problem. Anything in particular?"

"Just a couple tacos and a burrito," she said.

"How about you, Sally?"

"I don't want anything. I'll fix myself something from the refrigerator."

Geraldine glared at her. "Just be that way."

"I'm outta here," John said. "Have fun."

He winked at Sally. She bit her lower lip. Geraldine returned to her game show as if nothing had happened.

McDonald's wasn't crowded when John walked to the counter. To his surprise, his friends weren't there. He glanced at his watch and realized that the gang usually gathered on Tuesday. He was a day early.

John got a steaming cup of coffee and an egg biscuit and walked to the usual meeting spot near the rear. He watched customers come and go while thinking about the previous evening. He regretted getting looped, but decided there was no reason to agonize about it. He still had a light throbbing in his head. The lesson learned was not to do it again.

"Good morning, John" came a voice behind him.

He turned and smiled at Glory, who had come in through the rear entrance. "Have a seat."

"Let me place an order and I'll be right back," she said.

As Glory carried her tray with coffee and pancakes to the table, John noticed her strained expression, no doubt coming from her son's arrest. She was wearing a light blue dress and short heels, looking more business-like than casual in her attire. She also looked as if she had spent some time with her hair and makeup.

"You're all dressed up," John said as she sat across from him. "What's the occasion?"

"Did you read the newspaper?"

"I glanced at it."

"Then you know my son was arrested yesterday," she said. "We spent a little time in court this morning. And don't tell me you didn't see it."

"You guessed right," John said. "It wasn't something I wanted to bring up. I'm sorry about your son."

"Clayton has been such a good kid," she said. "But a year or so ago, he got involved with the wrong crowd. Drugs, mostly. And if you must know, that's the main reason I moved back here to Lexington. I wanted to get him away from those people. But it appears he's meeting similar lowlifes here. I don't know what I'm going to do."

"Where is he now?"

"In jail. I told him I wanted him to experience some time behind bars to get an idea of what it's like. I hope it sinks in his thick skull. I think people used to call it tough love."

John took a bite of his egg biscuit while Glory made a few stabs at her pancakes as she seemed lost in thought.

"Do you mind if I tell you something?" John asked.

"Hell, why not? After what I've heard from the police the past day, I'm ready for anything."

"Your boy robbed me several weeks ago at Shipley Park,"

Her eyes opened wide. "Why didn't you say something?"

"Because I didn't know who he was then. I recognized him when he was here with you."

"How much did he take?"

"Fifty-six dollars."

"Did you call the police?"

"I didn't. With that amount, I didn't think they'd be too concerned, having to investigate other crimes in the city."

"From what the police told me, he's only been taking cash. He thought he was being smart because they could trace him if he was using stolen credit cards. I guess he uses cash to buy drugs."

John took a sip of coffee. "Does he have a gun?"

"Not to my knowledge," she said. "Did he threaten you with one?"

"He claimed to have one in his coat pocket."

"I have a gun at home, but it's hidden away."

"You might want to check when you go home."

"This is so distressing," she said, tears filling her eyes. John handed her a napkin.

"I can imagine," he said. "We want the best for our children, but occasionally they can disappoint us."

"Have yours?"

"At times," John said. "I think a lot of folks go through a rebellious stage while growing up."

"Rebellious as in drugs?" she asked. "Not in social protest like we did in the '60s?"

"Yep," he said. "And our drug problems weren't nearly as serious as they are today."

"I assume you figured out that Clayton is Clay Rawlings' son," she said. "That's the reason I left town."

"Did he know he had a son?"

"He knew," she said. "He'd sometimes visit when he was at a convention or some sort of meeting near us. I never told Clay about his father. Perhaps I should have. It may have made him more grounded while growing up."

"You never know," John said with a shrug.

"To Clay's credit, he provided me with child support. It wasn't much because he had to keep it from his wife. But it was appreciated. Seems silly, but it's the thought that counts. I was making good money, so I put it all into a college fund for Clay. Now I'm not sure what the future holds for him."

"Maybe this will be a wake-up call for him," John said. "His first arrest?"

"First time behind bars. He's had some minor warnings in the past. I guess he thought he'd get another one."

"Let me know if I can help in any way."

"Maybe you can tell the guys in the group not to bring it up for a while," she said. "I'm still sensitive about it."

"That's normal."

"I'm glad I got to talk to you this morning," she said. "You've got a great ear."

John chuckled. "Thanks."

"Some folks don't have much patience with Glory B."

"You know about Glory B?"

"Of course, John," she said with a laugh. "Did you think I was deaf when I was at the paper? Believe it or not, I had a few sources who kept me posted on what was being said about me."

"A good journalist has her sources," he said.

"Thank you for being a friend I didn't know I had," Glory said warmly as she got up, touched the top of his hand, and left.

Forty-four

John stopped at Taco Bell and bought the Mexican food for Geraldine. And just in case, he went into Subway and bought a turkey sub and chips for Sally. But when he got home, Geraldine had left a few minutes earlier with her bridge friend Oscar to play bridge at the senior citizens center.

"Care for tacos and burrito?" John asked, placing the sacks on the counter. "I also got something at Subway for you."

"I'll put it in the refrigerator for her to eat when she gets back home," Sally said.

"You might want to eat the tacos and burrito now," John said. "I'm not sure how they'll do in the fridge. I can't believe she didn't think about going to play bridge when she asked me to pick up some lunch."

"She has senior moments like the rest of us," Sally said as she unwrapped the food. "How was your time at McDonald's?"

"Would you believe it was only me and Glory?"

"Really?"

"I got the day wrong," he said as he sat on a stool. "I thought today was Tuesday. With everything going on, I tend to lose track of days and time. It must be an age thing."

"What did Glory have to say?"

"About me being there today?"

"No, silly," Sally said as she spread mild sauce on the taco. "About her son."

"Needless to say, she's concerned about him, who happens to be Clay Rawlings' offspring."

"Oh." Sally sat across from him.

"That's what she told me. We knew Clay was a womanizer, so it doesn't surprise me. But I confess I didn't pick up on them having something going while I was at the paper. Most of the women gravitated toward him. I always thought it was more of a power thing, but he was a smooth operator, so to speak."

"Not as smooth as he thought," Sally said. "He flirted with me a few times."

"No way."

"What do you mean by that?"

"He was one of my best friends," John said, scratching his beard. "He'd be going behind my back to do that."

"It was nothing."

"Why are you telling me now?"

"Because it was nothing," she said. "I didn't give it any thought. Furthermore, I know you and Clay were close friends. I didn't want to interrupt that. Anyway, it didn't happen when you and he were buddies. I'm sorry for upsetting you. I didn't think you'd take it this way."

"This really pisses me off," John said, crossing his arms across his chest.

"Let's talk about something else," Sally said, biting into the burrito. "This isn't important."

John pursed his mouth a few seconds and let out a deep breath. "Okay, tell me about your mom's friend. Did you get to meet him?"

"Hardly," Sally said. "She was peeking through the front window and was out the front door when he pulled into the driveway."

"You didn't see him?"

"I looked out the window," she said. "He appears to be a few years younger than Mother. He was driving a nice, big car. When he got out to open the door for her, he wasn't much taller than her. He was wearing a sports coat. He seemed to be clean cut and had really dark hair, almost coal black."

"That's a pretty good description," John said. "You should have gone out to his car and introduced yourself to him."

"Mother would have had a conniption fit if I'd done that."

"You've got that right."

"Are you going to mow the lawn?"

"Maybe later this afternoon," John said. "What time do you expect your mother to return?"

"In a couple of hours. Why?"

"It looks like we've got the house to ourselves for a little while. That's a rarity."

"Do you have something on your mind?"

"Hmm, let me think," John said with a wicked grin. "Remember the song, "Afternoon Delight?"

"I think I could use some of that."

Without a word, John got up from the stool, walked around the counter, took her hand, and led her to the bedroom. They disrobed next to the bed, letting clothes fall to their feet, and tenderly kissed in the quiet of the moment. They pulled back the covers and sank into the bed in a loving embrace, touching and kissing, savoring their private time.

"Did you take your little blue pill?" she whispered into his ear.

"I don't need to," he replied softly. "Being alone with you is more than enough to arouse me."

"Let me get ready, then." She opened the nightstand drawer and took out lubricating crème. After applying it, she smiled. "I'm ready."

They explored each other's bodies, accented with warm kisses before John entered her, eliciting coos as she wrapped her arms around his back. He caressed her sensitive breasts and kissed up and down her neck as their bodies writhed in sharing their love. When it was over, John rolled over on his back, and she rested her head under his chin.

"We need to do this more often," John said as she put an arm across his chest.

"It seems we never have the time," she said. "There always seems to be something going on."

"One of these days, things may simmer down," he said. "But I'm not counting on it for a while, at least until Brody's situation is resolved."

"Do you think him having good job will help in getting parental rights?"

"It sure couldn't hurt, but you never know. The Garcias have money and probably a lot of influence in Louisville. Only time will tell."

"One day at a time."

"You've got that right."

They lay quietly for several minutes, cherishing the rare intimate physical encounter. They eventually dozed off until awakened by Whiskers' sharp barks.

They raised in bed, almost in unison, propped by their elbows. "I wonder who that can be?" John said.

"Mother is probably back. Either that or some delivery person dropping something off at the front door."

"Expecting something?" John asked.

"I don't think so."

John eased out of bed and slipped on his clothes. He gathered Sally's off the floor and handed them to her.

When he got downstairs, John walked into the living room, pants undone and tucking his shirt in. Geraldine was sitting on the couch with a man John presumed was Oscar. Whiskers ran to John's feet, wanting to go outside.

"Oh, excuse me," John said, turning his back to them for a moment as he zipped up his pants. He went over to the door to let Whiskers out. "I didn't know anyone was here."

"I don't want to know what you were doing upstairs," Geraldine said, then looked at Oscar and giggled.

"We were taking a nap," John said. "Sally will be down in a few minutes."

"Hello, I'm Oscar Bigelow," said Geraldine's friend, rising from the couch to shake hands. "It's a pleasure to meet you, sir. I've heard so many positive things from Geraldine about you and her daughter."

John shook his thin hand. "John Ross. Nice to meet you as well." John walked back to the front door and opened it to let Whiskers back in.

"That's the little mutt I've been telling you about," Geraldine said to Oscar.

"He's a cute little doggie," Oscar said.

Sally showed up, apparently hearing their voices beforehand, as she had brushed her hair, applied a touch of lipstick, and changed her top.

After Sally was introduced to Oscar, they exchanged pleasantries for a few minutes before Geraldine informed them she and Oscar were going out for an early dinner.

"I hope you can visit again," Sally said as she and John walked the couple to the door.

"I hope so as well," Oscar said, shaking both their hands.

"Uh, Geraldine," John said. "Now don't stay out too late. You know you have a ten o'clock curfew."

Oscar chuckled.

"I told you he was a smart aleck," Geraldine said as she grabbed Oscar's hand.

John and Sally stood at the door as they left, almost like parents watching their daughter go out on a date.

"What do you think?" Sally said as they went back to the kitchen.

"Seems okay for first impression," John said. "He was cordial, and he looked clean."

"Oh, John, can you ever be serious!"

"I am," John said as he sat at the bar. "You wouldn't believe all the dirty old men I've seen."

Sally laughed. "How old do you think Oscar is?"

"It's hard to say, with his coal-black hair and pencil-thin mustache. No doubt he's used a bit of coloring on it. I'd guess early seventies."

"And Mother is ninety. Don't you think that's kind of strange?"

"I never really thought about it," John said. "Do you think they're having a sexual relationship?"

"No!"

"Then what?"

"I don't know," she said. "There's something odd about it all."

"Can't they be friends? I mean, they're only bridge partners. What's so strange about that? Maybe they enjoy each other's company."

"You may be right. Maybe it's just my imagination."

"If you want me to, I can do a background check or something," he said.

"Just don't let Mother know about it."

"Yes, dear. It'll be between the two of us."

"I'm getting hungry," Sally said as she opened the refrigerator and took out the turkey sub. "Want to split this?"

"Sure thing," he said.

Sally cut the sub in half and placed them on paper plates. John removed the turkey from his sandwich and gave it to Whiskers, who was in a begging mode, licking his mouth.

"All you do for that dog," she said.

"Anything for dessert?" he asked with a big wink.

"Don't you get any ideas. You've already had your dessert!"

Forty-five

John finished mowing the lawn late in the afternoon. As he pushed the mower into the garage, Brody pulled up in front of the house. Whiskers was awakened from a lazy nap on the porch, lifting his head to see who was there, then putting it back down again.

"What's new?" John asked as they reached the front steps at the same time. They sat on the top step.

"I heard from George Garcia a little while ago," Brody said. "They're going to bring Sasha to me this weekend rather than me driving to Louisville."

"That's nice. It'll save you a little time and gas money."

"It seems kinda fishy to me."

"Maybe they have plans in Lexington?"

"Could be, but I think they have something else on their minds."

"Have you informed them about your new job?"

"Not yet. I'm not sure if I will. I may just spring it on them at the next hearing."

"You do what you think is best," John said. "I hope you consult your attorney about it."

"Oh, I will," Brody said, grinning. "We may have a few surprises at the hearing."

Geraldine and Oscar returned from their dinner, interrupting their conversation. Oscar parked his car at the end of the driveway and walked around and opened the passenger door for her. He smiled and waved at John.

"Who in the hell is that?" Brody whispered.

"Your grandmother's boyfriend."

"You've got to be kidding me. He looks like a dweeb."

Oscar gave her a quick peck on the cheek, then returned to his car and drove away as Geraldine strolled to the front porch like a queen.

"How was dinner?" John asked.

"It was divine," she said as they stood to allow her to go up the steps. "We had steak and lobster. I haven't had that in, I don't know how long. At least since I've been living here."

"Why didn't he walk you to the door?" Brody asked. "I would have liked to meet your boyfriend."

"Oscar is simply a friend, not a boyfriend," Geraldine said with narrowed eyes. "I don't like what that implies."

"It would have been nice to meet him."

"Maybe next time," Geraldine said as she opened the door. "He had business to attend to."

"Kinda late in the day for business," John said. "It's almost dark."

"Now why do you say that? You don't know what kind of business he's in."

"You're right. I apologize."

Geraldine went into the house without another word.

"His name is Oscar Bigelow, if you're wondering," John said as they sat again. "We don't know a thing about him other than being bridge partner with her at the senior citizens center."

"He looks younger than her," Brody said. "Is she robbing the cradle?" He snickered.

"Like I said, they play cards together. I don't believe there is any romance going on. And if there were, isn't it her business?"

"Yeah, I guess," Brody, shrugging. "It's hard to imagine old folks having any kind of sex life."

"Really?" John said as he thought about his bedroom adventure earlier in the day.

Sally stepped out onto the porch. "I didn't know you were here," she said to Brody. "How was your day?"

"Everything is going well at work." As Brody turned to look at her, the short sleeve on his arm pulled up slightly, revealing part of an etching.

"What is that?" Sally said as she bent down to get a better view. "Is that a tattoo?"

Brody blushed and gulped. John twisted around to see what Sally was looking at.

Brody rose and pulled up his sleeve to uncover a likeness of Ashley encircled by a heart. In script lettering, "Ashley My Love" marked across on top and "Always and Forever" on the bottom.

John and Sally stared at the tattoo for several seconds as if entranced by the artwork or at a loss for words. Then they looked at each other, still speechless.

"What do you think?" Brody said as he covered the tattoo. "I was going to surprise you."

"You certainly did that," John said. "I never expected anything like this. You've always been skittish about needles."

"It's a beautiful image of Ashley," Sally uttered, her head bobbing slowly.

"I need to be going," Brody said. "I've got to put in a couple hours at the diner."

"Diner?" John asked. "I thought you quit."

"Well, Dad, I thought about what you said and went back and told Mr. Alvarez about my new job. He understood and wished me well. But then he said he needed to find my replacement real fast. I told him I'd stop by and work a few hours each evening until he found someone."

"I'm so proud of you," Sally said, giving him a hug. "That was so considerate."

"I just couldn't leave him in the lurch like that. He's been good to me."

"Let me know if you need us when the Garcias drop Sasha at your apartment," John said.

"They're dropping her off this weekend?" Sally asked.

"I need to run," Brody said. "Dad can tell you."

They waved as Brody drove off. "It's nice out here," Sally said. "Do you mind if we sit a little longer?"

"I could use something to drink," John said.

"Ice water? Tea? Soft drink?" Sally asked. "Do you think you could handle a cold beer?"

"Are you serious or teasing me?"

"Maybe a bit of both."

"Ice water will be fine."

Sally returned a few minutes later with two large tumblers of ice water, handing one to John as she sat close to him. "Mother is watching TV."

"A reason you wanted to sit out here for a while?" John asked.

"Maybe so."

"Surprised by Brody's tattoo?"

"What do you think?" Sally said. "I couldn't believe it."

"I guess I'm a bit surprised, but honestly, nothing he does really shocks me anymore. I don't know if that's good or bad."

"He's an adult and it's his body."

"But that doesn't mean I have to like it," John said.

"You just have to accept it," she said. "It's not like or dislike."

"You are so wise," John said.

"You're being a smart aleck again."

"You know I'm kidding."

"I've learned through the years not to take you too seriously."

"But getting back to the tattoo, I wonder if he ever considered that one of these days he may be in a serious relationship and that gal may resent seeing Ashley's image on his arm," John said.

"Brody probably didn't give it any thought," Sally said. "He's in mourning and will be for a long time. As for a future relationship, maybe that person will view the tattoo as a sweet endearment to a past love and respect him for that."

"But—"

"John, just move on. I think younger folks are more accepting of tattoos and what they represent. What would you think if I got one?"

"With my image on your shoulder?"

"Sure, sweetie," Sally said, nudging him on his side with her elbow.

"Or on your butt?

"A couple gals in my book club have tattoos," she said. "Even a few in the retired teachers' group."

"You're serious about getting one?"

"I think they're somewhat interesting, but I doubt if I would do it. Some of the women have tiny dolphins, butterflies, and hearts on their ankles, wrists, and even their boobs."

"Whatever you want," he said. "It's your body and your decision. I'll love you, whatever you decide."

"No tattoo for you?"

"Heck, no," he said, taking a sip of water. "I've heard too many people regret getting them. I know some guys who got them while in the service and some them said theirs began to smear over time. My guess is tattoos today are probably longer lasting."

"I may surprise you one day," Sally said.

"I like surprises. Especially like the one this afternoon."

"Maybe if we find some private time again."

"Did your mother have anything to say about her date with Oscar?"

"Not really, other than she had a nice time. Mother mentioned something about a trip."

"A trip with Oscar?"

"She didn't say anything else because there was something she wanted to watch on TV. I need to ask her about it."

"Do you ever feel the roles have reversed?"

Sally sighed. "I do. But I don't want to be overprotective-"

"That's easy to do," John said. "Sometimes we do it without realizing we're doing it."

"We naturally protect those we love."

Forty-six

John and Sally were at Brody's apartment on Saturday morning, watching a news program on TV when the Garcias arrived with Sasha. Donna carried Sasha into the living room, ignored Brody and handed the sleeping infant to Sally.

"How are things?" John asked, attempting to break the chill filling the room as he muted the TV.

"They could be better," George said as he and his wife remained standing, their jaws tightening as they glanced at Sasha.

A deafening silence enveloped the room for several seconds as everyone seemed frozen in the moment. Then Donna blurted, "We're going to seek full custody of Sasha. We don't believe the current arrangement is working out."

"What?" Brody said.

"We feel it's an inconvenience for everyone," George said. "This back-and-forth every weekend isn't working."

"Perhaps for you," Brody said. "But I love being with *my* daughter. I wish I had her all the time."

"That's not going to happen," Donna said. "We're going to petition the court on Monday to gain complete custody."

"Why are you doing this?" John asked. "What has Brody done to make you want to do this? Sasha is his daughter."

"And she's our granddaughter," Sally added as she moved to the front edge of the cushion.

Donna began wailing. "If it hadn't been for Brody, we wouldn't have been in this mess to begin with. We would still have our Ashley."

"Please, Donna," George implored. "Control yourself."

"I don't care," she said, venting her rage at Brody. "You got her pregnant, then you tried to persuade her to get an abortion."

"That was her choice," Brody said, his face turning red with anger. "She wanted to wait until after she finished her studies before we started having children. But you pressured her to have the baby."

"And I'm glad I did because I now have Sasha. And I want to keep her forever. She's part of me."

"I don't think you understand what you've done," Brody said. "Either that or you're in denial. If she'd had an abortion like she wanted to, she would be here now. But you pressured her. It's your fault she is no longer with us."

"That's enough, young man," George said gruffly as his hands trembled. "We've heard enough."

"I'm sorry, Dr. Garcia," Brody said, "but you know it's the truth."

George took Donna's hand. "Let's go. We'll be back Sunday evening."

Sasha began whimpering.

"You better enjoy her this weekend because you won't be seeing her again," Donna bellowed.

George ushered her out the door, then looked back tightlipped.

"My goodness," Sally said as she soothed the infant. "What was that all about?"

"Now you know why she hates me," Brody said. "She blames me for Ashley's passing when she's really the one to blame."

"Why haven't you said anything to us about it?" Sally asked.

"Because I wasn't totally sure. I know Ashley was stressed about having the baby. I think her parents are some kind of religious nuts who believe abortion is a sin unless under certain kinds of conditions. Ashley was afraid to go against them."

"I wouldn't call them nuts, son," John said. "A lot of people feel that way. It's ingrained with some folks. I don't agree with them, but it's their religious right."

"Even if it kills someone?" Brody said. "That's totally nuts."

"That's what they call pro-life," Sally said. "We're pro-choice. Women should have a choice in these matters."

"They sound more like pro-death to me," Brody said.

"Can we let it rest for a while and just enjoy being with Sasha?" Sally said, biting her lip.

When Brody sat next to her on the couch, she placed Sasha in his arms. He smiled at the baby and the stress seemed to flow from his body as he cradled her and softly kissed her forehead.

"I don't know why Ashley's parents have to be so nasty," Brody said, looking up from the infant. "She wouldn't have wanted them to act this way. I've tried to respect them, although they haven't shown much to me. Especially Mrs. Garcia."

"You can't control what they say or do," John said. "You have to do what you believe is right."

"Did you see Dr. Garcia's hand shaking? She really had him upset as well."

"He seems like an okay guy, for the most part."

"Ashley told me he was at Camp Lejeune during his medical internship. He thinks he got Parkinson's from drinking the contaminated water. He's part of a class-action suit and could get a hefty sum over it."

"That's a horrible price to pay for your health," John said. "I hope it works out for him. I'm sure he had to give up a lucrative medical practice."

"Has Donna had any health issues?" Sally asked.

"Hell, no," Brody said. "She's too mean to get anything."

"Here we go talking about them again," John said.

"If you guys need to go, I understand," Brody said. "I'll be okay."

"Are you sure?" Sally asked. "I'll be more than happy to stay and give you a hand with Sasha."

"Why don't you come back tomorrow and spend the afternoon before the Garcias return to pick her up. I may need some support then."

"We'll see you tomorrow," John said. Sally gently pecked Sasha's nose as she rose from the couch. John bent down and lightly squeezed her bare toes.

Forty-seven

John was awakened from his sleep late in the evening with his phone vibrating on the nightstand. He picked it up and saw Brody's name on the screen.

"What is it, son?" he said, unsteadily.

"Something terrible has happened," Brody exclaimed, loud enough for Sally to hear.

"What?"

"It's not Sasha, is it?" Sally said with alarm in her voice to John. He turned and gave her a look to be quiet.

"The Garcias were in an accident going back to Louisville," Brody said. "Ashley's sister called and said they were involved in a big tractor-trailer accident between Frankfort and Shelbyville. Dr. Garcia died at the scene. Mrs. Garcia is in the hospital in Shelbyville in critical condition."

"Sasha is okay," John whispered to Sally. "The Garcias were in an accident on their way back home."

"Are you still there, Dad?" Brody asked. "Can you and Mom come over and watch Sasha while I go to the hospital?"

"We'll be right over," John said as he got out of bed. He told Sally what he knew as they got dressed. Sally peeked into

Geraldine's bedroom and informed her about the accident. They drove to Brody's apartment in meditative silence.

Brody was pacing back and forth between the living room and Sasha's bedroom when they arrived, anxious to leave for the hospital about 50 miles away. Sasha was asleep in the bassinet.

"Let me drive," John said.

"Thanks, Dad," Brody said. "I can't even think clearly, so I probably shouldn't be behind the wheel."

They sat in silence most of the hour-long drive, pulling into the half-empty parking lot, and scurrying into the hospital. They located the emergency room, where Ashley's sister rose from a bench against the wall and motioned to them. She was drained and appeared helpless and lost, standing there by herself in the sterile hallway.

"I'm so glad you made it," she said, fighting back tears as Brody placed his arms around her.

"I'm so sorry, Evie," Brody said stepping back. "This is my father, John."

John managed a weak smile. "We saw them earlier today. This is so hard to understand."

"Daddy died at the scene," Evie said, as tears began flowing down her cheeks. "I don't think Momma is going to make it. It doesn't look good."

"Is your brother on the way?" Brody asked.

"George should be here soon," she said. "He's flying in from St. Louis. A friend is going to pick him up and bring him here."

A nurse stepped out of the recovery room and walked over to them. She looked at Evie. "Would you like to speak to her?"

Evie smiled and followed the nurse into the recovery room. Several minutes later, Evie came back out, her arms tightly across her chest, and said to Brody, "Mamma asked to see you."

"Me?" Brody said.

Evie grasped his elbow and led him into the room. He was sobbing when he stepped back into the hallway a few minutes later.

"She asked me to forgive her," Brody said burying his head in John's shoulder. John held his son for several seconds then guided him to the bench to sit. Brody's hands covered his face as he leaned with elbows on knees.

Moments after Evie reappeared, her brother came rushing toward her.

"Momma's gone," she said, as he took her faltering body in his arms. He glanced at Brody with a teary smile.

George sat her next to Brody and went to the recovery room to spend a few minutes with his deceased mother.

"George is a pediatric doctor," Evie said. "We always called him Junior until he became a doctor. Momma and Daddy were so proud of him becoming a doctor." She burst into tears.

"Evie is a school psychologist," Brody said to his father. "Ashley was proud of George and her." He turned toward Evie. "You were always so supportive of Ashley, and she appreciated it."

"We sisters stuck together through thick and thin," Evie said, teary-eyed.

When George came back out, he walked to Evie, and they embraced.

"Let me know if there is anything I can do," Brody said, his eyes still reddened from crying.

"Just take good care of Sasha," George said. "And let us know if there is anything we can do for you."

Brody's mouth tightened, and his eyes watered. "I appreciate that. I'll do everything in my power for her. We're family."

John stood solemnly to the side as Brody hugged the brother and sister again. Several seconds later, John motioned to his son, and they left the hospital without saying a word and sat in silence most of the way back to Lexington.

"Evie told me she and George believe Sasha belongs with me," Brody said, breaking the quiet between them. "She said they won't be contesting custody. All they want is for me is to keep them part of the family and for them to have a bond with her."

"That's certainly a reversal of their parents," John said.

"Yeah, she even apologized for not saying much at Ashley's funeral. She said her mother was going through an emotional crisis and that she and her brother didn't want to upset her even more by disagreeing with her about how she and Daddy were treating me. They were hoping things would improve."

"I suppose that's understandable," John said.

"That's what I told her," Brody said. "You know, I would have let the Garcias spend as much time as they wanted with Sasha. I knew it was important for them. But I couldn't understand why they wanted to exclude me. It didn't make any sense to me."

"I guess it's time to move on and create the life you want for Sasha."

"That's what I plan to do."

It was nearly four in the morning when they got back to Brody's apartment. Sally was asleep on the couch and Sasha was in her bedroom.

"Let's let mom sleep," John said. "I'll be back later this morning."

"Thanks for everything, Dad," Brody said. "I don't think I could make it without you and her."

"We'll continue to do it together. Remember, we're family."

Forty-eight

Geraldine went with John to Brody's apartment to pick up Sally and visit Sasha. The senior citizens center was along the way and Geraldine asked him to stop so she could pick up a schedule of the upcoming week's events that included a city bridge tournament.

When John parked the vehicle in front of the building, she asked if he would mind going inside to the front desk to get the handout.

"I want to find out what time Oscar and I should be here to participate," she said. "We're both so looking forward to it. We think we have a good chance of winning."

John left the car running and walked into the facility. As he went to the front desk, he noticed several people with reading materials. At the far end, a group was playing Bingo. He smiled when the woman in charge shouted out the results of the pill spin, realizing that some participants were hard of hearing.

"Can I help you, sir?" a woman asked behind the desk. "Are you here to take part in our activities today?"

"I'm just looking for a handout about a bridge tournament this week," John said.

"So you play bridge, too?"

"It's for a mother-in-law. Geraldine Corman."

"We know Geraldine," the woman said. "She's such a delightful woman."

"While I'm here, do you know anything about Oscar Bigelow? He's her bridge partner."

"Oh, yes. Oscar and Geraldine make quite a team. Oscar has been coming here for a few months. I understand he's never been married. Someone told me he lived with his mother until she passed away a couple of years ago."

"Anything else?"

"I really can't think of anything," the woman said, smiling. "Oscar seems like a nice man. I know the older gals like him. I guess he can be a charmer."

John turned around and saw Geraldine motioning with her hand to return to the car.

"I need to go," John said. "Thanks for the information."

"Come back and visit. I think you'll find fun things to do."

When John got back in the car, Geraldine's eyes narrowed. "What took you so long?" she asked. "Did you join or something?"

"Hardly," he said as he handed the flyer to her.

"Well, you know there are people in there your age, some even younger."

"Thanks for reminding me," he said as he pulled the car on the road and headed to Brody's place.

Sally was sitting in the rocking chair feeding Sasha when they arrived. Brody was in the bathroom taking a shower. Geraldine went directly to the baby, touching one of her tiny hands.

"How's everything?" John asked Sally. "Brody doing okay?"

"He seems to be. He only got up a few minutes ago."

Sally asked Geraldine if she wanted to feed the infant. Geraldine sat back on the couch and Sally gently placed Sasha on her lap.

Sally told him she'd called Chloe earlier that morning and that Chloe and her daughter, Whitney would be flying in on Wednesday and would stay for several weeks to help Brody with the baby.

"Maybe Whitney can spend some time with us," Geraldine said.

"That's the plan, Mother."

Brody came out of his bedroom wearing jeans and a long-sleeved blue shirt, cleanly shaved and his hair combed back. He sat next to Geraldine.

"I still can't believe everything that happened," he said, glancing at John. "It all seems so surreal. I keep thinking I'm going to get a call from George, telling me that he and Donna will be picking up Sasha later today."

"It does seem rather strange."

Brody let out a deep breath. "I guess the next thing I hear about them will be funeral arrangements."

"Regardless of what has transpired in the past, it's still tragic," Sally said.

"And you know what came to mind while I was taking a shower?"

"What's that, son?" John asked, his brows crinkled.

"I'm a millionaire."

"Huh?"

"Don't you remember they set up a million-dollar trust fund for Sasha?"

"That's Sasha's trust fund," Sally said.

"But won't I be the executor?"

"You'll have to have a lawyer review it," John said. "For all you know, it may not even take effect until she's eighteen."

"Really?"

"That's why you don't want to jump to any conclusions."

"I wonder if they had her in their will?"

"I guess you'll find out in a few weeks."

"I was hoping that I, I mean Sasha and me, would come into some money."

"This isn't the time to talk about trusts and wills," John said.

"I didn't mean anything about it," Brody said with a shrug. "I was just wondering."

"Oh well, we need to be going," John said.

"Can't we stay a little longer?" Geraldine said as she lifted Sasha against her chest and patted her back. "We just got here."

John looked at Brody. "Do you mind if she stays? We'll come back in a couple hours and get her."

"No problem. She can take care of Sasha while I do a few things around here."

After they got into the car, John looked at Sally for a moment.

"What is it?" she asked.

"Can you believe Brody is already thinking about what Sasha will get from the Garcias?"

"I think it's a reasonable concern for him, but the timing is bad. But that's Brody."

"I'll never understand him."

"Do you mind if we stop somewhere and get a bite to eat?" Sally asked. "I've only had two cups of coffee. I'm famished."

"Any place in particular? There's a Frisch's up the road a little bit."

"That's fine."

They got seated and placed their orders; a Big Boy platter for Sally, and a salad for John. While waiting for their drinks, John scanned the restaurant and saw a familiar face in the corner. He studied the person for a few seconds until realizing it was Oscar Bigelow. And sitting with an elderly woman, at least several years older than him.

John whispered to Sally to look in that direction. She quickly covered her open mouth.

"I don't believe it," she said.

John told her about stopping at the senior citizens center and picking up a newsletter for Geraldine, and being told that Oscar was quite popular among the older ladies.

"Maybe Oscar and that woman are longtime friends," Sally said, looking back at him.

"Could be," John said. "But I'd like to find out more about him."

"I'll see what I can learn from Mother," Sally said.

"Good luck with that."

"I know, she gets defensive about it. But she mentioned going on a trip with him. Maybe I can get more details from her."

"Just make sure she's in the right mood to divulge anything about it."

"You're not telling me something I don't already know."

Their orders arrived, and as they were eating, Oscar and his lady friend got up and went to the cashier. They left the restaurant holding hands.

Forty-nine

Geraldine, exhausted after spending part of the day with Brody and Sasha, went to bed shortly after getting back home. She insisted on John stopping at a Burger King for a Whopper and fries. She went to bed with a full belly.

John and Sally said nothing to her about seeing Oscar earlier in the day. They decided there wasn't any need to upset her, especially after spending a pleasant afternoon with Sasha. After watching a program on PBS, they retired for the night.

John savored a quiet morning as Sally and Geraldine slept in after their tiring days. He drank two cups of coffee, perused the newspaper, and took Whiskers to Shipley Park, their favorite destination.

With Glory's son arrested for robbery, and maybe still in jail at her request, John felt relatively safe sitting on the bench near the pond while Whiskers aggravated the fowl. Several solo joggers pounded along the path behind him.

When he returned home, Sally and Geraldine were seated at the bar. Geraldine had tears in her eyes.

"What's the matter?" John asked while Whiskers went to the water bowl.

"You know what's the matter," Geraldine said, her voice breaking. "Why didn't you say something to me yesterday?"

"We didn't feel it was the right time."

"You should have let me determine that."

"Wasn't he going to take you on a trip?" John asked.

Geraldine glowered at Sally. "Do you tell him everything?"

"I only mentioned what you told me about going on a trip."

"That trip was to Berea to eat at the Boone Tavern. I've heard so much about that place."

"We can take you there," John said.

"I wanted to go *with him*!" Geraldine said. "Did you think we were going on some expensive cruise or something?"

"I don't know, Mother. We didn't want you to be taken advantage of. You always hear about people scamming older folks for money. We didn't want anything like that to happen to you. I hope you understand."

Geraldine's phone rang in her bedroom. "Would you mind getting that?" she asked John.

He hurried to her room, but the call ended before he got there.

"Here you go," John said as he handed the phone to her.

"I received a text message," she said. She had a puzzled expression after reading it. "It's from Oscar. He's letting me know he'll pick me up around twelve-thirty to play in the bridge tournament."

"Are you going?" Sally asked.

"I have to think about it," Geraldine said with a stern face. "Can I have another cup of coffee?"

After refilling Geraldine's cup, Sally left to make up the beds and get dressed for the day.

"Anything I can get you?" John asked. "I'm going to work out in the yard for a while."

"No, thank you," she said. "I just want to be left alone for a bit to think things over."

John left through the garage, grabbed a rake and lawn bag, and went to the backyard to gather dead leaves and twigs from the trees. He asked Whiskers to come along, but the pooch was tired from the walk to the park and went to his bed in the den to nap.

When finished with the yard, John noticed Bert laying down more mulch in his never-ending home beautification project and decided to visit.

Bert had worked up a light sweat and was leaning on his shovel, taking a breather.

"Looking good, Bert," John said as he walked up to him. "Best lawn in the neighborhood."

"Thanks, John. It's a lot of hard work, but it's worth it when you start seeing results. I have some flowers in the backyard that are blooming. I think I'll see some roses in the next few days from those bushes in front of the house."

Wilma, Bert's wife, stepped out onto the front porch with two large glasses of iced tea. "I got something to cool you down," she said cheerfully.

Bert and John took the drinks and sat on two dark green aluminum chairs on the porch while Wilma went back inside.

"We think Wilma's got cancer," Bert said quietly. "She's going in for some tests tomorrow."

"I hate to hear that," John said. "I hope it's not too serious."

"Cancer is serious."

"What I mean is, I hope the tests reveal she doesn't have cancer."

"The doctor is positive she does," Bert said dryly. He looked off into the distance.

"What kind of cancer?"

"That's kind of personal right now. I'll let you know once there has been a determination by the specialists."

"If so, let's hope it'll be in the early stages and treatable." John took a long swallow of tea, feeling uneasy while trying to think of something else to comfort his friend.

"Thank you, John. I'll keep you posted."

"I guess I should be getting back home. Sally is probably wondering where I am."

As John rose from his chair, he saw Oscar escorting Geraldine to his car in the driveway.

"Old Geraldine has a boyfriend?" Bert said.

"Bridge partners."

"He looks younger than her, unless that hair is fake. Does he wear a hairpiece?"

"I never looked that closely." John handed his empty glass to Bert. "Thank Wilma again for the tea. And I hope things turn out fine."

When John returned to the house, Sally was dusting furniture in the living room.

"Did I just see what I thought I saw?" he asked.

"Yep," Sally said. "Mother said she liked playing cards with him and that they were only going to be bridge partners and nothing else."

"Did he come into the house?"

"She met him at the door. He smiled at me, and then they left."

"Uh, did you notice if he wore a hairpiece?"

"What?" she said, arching her head.

"Never mind."

Fifty

John was telling Sally about Wilma's medical condition as they sat on the couch in the living room when Geraldine and Oscar returned from their afternoon of bridge. John could see them through the sheer curtains as Oscar walked her to the front porch, held her hand as she went up the steps, then smiled and waved goodbye.

"How was the tournament?" John asked as she came into the house. Geraldine looked tired as she sat in the easy chair and released her cane onto the floor.

"We advanced to the second round," she said with a drained look.

"Are you all right, Mother?" Sally asked. "You don't look like you feel well."

"I'm just mentally beat," she said. "There's a lot more pressure when you're in a tournament."

"Can I get you something to drink?"

"I'm okay. I may take a short nap in a little while."

"I'll prepare dinner while you rest."

"How come you haven't asked me about Oscar?"

"As you usually say, it's none of our business," John said.

"Now you're being a smart aleck."

"Well, then, tell us about Oscar."

"The gal you saw him with at the restaurant yesterday was his aunt," Geraldine said. "She's about my age. She was his late mother's sister."

"How sweet of him to take her out," Sally said.

"Oscar told me he occasionally takes old folks to places. Even men. And if you're wondering, even me."

"That's awfully considerate of him," John said.

"Oscar said he first got involved in it when his father was in a veterans' retirement facility. He began volunteering because he thought many were lonely and forgotten by others. So he would play cards with them, read to them, and take them to movies and other activities. He said he really enjoyed being with older folks."

"I don't know what to say," John said.

"You don't need to say anything."

"Mother, we just want you to know we love and care for you," Sally said. "We didn't want you to get hurt."

"Aren't you glad you know more about him?" John asked.

"If you put it that way, I suppose I am," she said.

"Did you find out any more about him?"

"You sure are nosy."

"Just curious."

"Like a newspaperman."

"You've got that right."

"If you really want to know, Oscar has lived in the same house all his life. He never married, even though he almost did. He worked most of his life at Sears where he sold shoes. Anything else you want to know?"

"Thanks for sharing, Geraldine."

"Maybe we can have him over for dinner some evening," Sally said.

Geraldine leaned over and picked up her cane, then rose from the chair. "I think I'm going to take my nap now."

"I'll have supper ready when you get up," Sally said.

Geraldine stopped on her way to the stairs and said, "Oh, by the way, Oscar is still going to take me to the Boone Tavern."

"Good for you," John said with a smile.

After Geraldine closed her bedroom door, Sally said, "Oscar sounds like a good person."

"Yes, he does," John said. "We could use a few more Oscar Bigelows in this world."

~ * ~

Two hours later, Geraldine sauntered into the kitchen and sat on a stool.

"Ah, you're up," Sally said. "Dinner should be ready soon. I've got a meatloaf in the oven. We'll also have mashed potatoes and peas. Anything else you'd like?"

"A glass of ice water."

"Comin' right up."

"Where's John?"

"He ran to the grocery store to pick up something for dessert," Sally said as she handed the water to Geraldine.

"Long johns?"

"Probably a cake or something. And maybe your favorite for breakfast."

Geraldine cleared her throat. "Sally, I want you to know I appreciate you looking after me. I couldn't ask for a better daughter."

"Why, thank you, Mother. I try to do my best."

"I just want you to know I'm not looking for a romantic partner. I'm too darn old for that foolishness. So don't you worry about this old gal falling in love with some old coot."

"I admit it crossed my mind a little. I've read about people taking advantage of elderly men and women. John and I didn't want that to happen to you."

"Oscar is a good friend," Geraldine said. "We enjoy each other's company, especially when playing bridge. But I've made other friends at the senior citizens center. That's something I've missed since moving here. I love you and John, but I do need to get out of the house occasionally. I can't sit in that squeaky recliner watching TV all the time."

"We understand," Sally said. "Just let us know whenever you need us to take you someplace."

"I will."

Sally walked around the counter and gave her a hug. "I love you, Mother," she said, then kissed her on the cheek.

Fifty-one

"I'm off to visit with my buddies," John told Sally in the kitchen the following afternoon after taking a short walk with Whiskers. "I shouldn't be gone too long. Anything you need while I'm out?"

"I think I'm good," she said, putting dishes away in the cabinet. "Oscar is going to pick up Mother to go play bridge. I may walk down and check on Wilma a little later."

John was surprised when he got to McDonald's. Glory was sitting by herself as the others hadn't arrived for their daily dose of gossip and whatever else was on their minds. He got a large coffee and sat across from her.

"I hope I haven't scared the others off," Glory said.

"They'll be here," John said. "There's no set schedule with this bunch."

"Since we're the only ones here, I thought I'd give you an update about my son. He's out of jail now. We have a lawyer who hopes to get him a lenient sentence since Clay is a first-time offender. Maybe get it off his record for good behavior after a period of time."

"I hope that works for your son and he can keep his nose clean."

"That's my concern, John. While I don't want my son to have a criminal record, this sounds more like a slap on the wrist. Clay is at that rebellious stage, and I'm not sure he can do it. I've seen what has happened to a few of the boys he runs around with. They've become serial thieves and druggies. I don't want that to happen to my son."

"I understand," John said. "Does he have a job?"

"We're looking."

"I'll ask around and see if I hear of anything."

"My big concern is drugs. I've seen and written about what they can do to people's lives, young and old."

"Maybe I can have someone get in touch with him. Do you think that would help?"

"I think he would be more receptive to listening to someone else than to me preaching about the evils of drugs," she said. "It's drugs that have made him a thief. I think it's only grass now, but it could be more. You never know everything your kid is taking. I want to stop it now if I can."

"If you don't mind me asking, what is he going to do about that tattoo on his neck?" John asked.

"Oh, you saw that horrible spider web?"

"At the park."

"Thank god, it's only a henna tattoo," she said. "It's already off his body. That's about the only good decision he's made in the past year or so."

John looked at the entrance and saw Curt, Mel, and Brandon heading toward the counter to place orders.

"It looks like the guys have arrived," John said, glancing toward the front. "I'll give you a call later today."

"Thanks, John," she said with a soft smile.

The morning huddle lasted less than an hour, which was fine with John because his friends didn't have much to offer to solve the world's problems or opinions about various sports. Mel had a doctor's appointment, Curt was going to play golf, and Brandon was taking his wife to a movie. Even Glory was ready to leave, as John believed she didn't want to be away from her son very long.

As John was driving home, he received a text from Chloe, letting him know that she and Whitney would be arriving at Blue Grass Airport at two-forty the next afternoon. Sally wasn't in the house when he got home, but he was greeted by Whiskers, eager to go to his favorite place at the side of the house. John knew it was also about time to grab the pooper-scooper to clean up the doggie droppings, something he'd finish before Chloe and Whitney arrived.

When John went back into the house, he replenished Whiskers' water bowl and fixed himself a cup of coffee. He flipped through the newspaper, noticing a three-day-old story about the accident that had claimed the lives of George and Donna Garcia as well as four other people. The article referred to the Garcias as a prominent physician and respected educator who left behind two children but didn't make mention of any grandchildren. John took a pair of scissors from a drawer and cut out the story, perhaps to share with Brody and Sasha at some opportune time in the future.

Sally came back from the Reliford's house, carrying two small flowering plants in large plastic cups.

"Bert gave me these to add some color to our front yard," she said with a laugh while placing them on the counter. "And, by the way, Wilma had a minor bowel obstruction that they were able to clear with medication."

"I'm sure they're relieved by that," John said. "Especially Wilma. Constipation can be painful."

She made herself a cup of coffee and sat at the counter. "I didn't expect you back this early."

"Too much going on. We drank our coffees, gabbed for a few minutes, and left."

"Did Glory show up?"

"She was there when I got there. She gave me an update about her son. I told her I'd try to help."

"What can you do?" she asked, then took a sip of her coffee.

"It won't be me. I'm going to talk to Brody. Since he's working at the rehab center, maybe he can offer some advice. I'm going to ask him to call her and talk to her son."

"That's a great idea."

"Kind of role reversal for him, which I hope would raise his self-esteem."

"I assume you got the text from Chloe," Sally said. "I'm so anxious to see them. I know Mother is looking forward to it."

"Me, too." John said. "I think I'll ask if she wants to go to the airport with me to pick them up."

"Hey, I want to go, too!"

John grinned. "No problem."

"Maybe things are beginning to look up after all we've been through the past few months."

"Only time will tell."

Fifty-two

Sally and Geraldine were asleep when John left the house barely after sunrise, a spur-of-the-moment decision he couldn't explain while walking with Whiskers to Shipley Park. Even the pooch seemed perplexed, as he usually returned to his bed in the den after breakfast.

John sat peacefully on the bench, the sky overcast, reflecting on what had transpired the past few months, while mindlessly watching Whiskers sniff along the edge of the pond in search of waterfowl to hassle. In the distance, he noticed three women jogging on a paved path, thinking there was safety in numbers in these trying times.

His phone vibrated, disturbing the calm. He took it from his pants pocket and saw the caller was Glory.

"Good morning, Glory," he said.

"I hope I'm not interrupting anything," she said. "I thought you might be an early riser from your newspaper days."

John chuckled. "You thought right."

"I'm calling to let you know how much I appreciate you having your son get in touch with me last night."

"That's good to hear. I didn't know if he had reached you yet."

"He talked to Clayton for nearly half an hour. I don't know what he said, but something surely clicked because Clayton is going to the rehab center at ten this morning to meet with Brody. I haven't seen my son this upbeat in months."

"That's great," John said, who couldn't help but wonder if Glory was talking about his Brody.

"You have a wonderful son," she said. "You and your wife must be very proud of him."

"He's been through a lot this year, and I think he's probably learned a few lessons along the way."

After ending the conversation, John called for Whiskers to go back home. Sunshine broke through the clouds. Several solo joggers whisked by, coming and going, as he was leaving the park. A young couple was pushing a stroller near the playground. John couldn't help but think that he and Sally might be spending similar time with Sasha Malia. And then he felt a sense of sadness realizing Brody wouldn't have Ashley to raise their daughter.

When he got home, Sally and Geraldine were seated at the bar eating omelets and drinking coffee. Whiskers went to his water bowl for several slurps, and after John handed him a treat, retreated to this bed in the den.

"Where in the world have you been?" Geraldine asked.

"I decided to go to the park," John said, standing at the end of the bar. "A good time to clear my head."

"I bet that didn't take long," she snickered.

"You might try it sometime."

"I'll let you know if I ever need to."

He grinned. "Okay."

"What's that supposed to mean?" she asked.

John poured himself a cup of coffee, sat across from Sally and recounted the phone call with Glory.

"I don't know what to say," Sally said, wide-eyed.

"I didn't either," John said, taking a sip of coffee. "Maybe he's finally grown up."

"It's about time!" Geraldine said, adding, "But I wouldn't hold my breath."

"Miracles never cease to happen."

"You sound like Libby," Geraldine said.

"God willing," John said.

"Now you're being a smart aleck."

"Would you two cut it out," Sally said. "We'll be here to support Brody. Like we always have. It's a family thing."

"Speaking of family," John said. "Chloe's plane arrives around three this afternoon. Everyone going with me?"

"Count me in," Sally said with a smile. "I can't wait to see Whitney again."

Geraldine lowered her chin. "I have my bridge tournament this afternoon. Oscar is picking me up at one. I can't cancel on him."

"You'll have something to look forward to when you get back home from winning your game," John said.

"We can ask Brody to bring Sasha over so Whitney can meet her new cousin," Sally said.

Geraldine beamed. "I'd like that."

"Maybe things are getting back to normal."

"Knock on wood," John declared, rapping the counter three times.

Meet Michael Embry

Michael Embry is the author of 16 books, including 12 novels, three nonfiction sports books, and a short-story collection. He spent more than 30 years in the news media, working as an award-winning reporter, sportswriter, and editor for two newspapers, a national news service, a regional magazine, and a book editor.

Embry is co-founder, along with fellow Wings author Chris Helvey, of the Bluegrass Writers Coalition. He is an active member of several environmental, human rights, animal rescue, and wildlife organizations. His interests include reading, travel, writing, and photography. He lives in Frankfort, Ky., with his wife, Mary, and rescue dog, Belle.

Other Works from the Pen of Michael Embry

Reunion of Familiar Strangers - John and Sally Ross venture off to attend his 50th high school reunion, a gathering of former friends who seem more like strangers.

Make Room for Family - John Ross returns from vacation to a big surprise when he is greeted by his brother- and sister-in-law, who seem to have made it their home.

New Horizons - John Ross and his wife Sally take a long overdue vacation, traveling to Budapest for a guided tour. It turns out to be an unforgettable trip, mainly for the wrong reasons.

Darkness Beyond the Light - John Ross and his wife Sally learn their self-centered son Brody has been leading a double life and must navigate uncharted territory during the Christmas season to lead him out of the darkness of drugs.

Old Ways and New Days - Retired sports editor John Ross discovers there are many adjustments he must make in this coming-of-old-age novel.

The Bully List - Dealing with bullies isn't an easy thing to do so Josh and Sam try to come up with a list of things to do to get even with a gang of bullies.

Shooting Star - Basketball standout Jesse Christopher finds most of his challenges away from the gym as he tries to fit in as the new kid in school.

A Long Highway - A random act of violence in the workplace forces sports columnist Micah Stewart to hit the road in search of meaning to his life.

The Touch - Sports editor Blake Williams, a widower trying to raise three children, is careful to open his heart to another woman, fearful of the pain he might suffer again.

A Confidential Man - Sports columnist Chase Elliott is known as a trustworthy friend who can keep confidences. But can keeping some confidences prove to be deadly?

Foolish Is The Heart - Sports columnist Brandon Wilkes discovers there are important things going on in his life other than covering the big games.

Dear reader,

I hope you've enjoyed reading this tale of family ups and
downs.

Your opinion is valuable to other
readers like you,
who may be looking for books like mine.

Please consider taking a few minutes to post a review,
however brief,
on the site where you purchased this book
or on the Wings ePress web page.

You may also want to visit my author page
at the Wings' website, where you can find
all the other books in my series.

Thank you!

Michael Embry

Visit Our Website

For The Full Inventory
Of Quality Books:

<u>Wings ePress, Inc</u>

Quality trade paperbacks and downloads
in multiple formats,
in genres ranging from light romantic comedy to general
fiction and horror.
Wings has something for every reader's taste.
Visit the website, then bookmark it.
We add new titles each month!

Wings ePress, Inc.
3000 N. Rock Road
Newton, KS 67114